11/3000

MR. WRAITH.

SARRATT

R. N. Berry

An Authors OnLine Book

British Library Cataloguing Publication Data.
A catalogue record for this book is available from the British Library

ISBN 978-0-7552-0708-4

Authors OnLine Ltd
19 The Cinques
Gamlingay, Sandy
Bedfordshire SG19 3NU
England

This book is also available in e-book format, details of which are available at
www.authorsonline.co.uk

FOR

DAWN

The map chambers

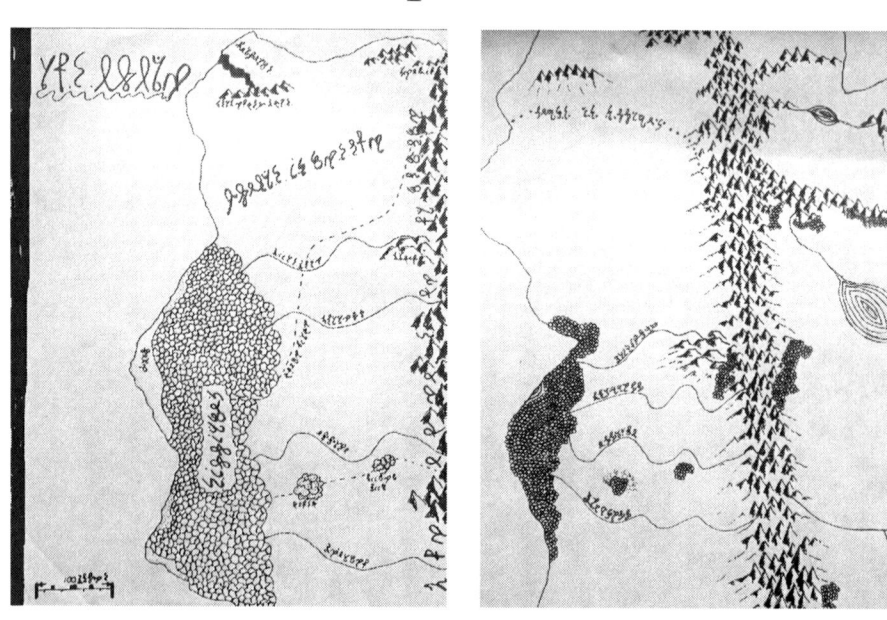

1   2

Map number one is probably one of the first hand- drawn maps of Ursalane. It is to be found within the book of Obsideon, the Elf scholar and prophet; he discarded all other lands, showing only what was then the boundaries of Follonday, home of the Elves. This was in the age of Hemplestar, the first king of the Elves. The map is over five thousand years old.

Map number two was drawn many centuries later; this

was the first draft. The Elves had started to recognise other races by this age, the time of Esslestar. It is to be found within the libraries of the Troll scholar, Denjolm; he studied this for months before setting out in the hope of finishing what had become an obsession when he was still very young.

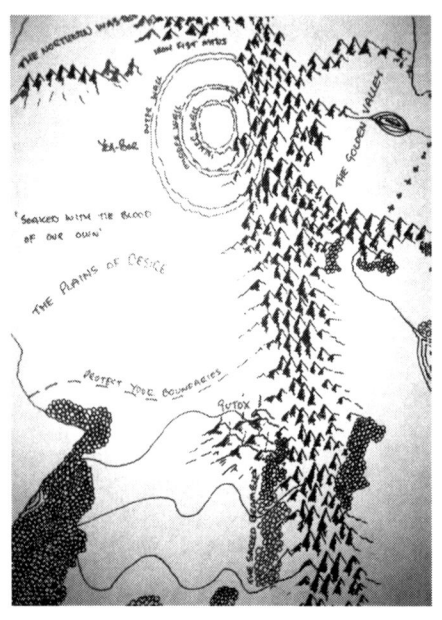 

3   4

Maps three and four are the finished maps Denjolm completed over a period of three years; he travelled from the far north to the southern coast, traversing nearly every mountain within the Great Eastern Divide. It was while he was travelling along the Great Eastern Divide that he came upon the Watch Wizard; they spent over three months travelling together,

URSALANE

The continent of Ursalane is the lost civilisation of the Atlantic. The Elves referred to this as the Mid Atlantic, they being the ones who gave us the earliest maps of the region. The drawings on this salvaged map though are from the scholar Denjolm. A Troll of great learning, he spent most of his earlier years under the guidance of the wizards of the Watch, a place in which he brought back to life the intricate ways in which the early Elf civilisations drew. The drawings were done by the Troll over many years of travelling the peaks of the Great Eastern Divide.

A WORD OF CAUTION

Please enjoy the experience just as Peter Miller did.
His life changed forever after listening to this tale, and
hopefully your life will change in just the same way.
But a word of caution: when you think you have
everything you have ever wanted, keep looking forwards
with more hope, for there will always be the shadow
waiting just around the corner, waiting to bring you down
into the depths of hell. The skies look clear tonight, so I
will run within your lands, making sure the darkness never
reaches you and your loved ones.

Travel well, my friends.
Acorn

The Chronicles of Ursalane

Sarratt
Prologue

Present Day.

Peter Miller looked at his watch and shook his head; he really did have to be somewhere north of the Watford Gap before six o'clock that evening. The time was now nine o'clock; he was within his study, a small room at the back of his house, which overlooked his rather small garden. He looked again at the letter he had received three days earlier.

Peter Miller

You do not know me and we have never met, but I do know of you
I looked upon you while you were growing up
The time has now come
We will talk in three days' time
The meeting place shall be

Motor way services
M6
CA4 0NT
I will be waiting within the Lorry Park from 6pm
Do not be late, for my travels are within your northern lands.

ACORN

"Peter," his wife shouted from somewhere within the house. "Thought you had a meeting in Manchester tonight, you realise that it is Friday."

"I just have to phone the office, love," he replied, putting the mysterious letter back within its envelope, which he stared at again, for it had been sealed with a crest; one acorn adorned the red wax. He was also perplexed by the fact that this letter did not have a stamp, which made him shiver. Had this strange person delivered it by hand?

"Peter Miller here. Can you put me through to Allison."

"Hold the line please."

"Hi, Peter, how are you?"

"Fine, just letting you know that I am going to the new studios this weekend, being shown round the future of broadcasting."

"You do know that you are reporting on the forthcoming defence cuts on Newsnight."

"Yeah."

"Well make sure you wear your long johns, Peter. I've heard it gets bloody cold up there!"

"Right, yeah, see you on Monday then, bye."

"Bye."

The reporter sat back in his chair and quickly went through what his meeting with the Minister of Defence was all about. He had already written out a rough draft; he would finish that on Sunday. He rubbed his balding scalp and felt his stomach, which was getting bigger by the year, and thought of the false promises he was forever making to himself. He was going to do it, he kept on saying to himself, but it was always 'tomorrow'. His wife of twenty years on the other hand was a fitness fanatic, forever at the gym. While he had her within his thoughts she popped her head round the door.

"Friday afternoon traffic, you had better get a move on; you don't want to be late, do you?"

"Going now, love. Come here and give me a hug," he said as he swivelled his chair to face her. She came in and sat on his knee, giving him a peck on the cheek; then she playfully slapped him on his balding scalp and jumped from his knee.

"Right, I'm off now. Come on, Peter," she urged. They both left their house at the same time.

Peter Miller put his overnight bag in the boot of his car with his briefcase; he took off his suit jacket and hung it in the back seat; he put his blackberry in the holder provided within the dash and put his Dictaphone in another holder. He climbed into his pride and joy, which was a Range Rover Autobiography sport; black exterior with the exclusive Cannes interior. He felt that this one thing in his life expressed his individuality; he always seemed to be happier once he got within his 4X4. He waved once more to his wife and was off. Just getting to a motorway had taken him over an hour and thirty minutes, from where he lived in Kew.

Many hours later and Peter Miller had just managed to crawl past Birmingham; he had been stuck in traffic for what seemed like an age, with no sign of anything changing in the foreseeable future. He thought of what this stranger might say; why did he want to meet within a motorway service station of all places? He definitely did not like the idea of meeting this stranger within the lorry park. He had dark thoughts that afternoon; his headache was turning into a migraine. Suddenly the traffic started to move; this always amazed Peter Miller and he always expected to drive past the emergency services tending to the crash that never happened.

When he eventually got past Preston, the traffic was free- flowing. He was cruising at around 85 mph; his mood though was still dark, just like the low, black clouds which had just come into view. They were the blackest clouds he had ever seen. The first drops of rain were big; it was three thirty and it had become very dark. The forked lightning was soon all around him, the great booms of thunder shaking his 4X4 to the wheels.

Eventually he reached the service station which the female voice indicated was the one. He pulled into the main car park and parked as close to the service station as possible. The rain was torrential, he switched off the ignition and started to unwind. He stretched his arms and legs and then checked the time. He was one hour early, so he then checked his voice mail. As normal there were at least a dozen messages from the last time he had checked it, just before he had set off on the journey north. Peter Miller was one of the few who always had his phone switched off when he was driving; he had seen too many accidents caused by people getting distracted by them. His phone rang twice and he answered as he always did.

"Peter Miller."

"Pete, its Dave. Listen, a few of the guys have tickets for the Arsenal game, fancy it?"

"Not this weekend, Dave. Up north with work, I'll phone you on Wednesday."

"This match is going to the biggest of the season, mate!" exclaimed his friend.

"I know."

"Oh well! I'll see you later then, mate."

"Yeah, see you, Dave," replied the disappointed reporter. After all, he and Dave were big fans of the Arsenal.

After some minutes he decided that he would go and get himself a cup of coffee and take a look at the lorry park. Whoever had wanted to meet there could even now be sitting within a massive articulated truck waiting for him. He put his jacket on and then his mackintosh. The wind was howling so he did not bother with his umbrella. The coffee was hot, but not to his liking. After a visit to the gents he made his way to the lorry park. Several lorries were parked up, all of them empty. He looked to the right where there was a small woodland area. He shivered at the cold wind and hurried back to the comforts of his 4X4. Peter Miller sat alone with his thoughts for the next thirty minutes or so and he was not liking the experience. From the outside looking in, his life seemed to be perfect, but he knew that everything was always on a knife edge. His work was forever challenging, just as was his wife when it came to his home life. He closed his eyes before turning the ignition key, This was it, he thought.

He pulled into the lorry park and parked his 4X4 facing the small group of trees which seemed before, when he had looked at them, like a woodland. It was a trick of the mind, he thought, as he could now see quite clearly the cars hurtling past, headlights on full. He glanced down at his watch and saw that the time was six o'clock. When he looked up his whole body stiffened with fear; he let a short brief scream form in his mouth. The hooded figure was standing right in front of the car. Peter Miller brought his knuckles up to rub his eyes; he was hoping that his eyes had played another trick on him. What happened next nearly gave the reporter a heart attack, for when he opened his eyes the stranger was sitting in the passenger seat, the green camouflaged hood hiding his face.

"Fucking Hell! Fucking Hell! Fucking Hell!" he swore at the top of his voice. His whole body had moved away from the stranger and was pressed up against the car door. He felt his hands start to shake first, then his legs. He wiped away the sweat from his forehead; he was very scared.

"Do not feel threatened, Peter Miller," said the stranger, the voice soft with musical tones woven amongst the words.

"How the fucking hell did you do that?" shouted the reporter.

"I have not got much time with you, Peter Miller. My travels this storm- ridden evening will take me into your northern lands."

Peter Miller never swore; he prided himself on the fact that on a Saturday evening in the pub after several drinks, he would not lower himself by using foul language, but he could not think of anything more appropriate for this situation.

"Fucking Hell! How did you get in the car that quick? It is a simple question, is it not?" His voice was still raised.

"You seem to be bothering yourself over nothing, Peter Miller. Look at me."

Peter Miller turned his head to look at the hooded stranger; the hood however was masking the stranger's face in deep shadow, but almost immediately he felt calm. He had stopped shaking and had slid back into his seat; the stranger though did not look upon Peter Miller for more than three seconds, his head turning to face the front of the car.

"I suggest that you take off your jacket, make yourself comfortable and close your eyes."

"Holy fuck! How the fuck did you manage that, for fucks sake? Give me a moment."

The reporter did as he was told, throwing his mackintosh

and jacket into the back seat. He then reached for his phone.

"You will have no need for these while I talk," said the stranger, who had within his hands, the Blackberry and Dictaphone. Peter Miller coughed awkwardly; the one thing he relied on was his Dictaphone, so he shrugged his shoulders and resisted the urge to swear again.

"Then I will begin, with the lost continent of Ursalane."

Peter Miller closed his eyes and drifted into another world.

Sarratt

Chapter One

The delegates of the Elvin race had been waiting in the grounds of Witches Watch for an hour, seated upon a round stone bench, which gave them views of the woodlands to the rear of the keep, a forest scattered with guarding spells to keep out those who were not welcome within the grounds of the watch. The sun was reaching its highest point in the sky and the temperature was not too warm and not too cold, for it was only the beginning of the springtime, a time of joy for most of the races. The small group of Elves had travelled a long way, for Follonday was to be found on the western coast, over the formidable mountain range which split the continent in two. Four weeks it had taken them: a trip they made each and every year.

"I think we will travel back by the way of the Plains of Desire, right up to the banks of the Moonshine," said

Allucia, who had once more told her companions the way she was going to take them.

"The Moonshine will be full this time of the season, my princess," replied Elian, a slender elf who was one of her personal guards.

"The plains could see us some sport as well," added Leandstar, a bigger Elf, who too had now risen, stretching his arms.

"You and your hunting Leandstar, do not breathe a word of this to the Watch wizard. This is why we have to come here, to make sure we are not breaking our pledges," she waved her hand at him, though her face was smiling at him.

The Watch wizard sat within his chambers at the end of the Corridor of Life, finishing off a very good pipe. His glass of ale finished as well, he stared out through the windows and at the blue skies. Everything looked calm and peaceful; he shook his head and looked up at the door just as it was knocked upon.

"Enter."

A young apprentice came into the room and bowed before the Wizard. He had in his hand a scroll, sealed with the crest of Esslestar.

"Thank you, Thomas. You can send them to me now, ask Sarratt to join me please."

The young apprentice bowed once more and hurried away, doing the tasks the wizard had asked of him. Sarratt had been within the gardens of the Watch, tending to the many different plants and vegetables which grew there. He particularly loved this time within the Watch, for he had many a spare day when he could garden. He looked up at Thomas and greeted him politely. Sarratt packed away his tools and made his way through the gardens of the Watch, all the time looking at the spring flowers which were in full bloom. The gardens of the Watch were a public place and many of the residents of the town came within for walks and picnics. The wizard though did not speak with anyone, his head bowed and concealed within his hood.

"Ah! Young Sarratt, take that seat within the alcove, and pull the curtain across. I will need your views on the state of the races after this day is done."

"The Elves are first then, should be interesting," replied the young wizard who had disappeared through the curtains.

Of the five Elves who had accompanied the Elven princess, only one came within the chambers of the Watch Wizard.

"Greetings, Wizard," offered Allucia, who had walked right up to the Wizard's desk. She did not offer her hand; she did not bow.

"Take a seat, Allucia. And you, Leandstar, please! Sorry for the delay, I was finishing off some very important business."

"As we can see!" replied the princess, who had pointed at the empty glass and smoking pipe.

The Watch Wizard looked upon the princess and his heart missed a beat. He had loved nothing the way he had loved Allucia. She was the image of timeless beauty.

Years ago she had looked this way upon him, but time had weathered the looks of the wizard. He wiped these thoughts from his mind and started the meeting.

"The Elves of Follonday are respecting the borders treaty between themselves and the Trolls of Yea Bor?" he looked up at the two seated Elves.

"The treaty signed by my father last summer still stands, Wizard."

"The boundaries have not been compromised in any way, shape or form, either by the Elves of Follonday or the Trolls of Yea Bor?"

"The boundaries you talk of, Wizard, are in our northern lands. We seldom venture upon the Plains of Desire, and our time is taken within our forests and southern farmlands."

The Watch Wizard continued through the list, nodding his approval, ticking each question when he was satisfied with the answer.

"Finally, can Esslestar assure the wizards of the Watch that he has put an end to the sport of hunting the race of Gnome?"

"You have to always make sure that rats do not become an epidemic; we show no hatred to the vermin of which you speak," replied Leandstar.

"I thought I could smell something going rotten while we were outside, Wizard. You would not put us anywhere near such vermin; we do not suffer that race as you well know," added Allucia, her hand wafting away the imagined smell.

"This is part of the treaty the king of the Elves promised, no, made into your laws, that not one Gnome would suffer at the blade of an Elf. Tell me this is so," said the Watch Wizard, who had put a cross against his question.

"Then why do we have to patrol the fringes of our forests? They are still raiding through our lands, homes within the third tier robbed of all valuables, livestock slaughtered. They do not care for the lands, they ruin the forest when and wherever they can," replied Allucia, who had risen, her battle dress holding the sword upon which she had put her left hand.

"This will be addressed, Allucia. I think that is all. We cannot afford for the Elves to think that they can rule all of the races; we do not want to go back to the dark days of Obsidian."

The two Elves never responded to what the wizard said of Obsidian, the Elf who was born of the stars. They talked with the wizard of when he was to visit Esslestar, that the house of her father would always welcome the wizards of the Watch.

The wizard remained standing as he waited for the second audience of the afternoon; this was to be the gruff, stout race of the Dwarf. Sarratt had remained behind the curtain, seated upon a weathered, torn leather chair. He had not stopped writing, every detail of the last meeting going down onto paper, and he felt that there was something not quite right with the Elves, but he could not put his finger on the problem.

The meeting between the Watch Wizard and the

Dwarves was heated, the Dwarves screaming at the wizard about the Golden Valley, a region in disrepute between themselves and the Trolls of Yea Bor. The riches within the valley were legendary; the war between the two races had been raging for years.

"Thorgehammer will not sign any more of your papers, he will not welcome any wizard within the walls of Pavelem. He says that if you do not listen, then the worst of your nightmares will come to pass sooner than you think," stormed the Dwarf, who had been reading the statement from a scroll he held in his massive hands.

"Tell Thorgehammer we will talk at the beginning of the last moon of this year," replied the wizard, his voice but a whisper, his hooded head bowing to the two furious Dwarves.

"He wants you to rid the Golden Valley of the Troll," added the Dwarf.

"See yourselves out, go and travel without rest until you reach the walls of your magnificent city. I hope that our next meeting is just as pleasant, be gone with you now," he said as he also spoke the spell with the words they could hear.

The Watch Wizard sat down and called for the young wizard to join him. The smallest of smiles was appearing, though with his hood still covering his face, Sarratt did not see.

"They will be cursing you by the time they reach Pavelem."

"Monsters, savages, they talk with no reason. I

remember, Sarratt, when the race of Dwarves was a decent race, offering help to all of the races. Now they have become a dangerous force which will need checking; dark ages seem to be only a season away."

"Do they know that they are within the Watch while a company of Trolls sit and wait their turn? A whole running unit arrived late last evening, I gave them the whole of the west wing," said the younger wizard.

"Twenty four Trolls, they do not trust anyone these days. I fear they are becoming isolated like the Gnomes of Gutox."

"Plus one," added Sarratt.

"Of course, the scholar Denjolm sits within our company. Denjolm will not say anything but the truth, unlike the Elf and the Dwarf, who conceal their thoughts away. I know more than some of their own, I fear."

There was a slight knock upon the door.

The sight of the scholar from Yea Bor was always a shock for the wizards. Standing in his running unit boots, he stood nearly eight feet from the ground, but Denjolm was different from any other Troll the wizards had met. He was the one who had managed to write down the guttural sounds of the Troll speech, this being many decades ago. Now, through his efforts, the Trolls of Yea Bor were becoming a race who valued the written word just as much as the spoken. His books adorned the shelves of the wizard's libraries; such was their importance in the evolution of a race.

After some good- hearted chat about what each of them

had been up to for the past winter, it was the Troll who changed the mood from light to dark.

"The council as I feared have brought up the king's position once more. He squanders his time upon the slopes of the Golden Valley, merely a shadow of his former self. I know of what Sarratt told him all those years ago. With your blessing this is true, but he refuses to sit within the debating chamber; he has not been seen within the walls of our city for five years."

"Sarratt will pay your king another visit this season, he is merely distracted," said the Watch Wizard, his hood now removed from his head; there was no need to conceal one's self in front of the scholar.

"The western and southern borders are being run by the Elves. We lost two running units just before the onset of winter. They have a continuous trade route with the Dwarves, just north of the river Moonshine. They are hemming us in, we are the guardians of the Plains of Desire, and this is the battle field where our blood flows." Not once did Denjolm raise his voice, or show any emotion other than a sadness at the way things were turning against his race.

"Denjolm, such is the way of the Elves and the Dwarves, we share your frustration, we share your sadness. We also care deeply for the wellbeing of your race. We will not falter from our course. The Dwarves will quieten down after the Elves see what is happening to the balance of life. Please, what of your northern borders?" asked the Watch Wizard.

"Shadows, rumours, we know that our distant cousins,

the Rock Trolls, have come to us for the first time in one hundred years, telling the debating chamber that the monsters from the shadows are appearing more often, mountain Ogres the most feared, Hobgoblins and Goblins, whisperings from the west, a darkness is growing, they say. Me! I think they exaggerate."

The Watch Wizard did not change his relaxed expression, he merely nodded his head. Sarratt though had leant forward, wanting to know more of the monsters from the north.

"You will stay for a while," offered the Witch Wizard.

"I would like nothing more than to spend this season within the libraries. Unfortunately I am being escorted in full battle dress by the second running unit. They are scouting the eastern borders of our lands when we leave. The council thought it would be wise if I saw what the Dwarves are preparing for this season's battles within the Golden Valley," replied the scholar, who had risen, his mighty frame towering over the two wizards.

When he had left, the Watch Wizard poured himself and Sarratt a glass of ale. He walked over to the map table, the whole of Ursalane laid out before them.

"Two more dignitaries to see then," stated the Watch Wizard, his finger wandering over the Golden Valley.

Next to walk into the wizard's chambers was the little figure of the Gnome, his yellow complexion matching his yellow boots, his red travelling cloak buttoned all the way to the neck. He did not look happy.

"Greetings from the lands of fire. My name is Flukkia.

I come with the thoughts of our King," he said as he sat down, helping himself to a swig of ale from the glass of the Watch Wizard, who almost burst out laughing.

"Sarratt, bring Flukkia a glass of ale."

Flukkia did not say 'thank you'. He blessed the glass of ale instead, gulping the contents down in one.

"My king wishes that you are being blessed daily. He says that you are good to those who live within the fires of Gutox, but he says he must tell you he lost over three hundred Gnomes the winter just passed, upon the Plains of Desire, hunted down like animals, killed without mercy or blessing."

"I will bless your dead; tell the king he must stop the raiding parties from entering the forests of Follonday. The Elves have had enough of the stealing, Flukkia. This will put an end to the needless loss of life. Tell the king that he does not need anything other than what lies within his lands," replied the Watch Wizard, knowing full well the king would send out just as many raiding parties this coming summer.

"The blessed king of our lands will listen intently upon every word you have spoken on this blessed day, but he will not be held a prisoner within Gutox. He will meet with you in person the next time you call for an audience."

"Well at least stay within the Bramble wood."

"Sacred Bramble wood," corrected Flukkia.

"Yes, sacred Bramble wood has saved hundreds of Gnomes over the years. Use it now more than ever; a darkness is falling across Ursalane."

"Darkness, I will make sure my king knows of the darkness; shadows can hide the most horrible things," the Gnome spat in disgust.

The Gnome and the two wizards talked for a while and then a knock came at the door. Sarratt jumped from his chair and rushed to the door. It was Allucia, she looked at the young wizard and simply pushed by him.

"I have left my purse," she stated flatly.

She walked over to the wizard's desk and waved her hand over its surface.

"You must be mistaken, princess," replied the wizard, who had remained seated.

"No! I remember putting it down there," she said, pointing at the desk.

"If I do come across the purse, I will send it at once to Follonday. Now I have business to conclude," replied the wizard, who had stood, his hand showing her the door.

"Make sure you do. I can smell rats. You do not want to find them, Wizard. They will cause you so much damage," she wailed as she stormed out of the room.

Saratt did try and be courteous but she shoved him out of the way. He felt anguish and bitterness within her as they touched. The door slammed shut, Sarratt locking it immediately.

"You can come out now, Flukkia."

The Gnome crawled from under the wizard's desk, dusting himself down as he stood.

"I think the Elf would have killed me, she scares me."

"Your passage home will be one of your safest. No one

or anything will come anywhere near you. Travel by the rainbow falls and be enchanted by the magic of the area."

"Then I will leave at once," said the Gnome who had put on his backpack and was walking purposefully to the door, but he was called back by the Watch Wizard.

"Flukkia, please empty your backpack," he asked in a soft voice.

The Gnome looked shocked. "Why?" he cried.

"We will see."

The Gnome gave the backpack to the wizard and hung his head.

"Let us see what we have in here then. What!" exclaimed the wizard.

He brought forth not only the purse of the princess, but his pipe, tobacco and matches. Sarratt looked on in amazement. How could he steal right in front of two wizards again?

"Sarratt, I believe this belongs to you," said the Watch Wizard as he handed the young wizard three pouches that had been in the pocket of his hooded robe.

"It is what we do, my blessed one. I knew I would never get away with it, but it is fun trying," said the Gnome, who had giggled to himself when he had heard the young wizard gasp out loud.

When eventually all of the Gnome's many pockets had been emptied, he was escorted from the watch by the Watch Wizard himself.

The evening was closing in and the sun had all but dropped from the western skies. The two wizards sat in the large dining hall of the Watch. It was full of apprentices all tucking into a hearty meal of bread and beef stew, ale being served in large tankards. The atmosphere as usual was pleasant, everyone present aspired to become a wizard. For many years they would try; most never succeeded.

"We have one more delegation to see, Sarratt. He is on his way. He will be here later this evening, seeing if we are doing what his Queen expects of us. Lord Tarique will test our patience, he will threaten our college, he will threaten our lives," warned the wizard, who had already started to make his way back towards the Corridor of Life. Sudden trumpeting and the sound of many horns being blown stopped the wizards in their tracks. They could also hear the hooves of many horses. The Watch Wizard went to one of the long windows which looked upon the approaches to the College of the Wizards and inhaled deeply. Sarratt was by his side, looking in wonder at the procession which was making its way towards them.

"It seems we will be in the audience of Queen Beatrice the Third. How very splendid!" said the Watch Wizard, more to himself than to Sarratt.

People had lined the long thoroughfare, coming out in their thousands, trying in vain to catch a glimpse of their Queen, who was being escorted in her royal carriage. Several huge horses with battle helmets were neighing loudly, stamping their hooves on the cobbled road, looking tired and agitated. No one would see the Queen, for she had the windows of her carriage closed over with ornate golden cloth, stitched upon it the crest of royalty: an Eagle in flight.

Right at the front of the procession was Lord Tarique, a huge burly man, famed throughout the lands as the Queen's champion, his moustache curled several times at its ends, his fingers forever teasing it. He brought the procession to a halt, bellowing out orders to the foot soldiers who had marched all the way from the city of Traxit. They moved into lines of fifty, creating a corridor for the Queen all the way to the imposing doors of the wizard's college.

"She has brought an army with her!" exclaimed Sarratt.

"Indeed she has," replied the Watch Wizard calmly, though inside he was in turmoil; an army within the grounds of his college was not permitted, the Queen knew this. He beckoned the young wizard and they made their way to greet their Queen.

The cheers had not stopped, people hailing her, chanting her name over and over, hands in the air; the atmosphere was like a carnival in the fading light of day.

"Bring right arms to bear," screamed Lord Tarique, who had by now dismounted from his black stallion.

The thousands of soldiers on foot obeyed instantly, stamping their left boot as one.

"Hail Beatrice the Third, Queen of all she surveys," his voice still booming out into the evening skies.

In one voice the whole of Queen Beatrice's army saluted her as she stepped from the royal carriage, within her hands two walking sticks. She did not acknowledge the screaming crowds which had rushed to see her; she kept her head bowed and with some difficulty limped to the steps of Witches Watch.

"We have urgent things to talk of, Wizard. Help me with these steps," she ordered, not once looking at either the Watch Wizard or Sarratt.

Eventually, after some struggling, they entered the main hall of the wizards. The fire was lit, huge flames licking at the inner walls of the chimney. The room was filled with leather couches, desks and tables where the residents of the Watch could study their orders. The walls displayed enormous tapestries of dragons, each one looking down upon their prey with a hunger in their eyes. The Queen sat upon a lone high winged chair which was by the massive inglenook fireplace, its height being that of fifteen feet. The room had been emptied of all the apprentices. The Queen looked up and down the hall, her fierce eyes studying the tapestries.

"Have you created real magic, Watch Wizard? Or are you still an illusionist?" she asked suddenly.

The Watch Wizard walked over to his Queen; his whole form hunched forwards, he suddenly looked thirty years older than his real age..

"Many think I have the words of real magic, my Majesty. Many believe I have the power of the lost fairy magic. Alas, these are but rumours; we study hard and one day a light will shine upon our college, and then there will be the power of the spoken word," lied the Watch Wizard.

"Time is running out for this college of yours, I need

you to have the power to bring me the wealth that true magic brings. Maybe now will be that time, Wizard," she threatened.

"We are so very close, your Majesty. Have patience and you will be rewarded with what you seek, the mighty red," replied the Watch Wizard, who had read the thoughts of the Queen as she had been looking at the tapestries.

She howled then.... howled like a wolf with laughter.

"You are good at the guessing games, ah! If only you could bring me a fleet of Dragons, then I would rule over the entire continent of these wretched races."

"We do not need the lost Dragons, my Queen. The army that awaits your orders will bring all the riches you desire from your northern lands," said Lord Tarique, who had strode up to the fire and removed his battle helmet, his long black hair tumbling around his shoulders.

"You know that our northern borders stop but within a few miles of here," replied the Watch Wizard, his eyes narrowing in disgust at the sight of the Lord.

"You will find that on the revised borders, Queen Beatrice the Third is now ruler of the Golden Valley," added Lord Tarique, who had brought out from his cloak a rolled- up map of the eastern lands of Ursalane.

"The treasure within that valley will be needed, Wizard. We will order the Dwarves of Pavelem that their stay within the Queen's lands is coming to a close, and they will see reason when you explain that the whole of my army is camped on their southern borders," ordered the Queen, who was rubbing at her sore legs.

The Watch Wizard walked away from the pair, his head whirling. This had been the last thing he had expected. The Golden Valley was already a battle field, a bloody one at that. He turned and faced them, his arms reaching out to them in friendship.

"My Queen, upon your journey home, do not sleep or replenish yourself with food or drink. I do hope you get over the illness before winter sets in," he spoke with interlaced words of magic. The Lord had brought forth his sword, his face had turned crimson with rage.

"Sarratt, can you tell the Lord of his travels this evening," suggested the Watch Wizard, whose right hand had placed itself upon the forehead of the Queen.

Sarratt walked from the shadows and opened his arms to the maddened Lord.

"My Lord, your journey home will be one of pleasure, but remember! Do not unseat yourself from your stallion, you will feel all the better for it," he said in the same manner as the Watch Wizard. Other words, words of magic entering the mind of the Lord, Sarratt placed the sword back within its scabbard and placed his right hand upon the head of Lord Tarique, whose features were still enraged.

"You will have no need of refreshments this evening for you are in such a rush to depart this place with your army, who will sing to you every day that you travel," said the younger wizard, who himself now felt drained of mind and spirit, for the will of the Lord was great.

The Queen and her Lord departed in haste; forgotten

were her dreams of conquering the northern lands. Lord Tarique was in a trance, he mounted his black stallion and shouted for the whole army of men to start the long march back to Traxit. Both would need medical assistance when they returned, for five weeks on the road without food, water or sleep would take its toll on both body and soul.

"They will come back prepared and knowing we have the power of the spoken word," said the young wizard, who had slumped into a chair.

"They will not bother us until autumn; many things can happen within a season, as you are going to find out," replied the Watch Wizard, who had also sat down, pipe in his hand and a mug of hot whiskey ale, brewed by the Tolls of Yea Bor.

"Wherever I travel, I will endeavour to seek out the persecuted and seek out those with evil intent. I will deliver your message wherever I am sent, Watch Wizard."

"Good," sighed the Watch Wizard, who had closed his eyes, thinking of how awful life had become within the lands of Ursalane.

Chapter Two

The four scurrying figures flinched at the crack of thunder, their yellow faces illuminated by the forked lightning which had struck a nearby tree, fire engulfing the entire trunk, its branches casting finger-like shadows towards the marauding Gnomes.

Treak slid down into the brook, his fingers clicking, his left hand coming up above his head. He was well aware of the dangers of travelling while in the midst of a Great Eastern Divide storm. Not many of the races within the continent of Ursalane risked their lives in the storm season. Those who did normally did not get to tell of the horrors of being hunted by the lightning, their charred remains the result of their foolishness.

"We need to find some bramble, otherwise we're dead, Crikken!"

Crikken had slid right into the freezing brook, his muffled swearing for his ears only.

"Two miles, west through Tarsit and being here isn't the brightest thing you have done, blessed one."

Kellek and the youngest of the four Gnomes had not followed the other two down into the waters of the brook. They had managed to stop near the top of the steep sides of the water channel. Akkia was the youngest of the four Gnomes, this being his first raid on the Elven city of Follonday, which still lay a good one hundred miles away. He was frightened and totally lost; he had spent all of his life within the Gnome homelands of Gutox, the volcanic region of Ursalane, a place in which only the Gnomes could survive. His homesickness was becoming acute.

Another thunder bolt of lightning streaked across the skies, this time a little closer to the four Gnomes, missing the woodlands and smashing harmlessly into the sodden earth. "Treak, are we going to die"? he asked, his whole body shivering in the cold of the night.

"Not tonight, young one. I, the blessed one, will steer us through whatever the Gods fire at us. Through this woodland we must go, as silent as the ghosts of the lost that wander these vile lands."

"He means the likes of us, who are hunted like a plague of vermin. You should be scared, very scared!" added Crikken, scrambling back up the steep slopes of the brook. His backpack drenched and dripping, though the contents would be dry, weighed heavily on his shoulders.

"We may be the smallest of the races, but we are the biggest of heart and soul. We do not kill for happiness, nor hatred. We kill others for our survival; we kill for fear, for the fear of a trapped Gnome is something you do not want to encounter, so! Akkia, stop your heart from racing and concentrate on the night before us. This woodland is ours tonight, let us go forward and rob and kill where we can," replied the leader of the Gnome raiding party, his fingers snapping and clicking with each word he spoke, his face contorted in hatred.

"This would be easier if we didn't have to travel in bright yellow trousers and a bright red cloak. The Elves dress in different tones of green and are virtually impossible to see and the Dwarves dress in browns, equally impossible to see within woodlands. We are like shining beacons for all to see, although you, my blessed one, are now a colour that may save your life this evening. You two, into the mud and slime, be covered with the slime that may save your lives," ordered Treak, ushering the two Gnomes into the freezing brook.

"It's freezing!" exclaimed the youngest of the four Gnomes.

Finally, after some swearing from Treak, the pair scrambled out of the brook, his fingers clicking and his hands slapping his thigh, which said even more than the spoken word, for clicks and slaps had always been part of the language of the Gnomes.

"Where are we?" asked Akkia, his whole body still shivering. His lips had actually started to turn blue.

"Tarsit, a strange place full of strange Dwarves. All they do is harvest the Wood Pearl trees. Only been here once and nearly died. Elves wander this place as well, horrible Elves, stinking Elves with long blades and arrows," came the abrupt response from Crikken.

In unison the other three Gnomes spat on the sodden earth, each cursing the race of the Elf.

"Crikken is right," added Treak, clicking his fingers in disgust. " No mercy will be given to four marauding Gnomes this night, so hush now and keep your eyes on me. I will lead, Crikken will bring up the rear. "

Treak scurried into the blackness of Tarsit, the trees looming into view, massive trunks with doors and windows, lights from within casting ominous shadows which flickered and danced upon the sodden earth. Luckily for the four Gnomes, the electrical storm which was still hunting things to kill was moving towards the Great Eastern Divide. The winds had died away but the rain was still heavy in its downfall.

They had moved quickly through the massive trees, their eyes forever looking out for movement. If they were to be caught now, their fate would be sealed quickly: a knife into the heart, an arrow through the eye - the preferred way of the Elf - or being caught by the invisible traps, which lay under foot, concealed within the ground. But these were mainly found on the outskirts of Tarsit and easily spotted.

Treak adjusted his backpack and looked into the woodlands of Tarsit. He could not see very much, but in the darkness he could feel the presence of the ancient mighty trees, some measuring eighty feet across, enormous trunks which could be and had been turned into dwellings of the resident Dwarves. Over five thousand of these trees grew within this area of Ursalane and nowhere else, but the main reason why the Dwarves had settled so far from their homeland was because of the fruits of the Wood Pearl tree, a small oval shaped wooden fruit, which when lit, burned for weeks, it's heat not diminishing. But it was the treasure of the golden Wood pearl which was most sought after. This pearl was rare, though much coveted, especially by the Wizards of the Watch, a college of Wizards who resided on the eastern side of the Great Eastern Divide, the mountain range which split the continent of Ursalane in two. They often visited the woodland, giving help to the residents and giving wealth to those who harvested the golden pearls, which were very rare. A golden wood pearl was a thing of magic, giving the Wizards insights into the world about them, a key to the possibilities of what they might control.

Treak set out through the smaller trees, his eyes looking for danger. He knew that if they were spotted, they would not return to their homeland, a land of fire and heat, a place only the Gnomes could survive, the sulphur giving them the yellow skin, the acrid atmosphere stunting the growth of a Gnome. The tallest Gnome recorded was five feet, but in the eyes of the wizards, they stood just as tall as the Elves, who stood several feet off the ground, with the Dwarf standing between five and six feet. The Gnomes were the smallest race which walked the lands, the biggest being the Trolls, who on average walked the lands looking down on everyone else.

Treak and his marauding group ran from tree to tree, utterly petrified at the thought of being caught within this strange settlement. The further they ventured into the woodlands of Tarsit, the brighter it became. Great lanterns which held wood pearls hung from branches, turning the night into day. It was here Treak stopped suddenly, his eyes catching a glimpse of a distant wood pearl tree, one which was being guarded. Two Dwarves with axes in their hands were stationed around this particular tree. He clicked his fingers and slapped his thigh three times, calling the other Gnomes to also stop in their tracks.

"Treasure awaits and it will be ours, my brothers, my kinsmen, my beloved. Bless me now and bless our homelands, and bless the ones we are about to kill."

The other three Gnomes gulped and felt their hearts race; all of a sudden they knew that these coming minutes could well be their last. The mighty wood pearl tree was indeed a monster of a tree, some one hundred feet across and circled by a white picket fence. No lights came from this tree, but Treak had noted that there were at least five doorways and countless windows carved out of the trunk.

Treak clicked his fingers and brought his left hand to his shoulder, his fist clenched. He nodded at Crikken and shook his head at the other two, his right hand gesturing that they crouch and await the result of the deaths of the two Dwarves, who were totally unaware of the presence of the four marauding Gnomes.

Treak actually smiled at his old friend as he brought

forth his thin daggers, one for each hand. Then he was gone, running with the knowledge that if Crikken did not do as he did at the same time, one of the Dwarves would most certainly call the alarm.

The white picket fence came hurtling towards Treak and he sprang through the air, his hands resting on the white fence before his feet hit the sodden earth. He was still fifteen paces away from his target, the Dwarf turning his gaze towards the noise of the Gnome's impact. He saw the Gnome at once and was about to cry out when the first of the two daggers entered his throat. He brought his hands up to clench at his throat just as Treak finished him off, decapitating him quickly. Treak looked up to see Crikken doing as he had just done, his eyes full of excitement. His breathing was heavy, but he smiled at Treak, and the smile was returned. Treak retrieved his daggers and wiped the blood from them. He waved for the other two Gnomes to come to him, which they did at once, helping them to drag the broken frames of the two Dwarves into the giant wood pearl tree. After Crikken had first picked the lock of the small door, within the tree they stared at each other trying to make their eyes adjust to the darkness. Then they separated and searched the entire tree, coming back empty-handed.

"There is treasure here; I know this because of the two guards, but where would you keep this treasure? Where would they hide wood pearls, Crikken?"

"If it was as you say, the wood pearl, then I would have left them upon the root, for the Wizards to harvest. Your treasure is below, blessed one," replied the Gnome, who had already walked over to the hatch that led into the bowels of the earth.

"But we must be swift. I would not want to be caught here. Come and let us see the wonders of the wood pearl tree," added Treak, his fingers clicking and his left hand slapping his thigh in excitement.

Kellek and the youngest of the Gnomes, Akkia, gasped out loud when they finally reached the cavernous room deep underground,for it was illuminated with the shine of the golden wood pearl, great swathes of them hanging from the root of this mighty tree.

"How can this be!" exclaimed Treak, wonder showing on his face.

"And they are ready to be harvested. This is truly breathtaking, blessed one. There is enough treasure here to change our race. To give this to the Gnomes will be the crowning glory of our lives," replied an open- mouthed Crikken.

Treak walked to the nearest drooping root and seized a handful of the golden wood pearls, tiny and oval in shape, but not solid gold, just golden in colour. He felt the warmth seeping into his hands. The others had also taken swathes of pearls from the roots of the monstrous tree, each marvelling at their beauty, but time was running out for the Gnomes. This tree would have others coming. Dwarves would be bringing Elves and Wizards to show them the wealth of this one tree.

"Empty your packs," ordered Treak, who had already

emptied his, though he did put back the life- saving sleeping wrap. This one item would keep him warm and dry during the wettest of nights. Eventually they had filled their backpacks with the golden wood pearls and had ascended the steep ladders which led them back to the ground floor of the tree. Crikken went straight to the window and peered out into the woodland. What he saw again got his heart pounding. Several Dwarves with axes on show were having a heated argument. One in particular was pointing at the tree; his whole stocky frame was shaking.

"We have company, blessed one," stated Crikken flatly.

Treak rushed to the window and looked at the Dwarves with hatred. He clicked his fingers and slapped his thigh four times. He then went back to the hatchway and descended the ladders. He was gone not more than three minutes, but when he did return he beckoned them to come and join him, which they did.

"Crikken, how far was the sacred Bramble wood? Did we pass it yesterday?" he asked urgently. Wisps of smoke had already started to enter the ground floor of the tree.

"We passed the wood this morning; five miles will see us to safety."

"What have you done?" asked Kellek nervously.

"I have given the Dwarves a fire which will burn for days. We leave now. Do not falter nor trip, for death will follow us all the way back home."

They left on the southern side through an even smaller door, Treak appearing first. He looked over at the group of Dwarves which by this time had realised that the most important tree within the woodlands was on fire. Treak heard panic within those voices, but even as he reached the white picket fence, he heard the voice of an Elf, higher pitched than the gruff deeper tones of the Dwarf. This worried the Gnome; an Elf would kill them with ease. Elves were his worst fear. The Gnomes feared the Elf more than any other race, mainly because of the way they hunted Gnomes relentlessly just for their own pleasure. Hundreds had lost their lives upon the Plains of Desire. Treak though could not afford to become distracted from his immediate goal, which was to find a safe passage out of the woodlands of Tarsit. After what seemed an age, the four Gnomes were back at the brook into which he and Crikken had slid.

"We need to get to the sacred Bramble wood, blessed one," stated Crikken flatly.

"The Bramble wood you speak of, my friend, is too far away."

"Then we are doomed!" cried the youngest of the Gnomes, who was still looking back at the woodlands, expecting at any moment an army of Dwarves to come charging at them.

"But you said we passed it, you said it was only a matter of miles away!" exclaimed Kellek, who was bent over trying in vain to get his breathing under control.

"I was mistaken; the Bramble wood we passed yesterday was lesser Bramble, though it did show promise," replied Crikken, who was wiping away some of the mud and slime from his face.

Distant thunder boomed and the skies to the east were illuminated by the fading storm, though the rain was still falling. Then another noise started to fill the skies around the four Gnomes, a sound that had them shaking with fear: war drums, pounding out the message that the four were now the hunted.

"Bless these lands, bless the animals which will help conceal us and bless ourselves," said Treak, who had not stopped clicking his fingers and slapping his thigh.

"Bless all that keep us from the stinking Dwarves," added Crikken.

Treak then set out, climbing over the first of many hedgerows that would stand in their way, before they would find safety within the lesser Bramble wood.

Within the wooded community of Tarsit, all hell was let loose; the Dwarves had swarmed around the giant wood pearl tree, trying in vain to put out the ferocious fire which was beginning to lick its way up the mighty trunk. It was during the panic that the Elf known as Arrun, spotted the footprints upon the sodden earth. He followed them all the way to the tree and sprinted around the tree until he came to the small doorway through which the Gnomes had exited. He dropped to his knees and again saw the footprints, heading away and out of Tarsit. He then sought out the Dwarf Chieftain, explaining what he had found. Within the hour, great booms of the Dwarf war drums signalled to every Dwarf , who was within the Dwarf age of fighting, to come straight to the eastern borders of Tarsit. Fifty hardened

Dwarfs and one Elf set out in pursuit of the vermin of their lands.

"Dwarfs build the most stupid of things," moaned Crikken, whose yellow boots were sodden.

"These streams feed the land within the summer months," replied Treak.

"You know what I mean!"

"In a way I do, but when the Dwarf decides to build something, he will not stop until it is done. Look at the cobbled trade route which snakes it way all the way to Pavelem. Now that is something to behold, my blessed one," added Treak, who thought of himself as a fountain of knowledge.

Crikken did not reply, just shook his head in dismay. He was cold and very tired; he looked around at Kellek and Akkia and saw the same look of despair.

"We are doomed if we do not reach the lesser Bramble wood, blessed one."

"We will not die on this day, for you are going to find the sacred Bramble wood before the stinking Dwarfs find us," replied the forever optimistic Gnome.

"Then let us make haste, for I can smell Dwarf on the wind," said Crikken, who had already started to run towards the east, the other three falling into line.

That morning proved to be the hardest since they had set out from their homelands all those weeks ago. They had not slept for two days, fatigue was beginning to creep into their bones, the youngest had fallen several times and was now some way behind the other three. He knew that they would not wait for him, nor would they offer assistance; such was the way of the Gnome. Even Treak was feeling dead on his feet; every small water channel seemed like a river and every hedgerow seemed like a mountain. On they trudged, the morning passing into afternoon. They did not stop for drink or food, and they knew that if they did not make the lesser Bramble wood, they were dead.

"We have missed the Bramble wood we saw yesterday. We have travelled southwards, my blessed one. Let us hope the farmers have been lazy and let Bramble wood grow," said Crikken.

The farmers indeed had to chop away at the dreaded weed every few months. Here it was known as Dragon weed. In places like the sacred Bramble wood, the weed stretched away for many miles, and grew to a height of fifty feet, a place the Gnomes had learned to use as a passage south from their volcanic homelands.

It was Akkia who spotted the Bramble wood, some distance to the north of where they were trudging. The sight of the weed brought them renewed vigour. They hurried as quickly as they could, smiling at each other. Kellek even managed to laugh out loud; such was his delight in seeing the safety of the Bramble wood.

"No thorns will harm us for we regard you as a sacred place. I cut you so that you will become stronger. I bless this Bramble wood with the first cut I make," cried Crikken, who had begun to cut a passage through the tangled mass of interlocking spiked vines. Kellek and

Akkia watched closely for this was a craft which took years to achieve. But the most amazing craft was being done by the leader of the Gnomes: Treak was replacing the cut vines in such a way, that even if a Dwarf was to pass within three feet of their opening, it would appear that the weed had not been cut. Treak had spent many years honing his skills; though the process was slow, it was worth everything, for when the Dwarfs failed again in their hunt, they would swear that the Gnomes were being given assistance by the Wizards of the Watch. It gave the Gnomes a magical presence within the southern lands of Ursalane.

The last of the sun's rays were setting the sky red in colour; the storm had drifted right over the towering peaks of the Great Eastern Divide, the sullen clouds giving way to large patches of the coming night sky.

The horns that broke the evening silence brought forth a fear amongst the four Gnomes. The drums which followed gave them an even greater fear, for this meant that the Dwarfs would not give up the chase and they were very close. Treak clicked his fingers several times, instructing Crikken to halt his cutting, which he did at once. But it was the youngest of the four Gnomes that was now shaking violently; Akkia felt like a trapped animal just waiting to be slaughtered. Another great booming horn sounded even closer still. Treak noticed straight away that Akkia had gone into shock; his eyes were closed and his whole frame was shaking violently. What Treak did next nearly cost the Gnomes their lives. As soon as

Treak did it he cursed himself for his stupidity, for he lay his hand upon the shoulder of the petrified Gnome, this causing Akkia to jump in fear and scream as loudly as he could. The scream was soon cut off, thanks to the lightning reflexes of Treak, who had clamped his hand upon the mouth of the youngest Gnome and had brought him to his knees. The closest of the Dwarfs though had heard the startled scream; he yelled for everyone to stop.

"It came from within the Dragon weed."

"Over there!" exclaimed another.

The Chieftain came at once, bounding over the sodden earth, the grasses long and tufted.

"Where is the Elf?" he yelled.

Arrun sprinted back from where he thought the Gnomes might be travelling. There were no signs under this grassland; too many cattle and sheep wandered around, masking any footprints the Gnomes might leave.

"The Dragon weed is home to countless vermin, but anything bigger than a field mouse would struggle to get within the twisted thorns. He was mistaken," pronounced the Elf confidently.

"I heard the scream of a Gnome; it came from there," replied the Dwarf, his hand pointing towards the hiding Gnomes.

The Elf walked towards the Bramble, his ears picking out various little sounds. Amongst these he swore he could detect heavy breathing, laboured; he waved his hand and called for silence.

Treak did not remove his hand from the shaking form

of Akkia; he knew now that the Elf was close to trapping them. He looked at Crikken who was pointing at a pair of roosting Crows. Treak nodded just the once and tried to hold his breath. Crikken reached inside his cloak and brought forth a hollow piece of volcanic rock; it was quite long and was a treasured weapon amongst the race of Gnomes. Crikken then loaded it with a small dart. Looking up into the bramble, he made sure he had a straight line of sight.

The silent group of Dwarfs were watching the Elf as he wandered ever closer to the Dragon weed. He could now definitely hear the breathing of something which was in fear. He stopped right in front of the mass of thorns and peered within. He knew nothing bigger than a mouse could be within this tangled mass of thorns, but there it was, the breathing.

The sudden shriek entered the ears of the Elf with such effect, that he had to cover them. He looked up into the skies to see a pair of Crows reeling away to the east. He shook his head and turned to see the Dwarf who had called the alarm being slapped around the head.

"Time wasted here is time we have not got; the thieving Gnomes will be halfway home if we have to stop at every little scream you hear. As you all know, the lands within Gutox are poisonous, we can not enter that place, so let us get going," he screamed, signalling for the horns to blow and for the drums to be beaten.

The Elf watched the Dwarfs for some minutes, his mind still considering the breathing he had heard, but he snapped himself out of his own illusion and sprinted after the hunting party of Dwarfs, his feet making no impressions upon the sodden earth, his long tied back hair whooshing behind, such was the speed he was running. Within minutes he was walking beside the Dwarf chieftain. He spoke quickly to him and was gone, heading towards the Great Eastern Divide.

The four Gnomes did not move a muscle for many minutes, such was the fear they had just experienced.

"Fool!" cursed Treak,, prodding Akkia in the back.

"Idiot!" added Crikken, who resumed chopping at the Bramble.

Kellek did not say anything, for he was exhausted. All he longed for was his body wrap. Treak clicked his fingers and slapped both his thighs.

"Let us bless the birds that gave flight."

"Bless their flight," added Kellek.

"I bless their screams which saved us from my stupidity," said Akkia, who had regained his composure.

"I have located the heart of the Bramble. Our dome waits," cried Crikken, who was chopping away even quicker. He burst into the dome with a laugh, for at the heart of the Bramble wood were the fruits of the vine, large berries, which the Gnomes would always eat whenever they entered a dome. They had a calming effect; something within them made the Gnomes extremely happy and talkative.

"Berries!!" exclaimed Treak, clicking his fingers in glee.

"Tonight will be a night to bless," added Kellek.

The four Gnomes arranged the dome. Crikken chopped away at some of the bramble, making the dome wider. Treak kicked away the dead vines which littered the floor. Kellek and Akkia had already started to harvest the berries, putting them upon the middle of the dome. They then stripped naked and got within their own body wrap, instantly feeling the warmth from the sleeping bag which had been made from within their homelands, each one retaining the heat of the volcanoes. The four of them sat within their wraps and started feasting on the berries, mushrooms and dried meats which they had brought all the way from Gutox. The talk that night was light and filled with laughter and memories, each of the Gnomes telling tales of their past. Though sleep was approaching, Treak decided with a few clicks that everyone would sleep that night with no watch set. However, as the others were soon fast asleep, he was calculating in his mind how to get back home safely; he was mapping out the way home when he drifted into a fitful sleep.

The party of Dwarfs had set up camp. When the blackness of the night became too much even for the Elf, the chieftain charged around the camp shouting orders and reprimanding his charges for the silliest little thing. Arrun had walked away and was looking east towards the Great Eastern Divide, marvelling at the sheer size of the mountain range, which stretched from the southern coast, right up into the lands of the Troll. It was while he was looking that he noticed far, far away small bobbing lights, many of them.

"I have a tent ready for you, Elf," said the chieftain, who had followed the Elf when he had seen him walk into the grasslands. What the Dwarf did not want, was for the Elf to decide he had had enough of the hunt, which had happened in the past.

"Can you see what I can see?" he asked quietly.

"Where are you looking at, Elf?"

"There!" he replied, pointing towards the bobbing lights.

"No, my eyesight is not what it was."

"I will be back when the new day dawns. Set watches. Be on your guard; I do not like what I see, Chieftain: many lights, many lights," said the Elf who had already started to run into the blackness of the night.

The chieftain charged back into the camp and shouted even more orders; he would have no sleep either that night.

The Elf returned just before the breaking of dawn, his face stricken with worry.

"Where is the chieftain?"

"Here."

"Forget chasing Gnomes, we have something which I never thought I would see!" exclaimed the Elf. "Pack up everything and go back to Tarsit, as quickly as you can."

"What madness do you speak of, Elf," growled the Dwarf. "We are hunting down Gnomes who have stolen the rarest of all our harvests; we are going nowhere."

The light was seeping onto the lower grasslands of the Great Eastern Divide, rolling grasslands that were inter crossed with fences and water channels, all of them built by Dwarf craftsmen. The chieftain was walking away from the Elf when he heard a low deep rumbling within the sodden earth. He stopped dead in his tracks and looked east, then stumbled backwards a few paces.

"What is this madness I look upon!" exclaimed the Dwarf.

"It is madness born of evil, marching straight towards where we are standing," replied the Elf, who had loosened his bow and brought forth several arrows.

"What of the Gnomes! Do they get away with such treasure?" he asked in a foul manner.

"The Gnomes are probably dead, the wood pearls scattered amongst the lower farmlands."

"Then what are we to do?" screamed the chieftain, his battle axe falling into his enormous hands. By now nearly all of the Dwarfs were staring at the distant army.

"Protect where you live, Chieftain, though I fear the worst from that which I am gazing upon," replied the Elf, who had already set off to intercept the front of the massive army.

Chapter Three

Within the Fingertip Mountains stood the crumbling ruins of an ancient castle. Long since had its roof gone, long from the memory of everyone except the three wizards. Three weeks earlier, they strode as one, out from the darkness of the ancient mountains and into the twilight of what appeared to be the end of a normal day. But as historians would write in the future, this would pinpoint the beginnings of the Wizards' Winter, for behind them on the western horizon, a black storm was brewing, though no lightning or thunder would emanate from its swirling clouds until the wizards decided that the moment had come for them to take the lands of the Troll.

The three wizards knew that this was the beginning of a new age, a time of such evil; even they would risk their lives in the pursuit of total dominance of the continent of Ursalane. Each of the different races were unaware of the wizards, such had been the time they had spent within the crumbling keep. Even they had lost count of the decades they had worked within the dungeons, casting spell after spell, creating new hideous forms of life. But the one they sought had remained hidden deep within the bowels of the earth, avoiding the traps which had been so carefully woven by the three wizards. But even he, lord of everything he ever touched, could not run away forever. His decision to be caught had been an easy one in the end. In the coming years though he would grow to hate the wizards as he had hated no other.

The wizard who went by the name of Prestersfordle had estimated that they would need to ensure that the evil being would have a countless supply of blood. The empty caged areas would have to be filled and kept full if they were to have any chance of bringing the one into their world. He walked with a stoop, his back hunched, his awkward limp making him look like he was in some pain. The other wizards walked upright. The one next to Prestersfordle was known as Fastanes, the physician. Shorter than the other two and carrying some weight, his stomach bulging out from the confines of his black robe, he was the one who had successfully worked out how to transfuse blood from one animal to another. His secret experiments though had already killed dozens of hapless Gnomes and thousands of small animals. His wobbling face was constantly on the lookout for more victims. On the end was the master of the Keep, the most powerful wizard that had ever lived. Marsukia knew he had turned away from his brotherhood at Witches Watch many decades ago. The path had always been the dark one. He had the power of many things; his thoughts could control the masses and his fingers knew the signs that could kill without a spoken word. His eyes burned a bright red; gone were the green ones he had been born with. In fact, the whole physical appearance of the wizard had dramatically changed over the years. If he had allowed his two fellow wizards to look upon his head, they would surely gasp. So the hood which covered the wizard's face, covered up many hidden things he had kept from the other two. He walked with purpose and a focus so intense that his whole body pulsated with energy; the air around him crackled and popped as he passed.

Down the grassy banks they marched, their thoughts as one. The three stepped onto the flatlands with a crunch, for this was a land made up solely of rock, great sheets of granite, twinkling in the fading light. Like vast steps they fell onto the legendary Plains of Desire, a desert of grass, completely flat and lifeless, save for the grasses. It stretched for thousands of miles to the south. The only things which cut through its dominance of the landscape were the great Elf rivers, four in all, their destination the magnificent falls of Follonday, the forest lands of the Elf.

Marsukia looked upon the heaving masses which stood on the Plains of Desire and knew that this would be the army that would crush the Trolls of Yea-Bor, and then crush all of the other races that lived within his world, a world that would be as black as the stormiest night, a world devoid of life. The Goblins had travelled great distances, coming with their cousins, the bigger Hobgoblins, from the northern wastes. They had fallen under the spells of the wizards, but even without the controlling spells, they would have come; such was the hatred they felt for the fairer races. Even bigger in size were the mountain Ogres. Again, these had travelled with the Goblins. They numbered less, but such was their ferocity, they were indeed a formidable fighting machine. But standing right at the front of the thousands of creatures were the Brethren. Small in number, less than a hundred, these had been created within the dungeons of the Keep, in front of the mighty furnaces which some of the Hobgoblins had repaired. Spells never before spoken had been thought up by Marsukia; the Brethren had come into the world screaming. The wizard had granted them simple protective spells, ones they would need if the wizards were to keep control of the creatures which even now were starting to chant deep guttural noises, their heads bobbing up and down. To look upon his sea of destruction was the culmination of years of sleepless nights, years spent within the deep dungeons. Now he spoke silently and rose into the failing light of the day. Marsukia lifted his hands high above his head, his black robe billowing about his slight frame. He spoke to each and every one of them, though no words came from his lips.

"Remember the days you were the hunted. Remember the years you have spent in exile. Today is the first day of a new age; a winter is coming to the races you hate so much. Go forth as one. I am the master of all the lands you walk upon. Failure is death; success is immortality. Let the storm begin."

The noise created by the thousands actually shook the lands. Simple handmade drums had started to beat to the rhythm of the marching armies. Long trumpets blew into the night skies. The floating wizard watched as the heaving masses slowly trudged past him. The hours passed into a full day and still they marched past the point the wizard had been the previous evening. He had stayed for a few hours, but such was the work he still needed to do that he left the Plains of Desire and returned to the ancient crumbling fortress with the other two wizards.

Marsukia had felt free while he was within the sky. How he longed to travel to other places, sit within the Troll kingdom, stand within the mountain city of the Dwarfs, walk within the forests of the Elf, claim his right to be the master of all he desired. The human race of Traxit was of great importance to the wizard. He had once been one of them, had been taught by the wizards of Witches Watch, a place he would personally crush, for his hatred was great for the wizards who taught there. But time was running out for the races of Ursalane. Marsukia knew he had to be patient, for even he, with all his power, could not hope to conquer all without the help of the one he and the other two were trying to bring into this world. As the three wizards entered the roofless hall of the Keep, Marsukia told of how pleased he was with the progress of the armies that were now on the first stage of Marsukia's master plan of the total destruction of all the races. He bade Fastanes a good evening's toil and waited until the squat figure had disappeared until he spoke with Prestersfordle, who was hunched over as if in pain.

"I have an errand for you," he said flatly, his voice quiet.

"Yes, dark one!" exclaimed Prestersfordle, his head tilting upwards to look at the blood red eyes of Marsukia.

"I would have travelled there myself, but I fear that I would become distracted; my work here is too important."

"Where?" It was a simple question, but said with venom.

"The halls of the Trolls. Tell them of what approaches them. Order them to send to me a thousand of their young. Give them some hope, though none will be in the offering."

"Hope is the word all cling onto. I will offer them hope, dark one," wheezed the stooping wizard, who had started to cough violently, a spattering of blood coming from his lips.

"Kill one while the head of the hall looks on," ordered Marsukia, who turned and made his way to his dilapidated rooms.

"But what of the evil one?" asked Prestersfordle, wiping his bloodied lips with a grin. "Nothing can be done while there is no blood," replied Marsukia.

The doorway to the rooms of Marsukia was without any doors, the rusted hinges hanging limply on the rotting framework. The windows were open to the elements and in the far left corner, part of the actual fortress had collapsed, exposing the inner courtyard. The wizard did not need to be within any structure, for the cold he never felt, such was the heat within his being. He walked within the room and looked upon the mass of guts that lay on the cold slabs. The room had once been a torture chamber. Still within, there were machines of horror. All had long since stopped working, rusted up and many broken, but the wizard had rebuilt one and had amused himself for some days with the Gnomes he had captured. But he had soon become bored with the screams and the sound of bones cracking. He walked to the desks, which were full of maps: maps of the continent of Ursalane that he himself had drawn. Each mountain peak he had clearly named, each valley had a number. It was like a grid and his finger was resting on the peak of Mount Thor, the mountain of the Troll.

"Little do they know of the terror I am planning," he said to himself.

Meanwhile, Fastanes the physician was staring out of the small window from within his room. This had once been a room where the evil Troll had kept his large collection of weapons, though none remained. The physician had turned it into a laboratory. There were steaming jars and bottles stacked high on the shelves which had once held swords, axes and bows and arrows. Right in the middle of his room, there was a long table, which had turned a dark red at the edges. This was the spillage of the countless ruptured innards. The blood had soaked itself within the wood. Clamps of various sizes were arranged about the table. These were for the different species of animal which had to be strapped firmly down. His thoughts of what he was doing were playing havoc with his emotions. He knew he had the power of life or death with the animals and more recently, Gnomes that were strapped upon his table. But something had always been within his heart and soul; be it small, life was precious. The clerics of the Rainbow Falls had taught him the skills of the knife; little did they realize that he would follow one with so much evil within his soul. The smell of the roasting pig brought him to his senses. His appetite was enormous; the other two ate seldom. In fact he could not remember seeing Marsukia eat for the last year or so. Shaking his head, which made his cheeks wobble, he made his way through to the kitchens. This was his place; this was where he was happiest, eating until he could not eat anymore. His mouth watering, he prepared the roasted pig for the feast that was going to see him through the coming night.

"Fastanes," came the voice of his master. It was not a shout, for the wizard had no need. The voice simply went within the physician's head.

"I am trying to eat!" he whispered.

"Forget the pig, I need you to come and work on the body."

"Coming," came the disgusted reply. Fastanes' thoughts, if they could be read by his master, would have caused him serious trouble.

A small bird was chirping from within a small cage, its

little body still shaking from the shock of being caught earlier that day. Fastanes did something then that would never leave his thoughts for the coming weeks - he let it go.

Marsukia was still bent over the maps, his finger moving down the Great Eastern Divide, the mountain range which was also known as the backbone of the continent.

"Marsukia," said the physician quietly as he walked slowly into the room. He did not like to spend that much time here. The heaving mass of guts on the cold stone slabs gave him shivers; he knew it to be the most evil thing with which he had ever been in contact.

"You eat too much," remarked the bent wizard.

"Unlike you, I have kept my taste for the cooked meat of the land."

"You have some new blood for me, I hear?" Marsukia asked, knowing this to be the case.

"Blood!" replied Fastanes, his thoughts still on the food he was craving.

This caused Marsukia to turn, his blood red eyes staring at the rounded figure of the physician. Fastanes quickly explained that the Brethren had indeed brought some new blood; it was the blood of an Elf.

"The Brethren have done the unexpected. The Elf, even for me to catch, is nigh impossible. How was this so?" he asked.

"The Brethren we sent to the northern forests of Follonday, said they ran and ensnared the bewildered creature. They did not kill the one, but brought him to the dungeons. There he waits. He does not talk; he looks scared," explained Fastanes, who was rubbing his stomach.

"Then we have the hot blood of an Elf. The signs are indeed improving. Fetch the Elf to me," ordered Marsukia.

"But what of the food that awaits me? Can the slaughter of the Elf wait a few hours?" moaned the physician.

"You know I wait for no one." It was a simple response, but the physician said no more. He scurried from the stinking room where the pile of guts lay and called for the Brethren to fetch the poor Elf. He thought of the Elf and felt pity. He stopped then and realized that he had a problem. He did not go back to the wizard's room at once. He was starving. The roasted pig was soon within his bulging stomach; his grease ridden face seemed happier now he had eaten. The screams that filtered down the stone walls of the corridor reached the ears of the physician on his way back to Marsukia's room. The Elf had died quickly at the hands of the evil wizard, the blood pouring into the glass jars which stood next to the dark one. Fastanes entered and tried not to look at the limp, lifeless figure of the Elf, who had obviously been thrown into the shadows of the room. He kept his gaze downwards and proceeded to inject the hot blood directly into the guts. A figure suddenly appeared before the crouching figure of Fastanes, its head looking past him and directly at the standing wizard. Thirty seconds later, the figure was once more a pile of bloodied guts, heaving up and down. But before it had returned to the twilight world, where it neither lived nor died, it spoke a language never heard before. The actual floor and walls vibrated with each syllable spoken.

"What was all that?" asked the retreating physician, who had pulled the black robe tightly around his body. The wind had howled through the open windows, sending a shiver through the body of the physician.

"He requires more than blood. 'The seeds of the living' is what I think he said. His talk though is hard to understand. The seeds of the living, Fastanes, I want to find the seeds of the living. Give this your time for the coming hours. Tell me where we can find them before the Sun shines down on the Plains of Desire," ordered Marsukia, who knew that if anyone could solve riddles, it was the physician.

Marsukia felt that the time he had spent over the past few months was at last reaping rewards. The demon had spoken to him, not to the physician, but to him. He would not sleep that night, for sleep as was the need of food, had long since proved to be a burden for the wizard. He stood before his desks and let his fingers run down the Great Eastern Divide. He studied each and every mile. His fingers stopped just past a wooded place and he tapped his index finger on the small farming community of Tarsit.

Fastanes also spent the night awake, though he longed for his bed. He needed his sleep, but the wizard had made it quite clear that he expected an answer by the morning. The hundreds of books lay scattered everywhere, small piles near the window and extremely high piles near the stone walls. His shelves were all being used for the experiments he had been conducting. Dawn wasn't far away and the physician had just started to read another book on satanic rights and myths of the past. These had all been written years previously, within the walled city of Traxit, home to the human race of Ursalane. He sensed the rising of a new Sun, knowing that Marsukia never slept. The pages were turned at speed, the physician taking information into his mind at an alarming rate. Suddenly he stopped; his chest rose as his heart started to beat more quickly. He turned back the few pages he had seconds earlier scanned. There it was, a recipe entitled 'THE DEVIL'S SEED'.

Marsukia watched as the physician entered his room. He did not smile, for that emotion had long since left his being.

"You have found the answer to the riddle," he stated flatly, his red eyes showing no emotion.

"Long hours I spent and no sleep have I had," moaned Fastanes, his face showing the signs of fatigue.

"Sleep is not important."

"Not to you, but I relish the dark hours," Fastanes replied sternly, his patience wearing thin.

"Then hurry and tell me of what you have learned," said the wizard calmly.

"That the seeds of the living are the very seeds we have been using for years; wood pearls are the seeds of the living," explained Fastanes, happy to see that the figure of the wizard stepped back a pace.

"Then we have what we need; we have plenty," said Marsukia, who had rested his hand again on the maps of Ursalane.

"We do have plenty, that is true, though we require the golden ones, and these are very rare."

"I thought of the wood pearls, but I too have never heard of the golden wood pearls being harvested. I will have to send the Brethren to search the place they are grown."

"But Tarsit is the only place where the seeds are grown. The trees are unique to that area. I have heard stories about the Dwarfs of Pavelem; they have unsuccessfully tried to reseed the pearls. Tarsit is a long way from where we stand. You cannot afford to leave the army that needs your spells," said the physician, his thoughts on his bed.

"Have you not listened? I will remain here. The Brethren will escort three thousand Goblins and Hobgoblins. They will have to travel the way of the Great Eastern Divide. The rivers that cross the Great Eastern Divide are too wide and their current is strong. The Elves would surely massacre such a small number. A messenger will be sent to the army that marches upon Yea-Bor, now you sleep," ordered Marsukia.

When the physician had left, the wizard looked again at the map. Tarsit,he knew, was an important trading post. Even he traded with the Dwarfs who mined the trees, though they knew not of his identity. He felt no pity for the fate of the Dwarfs who lived there. Within weeks, they would become his livestock, livestock which would help to satisfy the hunger of the demon which was waiting for its freedom.

The three Brethren stepped into the room of the wizard without looking at the pile of guts on the floor; they looked at their creator and waited until they were spoken to.

Marsukia looked at the seven foot figures entering his room and raised his hand. They stopped instantly, their faces blank of all emotion.

"Control the ones who travel with you. As you know, they treat death with pleasure. Pick three to four thousand. No Ogres shall go with you though, they are needed at the walls of the Troll city. Do not kill all that stand in your way, bring back as many prisoners as you can, collect the blood of the dying. The task I set you three is to seek out all the wood pearls within Tarsit, every single one. Go!" he ordered calmly. Not once had he ever raised his voice to his creations, they always did as they were told.

Fastanes though did not sleep for many hours; he could not rid himself of the thought of the little bird he had released earlier that day. He let the surge of happiness come from the depths of his soul; he let it stay with him for some minutes before he swore at himself. for he had chosen his path. He was the one who had killed countless creatures. He laid down and knew however that something was changing. Some goodness had found its way inside him; he cursed several times at his own weaknesses before falling asleep.

Chapter Four

The Troll army was in definition made up of small battle groups, which were known as running units, each unit consisting of two dozen Trolls. During times of war, each unit ate, slept and fought together; the bonds which were struck would last a lifetime. All in all, there were twenty four thousand running units, making the Trolls of Yea-Bor a formidable fighting force. Two hundred and twenty four units were at present fighting a fierce battle on their eastern borders. Their enemies were the Dwarfs of the mountain kingdom of Pavelem. The land they both claimed to be their own was the Golden Valley, a place each race depended on for both the ideal farm land and the Gold which was to be found within the Golden river, or as the Trolls would say, the river of yellow light. Right in the middle of the Golden Valley was the lake which held treasures that each of the races were desperate to claim as their own. Twenty years of battle and thousands of lost lives and still not one of the races were any closer to defeating the other. The main reason for this was down to the wizards of Witches Watch. They had managed to stop the two antagonists from all-out war. This had been possible because of the young wizard who went by the name of Sarratt. He was still learning his craft, but even so, he had nearly brought the war to an end on several occasions. His virtues were good and his mind was still an open book. The thin line he walked each day had not yet shown him the dark powers that were available to him.

Thengost walked to the front of the running unit, his braided hair bobbing up and down, the animal bones knocking against each other with each step; these were a sign of how many battles had been won by that particular running unit. Around the shoulders of Thengost, there were exactly forty nine. The animal bones were light and each was tied near the end of Thengost's hair. This gave the King of the Trolls a menacing look. To some, the sight was almost too much, though he had piled the weight on since the late King had died. He still held the respect of many, but not all. The new King had forty nine bones representing forty nine victories, but his last battle had been nearly five years previously. That had been his first as the new King and very nearly his last as King, for he had argued with the debating council that he should be allowed to continue fighting within his running unit. To this the council had reluctantly agreed, but as the King of Yea-Bor ran into battle on that sorrowful day, he did so wearing the King's feathers within his hair: the feathers of the Golden Valley dragon. They were the symbol of absolute power within the Troll race and only one was allowed to wear them. The Dwarfs instantly realized that the King of the Trolls was upon the battle field and ordered each and every dwarf to attack him. If not for the passing of the wizard Sarratt, the new King would surely have met his death, such was the ferocity of the attack made by the Dwarfs. Sarratt had looked down on the raging battle and had decided that he would not get involved as he was on his way to see the Elves of Follonday. But on seeing the black feathers of the new King, he had rushed to the side of Thengost, knocking aside dozens of fighting dwarfs, not killing any as he did so. The wizard strode right up to Thengost and slapped him hard on the side of his face, causing the new King to squeal out in pain.

"You play with the lives of Yea-Bor. Be this your last foray onto the battlefield. Rule your race as your father did, or I will stand before the council of the Trolls and say they were right all along."

Thengost did as the wizard said; he watched from afar the battles he so desperately wanted to be part of. Even now as he watched several Trolls fighting with the oncoming Dwarfs, he wanted to run down the gentle slope of the Golden Valley and fight alongside his soldiers. But he knew he was carrying too much weight and his stamina was nothing compared to the Trolls he was now applauding. A dozen Dwarfs lay within the swiftly moving river, their swords joining the hundreds of others at the bottom of the river bed. The running units then smashed the hastily built bridge, shouting as they did so. Thengost then saw that another bridge was floating its way across, the several dozen Dwarfs guiding it to the shore. The King shouted behind him and ordered four more units down onto the river's shores. The Dwarfs on the far bank watched as the running units split into formation. They knew that the Dwarfs they had sent across would suffer horrible deaths at the hands of the Trolls, but these sacrifices had to be made. Sooner or later they would breach the Troll defences and claim the Golden Valley for their own. Thengost watched with satisfaction as the attack ended like all the previous ones. The Trolls liked this form of battle; the Dwarfs did not use the bow, only the axe. They did possess small daggers, but they were no match for the mighty swords of the Troll. The Dwarf catapults were dangerous enough, but not many Trolls had died that way. The victorious running units ran back up the slopes to the cheers of the spectators, but as the cheering crowds quietened down, Thengost shouted for another four running units to enter the battle, for yet another bridge was on its way. This continued until the booms of the Dwarf drums signaled the end of their siege for the day. For reasons only known to the Dwarf chieftains, they had given up the night raids some years previously. Some did say though that the river was just as treacherous as any running unit during the dark hours of evening.

The camp fires of both the Dwarfs and the Trolls reflected against each other upon the flowing river. The Dwarfs' camp on the eastern side held thousands of tents and stretched away into the lowlands of their mountains. They had been camped within this valley for three years, but the river had,up until now, proved impassable. The Trolls on the other hand had two hundred and twenty four tents, some of these erected for the frequent visitors who made the long trip from Yea-Bor to look upon the battles. Thengost, being the King, had a tent of such size, that within it were twelve bedrooms, three changing rooms and a vast circular area where he entertained the visiting Trolls. In its centre was a large open fire, encased by rocks which had been carried all the way from Yea-Bor. There was even a large kitchen, where the King's chef was kept busy for long hours each day, preparing the feasts that had become somewhat of a legend back within the city.

Thengost sat amongst a dozen cushions, smoking on the long pipe Sarratt the wizard had given him shortly after they had met, The wizard had said the pipe would help him with his thoughts, for that was as important as anything in life, the power of thought. So as the King smoked on the long pipe which had become his trademark amongst the race of Trolls, he looked at the many servants busy dealing with the arriving guests. His personal guard stood directly behind and would remain so for the rest of the evening. Thengost's favourite servant was the huge pot-bellied Troll known simply as Pig, for that was the animal he most liked to cook, spit roasted for hours on a low heat, with honey poured over the skin at regular intervals. All the vegetables were roasted with honey also. The King had not once complained about the food that was cooked for him by Pig, his real name long since forgotten.

The evening within the King's tent would always start with a ballad, the same one, though the ending would always be different, reflecting on the day's battles. To be mentioned within the song was an honour. The singer watched each day from the slopes of the Golden Valley and was quick -witted enough to recall events that happened. This usually had the assembled guests laughing, but the laughter would not last for long, for the food was in such quantities that each of the guests struggled to finish. As the cook joined the King, he looked on with a pride that was plainly clear for all to see. He always sat next to the King, though he did not eat within the tent. He would eat after all the guests had retired, such was his way. When the food had been eaten, Pig the cook would clap his hands and retire from the service of the King. The many servants would quickly enter and leave with all the soiled plates, the long task of washing up awaiting them before they ate.

The King of the Trolls sat back upon his large cushions. His huge belly felt close to bursting, such was the amount he had eaten. The pipe was lit once more and he looked around at the faces he had never seen before. This was the worst part of the Kingship, having to be pleasant to the dignitaries that had made the long journey through the mountain passes. They all wanted their own time with the King. Each asked the same questions, each thought that he was as important as any of the hundred strong council, none of whom ever bothered to travel away from the city. However, as the King knew, this was actually part of being within the council, for the debates which were held each day of the year, required that all of the hundred attended. He no longer felt like a warrior, no longer felt he was needed. He listened with a blank mind. The King of the Trolls had become what he always said he wouldn't: a mere symbol of power, a power which had control of two hundred and twenty four running units. The King thanked his guest as the next was waiting to be seated with him.

The guests though seemed happy enough. They, like all the rest who had made the journey, had not said anything during the course of that day, watching with a sick fascination as they witnessed the deaths of one hundred Dwarfs or more. Only after a few glasses of mountain whiskey did they loosen their tongues.

"How many did we lose?" asked one.

"How many did they lose?" asked the other, shaking his head in wonder.

"I saw one of the Dwarfs get his head chopped off, it will give me dreams of the worst possible kind," said another, leaning over to join in the conversation.

"I saw at least three beheaded, but the one which will give me bad dreams was the one who managed to stay upon his squat legs whilst his arms were cut from his body. He was simply left to run in all directions like a headless chicken," said yet another, his eyes showing pity for the fallen Dwarf.

Amid the rising conversations, the King greeted yet another.

"Why are the Dwarfs so hell-bent on crossing here, my King?" asked the Troll who had sat next to her King. She had hair braided in exactly the same way as her King's, the only difference being that instead of the animal bones that adorned Thengost, she had feathers, lots of them. All of them were pure white, a sign amongst the she Trolls that stated that they were single and unattached. This did not go unnoticed; the King had still to find a suitable partner.

"They know that this is the weakest point of the river, but even here they cannot defeat us."

"Are you certain of this?" she asked, flicking her hair over to the right hand side of her head, this giving the King a clear view of her beauty.

"I know something of the Dwarfs of Pavelem, do you not, Lady?" replied Thengost, his face breaking into a small grin.

"And of what do you know, my King?" she asked, leaning ever closer to the King.

"Why! My Lady, one never speaks of one's secrets to a stranger," stated the King, shaking his head at her. Sabrina looked away from the King then, not knowing if she had said the wrong thing; her cheeks had begun to blush. Thengost noted this and added:

"If you were a wizard, you would have no need of these questions, for you would know what I was really thinking."

She turned her gaze towards him, her face breaking into a smile.

"I see that there are others that await your company; I will depart to my bed."

"They can wait, my lady. Tell me! Do you know of the hill behind the bell tower within the square?" he asked, his hand coming to rest upon her shoulder.

"Of this place I know well, my King," replied Sabrina, her face lightened by the touch of her King.

"Then make it your duty to meet me there on my return," ordered Thengost, his hand tightening ever so slightly.

"I will long for that day. Now I really must leave your company, I am all but asleep," she said as she slowly rose to her feet. Thengost was sad to see Sabrina leave. He had felt something between them, and he smiled at the next guest as he sat himself besides the King. The night seemed to go on for an eternity, but end it had to, so with the King bidding a goodnight's rest to the last of the guests, he slumped back amongst the cushions.

"Pig!" he shouted.

"My King!" replied Pig, the sweat pouring out of him.

"Is the drink not yet prepared?"

Pig the chef entered the large area where the King had sprawled himself out. In his hand he carried a hot steaming mug of honey whiskey; the King thanked the chef and relished every mouthful of the strong liquor.

"Is it to your liking?" asked the chef, knowing that the answer would involve the King's weight.

"You look after me too well, Pig. I will never fight again if you have anything to do with it, but I can sense a change within me tonight; a lady may have saved your King from becoming a pudding of a Troll."

"Food is the backbone of the Troll race," argued the chef.

"But you are not meant to give all the food to only one of our race, Pig!" exclaimed the laughing King.

"Bah!" spat the chef, known to all as the Pig.

Thengost had closed his eyes only for the briefest of moments, but he fell asleep as he always did, amongst the cushions in front of the roaring fire. As he slept, he dreamt of battle, dreamt he was part of his running unit, sprinting for the whole day. He felt light- headed as he was suddenly awoken by one of his personal guard.

"What is it?" asked the annoyed King.

"A Troll by the name of Henthorn wishes to speak with you. We ordered him to be on his way, but he would not wait for the breaking of a new day," replied the guard, aware that the King had not yet erupted in rage.

"Henthorn!" said the King to himself. The guard had not heard the King speak the name of the waiting Troll.

There was a nervous coughing from the guard.

"Send in the said Troll," ordered Thengost, who had rubbed his tired eyes. The guard quickly departed, glad he had not been yelled at.

Thengost brought himself up, so that he was sitting with his legs crossed. The flap of the outer lining of the tent could be heard as it was flung open. The King watched as the inner flap was given the same treatment; the Troll that came storming into the King's tent was not looking happy. He stopped some distance away from his King and swooped with his left fist coming to rest upon his forehead.

"My King," rasped Henthorn.

"My friend," replied the King softly, suddenly aware of just how fat he had become.

"Long hours have I been waiting."

"My personal guard does their job well."

"Even when they know that I travel with the scroll of the council, even when the crest of the western running units is quite clearly displayed for them to see... what world are they living in, my King?" he asked, a look of disgust upon his scarred face.

"They serve the King, not the council, as you well know. Come, the hour is indeed late. I wish to continue my rest," said the King, who had not liked the way in which Henthorn was talking.

"Time for rest, my King. I think you had better read the message from the council first, then decide if sleep is needed," replied the hardened, fighting Troll, who had stepped forward and had given the King the scroll.

Thengost took the scroll from the leader of the second running unit. He opened it slowly, dreading what the council might have to say. It was well known that the relationship between them was a bitter one. He read the message slowly, then read it again, this time stopping to look at the standing figure of Henthorn.

"You have seen these creatures for yourself?" he asked suddenly.

"No, but I trust what the scouts report. They have no reason to make this up."

"Have any of the wise council acted upon these creatures, sent out running units to face them?" he asked sarcastically.

Henthorn shook his head; he looked down at the enormous figure of the King and wondered where the Thengost of old had gone.

"Read the scroll again, my king," he ordered, his voice becoming tense.

Thengost quickly looked at the message again, screwed up the scroll and threw it away in disgust. He uncrossed his mighty legs and with some considerable effort, rose up onto his feet.

"You bring me tales from another age. The scouts are mistaken. The western plains are empty of all life except for the wild horses. Within that scroll is a fantasy, I dismiss it with the least effort."

"Then what the council say of you is true. You have deluded yourself for too long within the Golden Valley. You have lost the grip of leadership. The scouts have seen not hundreds of these creatures camped at the western Plains of Desire, but thousands upon thousands. I travel back to the council with the news of which they forewarned me. Thengost, for pity's sake, listen and travel back before it is too late," came the harsh reply.

"Too late!" exclaimed the King, his voice bellowing out of the confines of the tent.

"Yes! Too late, my King, for if you intend to stay upon the banks of the yellow river for any length of time, your Kingdom might not exist anymore. I give you my leave," replied Henthorn, who had bowed quickly as he had finished what he was saying. Before the King could grab hold of his old friend and shake him, he had left.

Henthorn had just about reached the inner flap of the tent when three of the King's personal guard came running in, their expressions those of fear for the shouting King. Henthorn picked the first startled guard and flung him aside.

"Out of the way! Here passes Henthorn, leader of the second running unit. I have no time to waste," he warned, his sword drawn menacingly. The two remaining guards stepped out of his way, before carrying on to see their stricken King.

Henthorn left the King's tent in one foul mood. His sword was still within the tight grip of his right hand, but his way was blocked by yet another of the King's guard: this Troll though was huge, standing eight feet in height.

"The sword has no place near the King," warned the deep booming voice.

"Denth!" exclaimed the shocked Troll.

"Put away the sword," ordered the guard, his voice becoming more of a threat.

"It is, isn't it?" Henthorn asked, this time doing that which the bigger Troll had ordered.

"By the blood of a thousand Dwarfs, it cannot be you!" exclaimed Denth, his tone of voice changing to that of excitement.

"Five years have obviously made you forget your friend," Henthorn replied sarcastically, his hand grabbing the Troll's hands.

"Henthorn, forever the trouble maker, what brings you within the Golden Valley?"

"Messages from the council, though I fear it was as I said it would be, a waste of time."

"A waste of time?" Denth looked puzzled.

"Time we do not have."

"Now I am completely lost," said Denth, his hands coming to rest on his hips.

"Sorry, Denth. This is not the time nor the place to be talking riddles. I though must be on my way; my paths are both long and dangerous."

Two Trolls suddenly appeared from within the shadows of the other large tents, their faces dark with emotion.

"Bugram, Browfell, I will not keep you waiting. The time has now come, my dear friend, for I too depart. I long for the day when the King comes to his senses and I long for the day when you and I can sit and talk of our younger days," said Henthorn, who had started to walk away from his old friend.

"Henthorn!" called Denth with a smirk on his face,"

What became of the red haired vixen you were always chasing?"

"I chased well," he laughed.

Denth's face split into the broadest grin he had had in years. But as the Troll was departing, the huge Troll went after them.

"But our homeland lies to the north; you are heading towards the south and Dwarf country."

"Dwarfs are not our concern, we head south for other reasons. Like I said before, time is against the Trolls."

"Then make haste," replied Denth who had given Henthorn a slap on the back.

The three Trolls headed through the tented village and were hindered no more. Like Henthorn had explained to Denth, their route was indeed south, through the mountain pass the Dwarfs had built. Pavelem Pass was part of the trade route between the city of the Dwarfs and the Elves of Follonday. No other way was possible for a hundred miles and that was nearly impossible to find. The Great Eastern Divide was all empowering over the continent of Ursalane, splitting it right in two. The council of the Trolls had been ordered by the wizards of Witches Watch to leave alone the trade route, saying that all-out war would be the consequence and the council would not want both the Dwarfs and the Elves knocking at their southern defenses. But this did have its own price to pay. Like the Gnomes, the Trolls had been cut off from the other races. It was only the wizards that spoke with the Trolls and offered them advice on how to manage without the resources that were so readily available to all of the other races.

The three Trolls walked for sometime, clothed in the running battledress of the second running unit. Knee length boots protected them against twisting their ankles, while the two belts carried several large containers of water and one of whiskey. Within the same two belts, there were various other compartments. Certain ones held hunting knives whilst others contained personal equipment, like cleaning aids, a razor, a spare running vest and most importantly a waterproof sheet. Each Troll looked after himself as much as he could while away on long journeys. Trolls took particular care of their feet, for these kept them going at a furious pace. The mighty sword was slung around the back along with the bow and arrows and the shield was always carried within the left hand. Members of the running units did not wear any headdress, and the only decoration was that of the animal bones.

With the coming of the new day, the three Trolls stopped at the foot of one of the mountains which made up the Great Eastern Divide, its snow- capped peak clearly visible, the scattering of clouds moving swiftly on towards the east. Here they drank some of the water and ate some cooked beef that, Browfell and Bugram had collected the previous evening from the King's chef. He had been only too happy to oblige.

"How are you two feeling?" asked Henthorn, smacking his lips together after drinking some water.

"Tired," replied Bugram for both of them.

"I would like to cover as much distance as possible before we sleep, especially now, seeing that the weather looks like it may stay dry, though within these mountains, an hour can see a great change."

Neither Browfell nor Bugram replied. They continued doing what they had been trained to do, checking to see that all of their possessions were in order.

"The pass we seek is still five days away. I hope we see some deer or pig on the way," continued Henthorn, who realized what a challenge the three of them had been given by the council of the Trolls. Bugram was the scout of the running unit. His skills with a pencil were said to be a gift, for when he drew something, it was like looking at the real thing. He was quick too; his hand raced over the sheets of parchment, his eyes only looking down once or twice. On the other hand, Browfell was like Henthorn: a warrior. He wanted to fight, wanted the fields of battle, he had lost count of how many Dwarfs he had slain.

"Dwarf would be nice," added Browfell, his sly grin making Henthorn laugh out loud.

"But they take too long to cook!" exclaimed Bugram, tongue in cheek.

All three broke into laughter, their deeply tanned faces tilting skywards. The sun was now casting shadows on the side of the mountains; it was time to head south. If the council was right, the three Trolls would get cut off and see the thousand or so creatures that had been spotted leaving the huge army on the Plains of Desire. What the three Trolls did not know however was that away to the east of them, past the Rainbow Falls, within the magical place the humans had named Witches Watch, a young wizard was also preparing to set out on the very same trade route; his name was Sarratt.

Chapter Five

It was the beginning of summer: the time of year when the place known as Witches Watch came alive with the annual festivities that had thousands of the human race gathering to see the magic on display. They travelled far to witness the new wizards performing their breathtaking spells and illusions. Most came from the great southern city of Traxit, ruled by the head of state, Queen Beatrice: a woman of great inner strength who believed that her armies were the greatest upon the lands she surveyed. She knew of the other races, but dealt not with them, but with the wizards of Witches Watch. She had never seen a Dwarf, Elf or Gnome and had no wish to. She suffered the wizards only because of the power they possessed; the wizards knew this and made sure that her huge armies came nowhere near their place of learning. This did not stop the thousands of Traxitians from going, for the period of one whole month in which the the trials took place, but some came as early as two weeks prior to the opening day. The once small settlement had grown over the years into a sprawling town, stretching as far as the Rainbow lake, some fifteen miles away. The inns and hostels were abundant, each making a good profit from the travellers.

The young wizard had kept his hood tight around his head. He walked within the shadows, unnoticed by the throngs of people that were intent on making their way to the buildings of the Witches Watch, a collection of buildings like no other. A hundred tall turrets and spires dominated the sky line, the tallest to be found right at the centre, golden in colour. Below these were the buildings, some at least a thousand feet in length. The Dwarfs had built them two storeys and three storeys high, but some of the buildings were empty shells. The wizards had asked the Dwarfs to build these for the simple reason of containment; some of the real spells that were practised there were dangerous and the wizards did not want to harm any of the people that had made these lands their home. A later addition to the Witches Watch had been the moat. This was to stop the prying visitors from getting inside., The young wizard turned the corner, into the main square, which was crowded as usual. On another occasion he would have let the people gasp at the appearance of a wizard, but he was in no mood to be delayed. So with a single word of magic, he vanished.

The outer wall of the Watch had several secret doorways; the young wizard quickly opened a door and emerged onto the closely mown lawns which meandered for sometime until they reached the first building of the Watch.

Sarratt looked back from where he had just come and sighed; even this small spell had taken its toll on him. He shook his head and hurried on towards the outer spiral stairway of the library. He made his way into the library, a quiet place of learning. Sarratt walked towards the east facing windows, passing row upon row of books. Thousands were to be found within the wizards' library. The musty smell seemed reassuring to the young wizard, for nothing seemed to disturb the air; none of the many windows had ever been opened. The enormous leather bound volumes of Ursalane, detailing in minute detail every settlement, town and city, every forest, wood and grassland, every slope, hill and mountain, gave off the strongest of the smells. Sarratt actually paused for a second, taking in the strong scent. His desk was situated right in front of one of the windows; the view of the distant mountain range was slightly obscured by one of the many turrets from within Witches Watch. He sat down wearily; his travels had been far. He thought of the Elves he had been to see, the wondrous forests that stretched for hundreds of miles, the heated arguments the King and he had had about the two warring races of the Dwarfs and the Trolls, how his path had taken him to the wooded settlement of Tarsit, where he had bought the treasured wood pearls, the long and winding road that led to the north, passing the Gnomes' homeland of Gutox:

a dangerous place even for a wizard, for the poisonous gases could kill without reason or notice. He thought of the Plains of Desire, a desolate place of grasses. The days and nights he had spent alone walking these lands had taught him to be at peace with the lands he tread, though when he entered Yea-Bor, he was aware of the tension of a race at war. Sarratt had used his magic then, making sure none of the running units intercepted him as he made his way to the city of the Trolls. Here he had his council with the head of the council. Again, the tone of the meeting was heated. The Trolls felt betrayed and vowed to fight the Dwarfs to the bitter end. Surratt's words of wisdom had calmed the mighty Troll down. As the wizard went over his words, sat within the library, he smiled to himself. The Troll had promised that the debating chamber would be used for peace as well as for the planning of war. The wizard had then travelled far into the east, over the Great Eastern Divide, using the Troll pass, which was called simply Yea. He saw the encamped Trolls on one side of the Golden River and the Dwarfs on the other. He felt dismay at the thought of how many lives had been lost over the valley, but such was his haste, he did not think for too long on the matter. Finally he walked within the lands of the Dwarf, a barren place, devoid of tree and shrub. The bitter easterly winds cut into the very being. If he had not been a wizard; he would have surely died amongst the strewn rocks of Pavelem. But the young Sarratt had strode up to the stone doorway of the mountain city and demanded he be let in. The doors were opened by the frightened Dwarfs, fearing the wizard as they feared no other, such was the spell the wizards had over the race of Dwarfs. The passage through the mountain was not a pleasant one, even for a wizard. Several times Sarratt had to cast one-worded spells, protecting himself from the rocks that were been hurled at him. Eventually he found his way into the King's hall, a vast hall that had been cut from within the mountain. Here the wizard had encountered even more abuse, the King of the Dwarfs being protected by a fanatical personal guard. The wizard spoke words of ancient spells that none heard, the attacking Dwarfs vanishing before they got within ten feet of him. His voice booming off the shiny, wet rock walls, he demanded that the King see him. But as Sarratt remembered, the meeting was brutal in the extreme; he was given no kindness, but told of the alliance with the Elves and that they would help them rid the lands of the Troll and the wizards. Sarratt did not argue the fact. The magic of the wizards did not hold with the Elves, for they possessed something within their ancient beings that shielded them from the spells of wizards. This was the first time the young wizard had felt hatred of a kind. As he stared out of the window of the library, he remembered how he had spoken under his breath, how the King of the Dwarfs had been suddenly lifted into the air, his body stiff with fear.

"You underestimate my power, Dwarf King. I, a mere messenger, feel loathing towards you and your race."

The mighty King was thrown against the rock wall,

his heavily built frame falling with an audible thud onto the marble floor. The king looked up to the wizard with a look of hatred; he shouted for help.

"You call for help when you plan the deaths of thousands. I give you the message I was sent to give you. Be content with the lands you hold; the wizards of the Watch will come against the Dwarfs if war is proclaimed."

Seated within the library, Sarratt the wizard rubbed his head, wondering if he had gone too far. The high wizard would want an account of all the meetings he had had. Would he take seriously what the Dwarf King had told him, that the Elves were ready to join forces with them and conquer the Golden Valley? He looked at the darkening skies, his mood darkening also. The time was fast approaching when he would knock upon the door of the high wizard.

Sarratt suddenly remembered the wood pearls that he had carried for so long. He hauled up the heavy sack and delved his hand into its contents to grab one of the so much sought-after treasures. He brought it up so as to look at its surface. Almost black in appearance, it gave off a whitish glow. This was not through any reflections from any other light source; the wood pearl would glow in the blackest of nights. This was probably the only thing the Watch wizard would be happy about, for as the young wizard deemed, the rest of his travels had been a disaster in one way or another.

The relative calm of the library was broken by the sudden appearance of the Watch Wizard himself. Sarratt looked up at the old wizard, his face concealing the shock of such an entrance.

"I wondered when you might return. Many weeks it has been."

"So I sit before you," said the young wizard.

"You have done all that was said of you?" asked the Watch Wizard.

"I have counseled the three races I was told of."

"The Dwarfs and the Elves are as one, as I feared?"

"The Trolls do not know of the great danger they are in. They want peace," replied the young wizard, his eyes firmly fixed upon the pile of wood pearls he had put upon the desk.

"The Trolls of Yea-Bor have another enemy," said the Watch Wizard, turning away from Sarratt.

Sarratt turned around to face the Watch Wizard, only to see him depart from the library. He followed, his thoughts darkened by the wizard's comments.

Once within the Watch Wizard's rooms, Sarratt sat upon a simple wooden chair, albeit carved intricately with the Elven flowers of Follonday. He watched as the older wizard busied himself in front of a golden bookcase, the bright glints of light piercing his mind. He thought then of Tarsit for some unknown reason, be it for a fraction of second: the treasure of the wood and the fuel of an age. Wars had been fought over its potential. The Watch Wizard brought forth a book, golden in colour. He turned some of the pages, as if he were reading them for the first time. No words were exchanged as the book was handed to Sarratt; the intended page was there for the wizard to see.

Sarratt looked at the page and gasped, for written down in the ancient writings of the Elf was a prophecy of doom. He looked at the ancient writing, his mind swirling as he thought of the Trolls of Yea-Bor. He laid the book down, his right hand ruffling his long black hair. The Watch Wizard took hold of the book and returned it to the golden bookcase.

"I felt the one stirring, he is one of such evil. I fear for the races that live upon Ursalane," said the Watch Wizard, who had remained with his back to the younger wizard.

"You speak in riddles," he replied distantly.

"I fear the three are behind this. They mean to bring a wizards' winter onto the races. We have much to do," said the Watch Wizard quietly.

"More riddles, who are the three you speak of?" asked the bewildered wizard.

"Riddles from my mind. You are right of course, but the three are a sad reality. They were once part of the Watch, good wizards, driven by the need to create life, but such is the thin line we wizards tread, one of them grew disillusioned with his faith."

"But I have never heard of the three!" interrupted Sarratt, who had risen and had walked over to the large window.

"Forty years have passed since they left here; you were but a snip of a boy. I removed all evidence of their presence. The Watch cannot afford to remember the ones which turn their backs on our learning. Maybe I was wrong to do this; time is proving it to be so," spoke the wizard in but a whisper. Sarrat remembered his parents crying as the Watch Wizard had taken him from his home.

"Then what are we to do?" asked Sarratt, his thoughts still on the council of the Trolls. Even now they felt that they had become a persecuted race. If it were true about the three wizards, then the Trolls would have good reason to feel persecuted.

"We have lots to do, but the three are all powerful, I fear. We are but two; let us hope that we find another wizard who has the power of the spoken spell. The signs are not on our side though. The festival must continue. After it has finished, I will travel to the Dwarf king and you will ride to the Elves. Esslestar will have to be told of the threat of the north. Let us hope he sees sense."

"But what of the one? Time passes by and we must remain within the Watch. To do what? Entertain the masses!" argued the younger of the two wizards.

"The wizards' winter will not happen for some time. The one has not yet entered our world. The three put themselves in great danger, for what they bring into the mortal world is a being that has no goodness whatsoever. I fear for them, Sarratt," replied the Watch Wizard.

"Pity for the three, would they show you the same?"

"It does not matter what feelings they have, Sarratt. I can only show mine, but it is the Trolls who need our help the most. Come, let us see the new arrivals, though I fear they will only be mere illusionists," replied the Watch Wizard, his hand coming to rest upon the shoulder of the younger wizard.

The festival was held within the grounds of the Watch. The wizards' council was made up of academics, men who had chosen to serve the ideals of the Watch. It did not matter that all of the council were mere mortals. It was and had been this way for at least eighty years, though the curious thing was that the people who made the pilgrimage each year, actually thought they were. Twenty four men made up the council, dressed in the black robes which were ankle length, their faces hidden by the large hoods. Witches Watch stretched up into the lower slopes of the Rainbow Mountains, with some of the buildings concealing secret caves which went all the way through the mountains. Hidden doorways opened up on the northern slopes, facing the Golden Valley, though it must be said, none had been used for years.

There was a buzz of anticipation amongst the hundreds of people who had managed to get within the main square; it was day one of the trials. Men who thought they had the power of the spoken spell came forward and gave their name and age. This was written within the book of the Watch. It was deemed an honour just to be able to get ones name within the large leather bound book. First upon the recently erected stage was a man of tender age. His manner suggested to the crowd he was indeed a wizard. He waved his arms energetically as he spoke. The dove which appeared as if from nowhere delighted the throngs of people. Next he produced ten golden coins. He walked up to the front of the stage and made sure all could see that they were real. He clenched his right fist about the coins and spoke what he thought was the ancient tongue of the Elves, long sentences that had the crowd cheering. When the climax of the spell came, he gestured that he was going to throw the coins high into the air. This he did. Ten golden coins tossed high into the air, the morning Sun glinting off the shiny golden surfaces, but it was not ten coins which came fluttering down. To the utter astonishment of the crowds, ten white feathers came to rest upon the stage. The round of applause lasted for some minutes. The man, who had spoken well, stepped down from the stage. He nodded at the wizards who made up the council. They in turn nodded back. This meant that the wizard-to-be would be called back the following day. All in all, there had been five hundred conjurers, illusionists and plain pranksters that first day.

Sarratt sat in on some of the displays and was made to both laugh and nearly cry. Some were indeed good with their hands, deceiving most who watched, but the true wizard watched and knew instantly that not one of the ones he had seen had the power of the spoken spell. At the end of the first week, one hundred of the so-called wizards had been told that they were simply mortal men: gifted, but still mortal.

The Watch Wizard came forward at the start of week two, his towering frame causing some of the children present to hide behind their parents' backs. He talked of the ways of the wizards who served at the Watch, how they learned that life was a special thing, how they had to travel the four corners of the continent making sure each of the different races abided by their rule. He spoke at length on the virtues that made the wizards of the Watch such a respected institution. But at the end of the brief speech, he performed the kind of magic only a true wizard could. Seemingly only one word was spoken, whereas in reality it had been several. The Watch Wizard floated into the air, the expectant throngs of people gasping in wonder and when the Watch Wizard spoke into the minds of each of the people present, they all jumped up at the same time, proclaiming that it had been he or she who had received the message to jump. On realising that everyone had heard the silent message, they roared with laughter. To finish one of the highlights of the four week festival, each watching person found that they had suddenly been given a refreshing cup of apple juice. They raised their paper cups as one, wanting to thank the Watch Wizard, but he was no longer there. He had apparently vanished into thin air.

At the beginning of the third week, the hundreds had been whittled down to fifty: young men who desperately wanted to be one of the twelve to continue on at the Watch. Sarratt had watched with some interest for the first week, but his mind was on the fate of the Trolls. He had become tired of the trials by the end of the second week. On the first day of the third week, he had been making his way to the square; he was to be the judge on that wet and windy day, but as he was about to take his seat, a message was given to him by a younger wizard, his face concealed by his large hood. Upon reading it, Sarratt felt his heart race. His whole spirit seemed to have been lifted by the contents of the scroll, and he slipped away from the crowds which had come in large numbers to watch.

Quickly he made his way to the rooms of the Watch Wizard, the door to the wizard's rooms already ajar.

"Enter," said the Watch Wizard.

"You sent for me?" asked the young wizard as he entered the room. Sarratt though was taken aback at the sight of a Gnome standing next to the Watch Wizard, his stained yellow face looking tired and exhausted.

"As you can see, we have a visitor from Gutox," said the Watch Wizard, his hand coming to rest on the shoulders of the Gnome.

"I came as quickly as I could," replied Sarratt.

"I will let Flukkia tell you why he has come to us."

The Gnome clicked his fingers nervously before he spoke.

"The creatures came to our lands and took as many of my kind as they could. Many died trying to stop them, but a magic seemed to have a hold over them."

"Magic of what kind, Flukkia?" asked the Watch Wizard, trying to urge the little Gnome to open up his feelings in front of the other wizard.

"Some of the horrible creatures made no attempt to

stop us from hurling spears and arrows at them. They seemed to want us to attack them, it was frightening."

"Were they avoiding the arrows, Flukkia?" asked the Watch Wizard.

"No! They stood there as our spears and arrows bounced off them, well, not bounced off them. I mean, they hit something just in front of them. We never even scratched their belts. That is why I have been sent to you, for your help!"

Sarratt sat down and thought of what the Watch Wizard had told him only three weeks previously. Was this the beginning of the winter he had said would come to the four corners of the continent?

"Help you we will, Flukkia. Now you must rest, eat and drink as much as you desire while you are here. Your room is now ready for you. Once more, may I thank your King for the messages he has sent us. They are, as always, much needed and appreciated," said the Watch Wizard, who had walked the Gnome into the corridor, where a servant was waiting to take the guest to his room.

"Sarratt, you will travel immediately to the forests of the Elves. The King of the Elves must be told of the evil which is stirring in the north. Then I want you to head north, go onto the Plains of Desire and search for the taken Gnomes. It is our duty," ordered the Watch Wizard, his face showing signs of anger: something Sarratt had rarely seen.

"Esslestar will not be seen easily," said Sarratt.

"That, my dear friend, is your problem. Now leave

while you still have the rest of this day in which to travel."

"I would check Flukkia's pockets before he leaves."

So the wizard left the company of the Watch Wizard and collected his belongings. It would be a long time before he set eyes on the Watch again.

Chapter Six

Treak put his body wrap away within one of the many pouches he carried and strapped his backpack on to his shoulders. The other three had not known of their leader's mistake and that was the way it would stay. But within Treak's mind he was still furious at the way in which he had lost so much valuable ground. He watched as the last of the backpacks was strapped onto Akkia's back and instructed Crikken to make his way due west out of the bramble. The Gnomes always left the bramble the way in which they had entered. With great care, once more Crikken expertly cut the vines so that they would quickly grow again; each of the four Gnomes blessed the bramble within which they had spent time.

Once upon the rolling meadows, they all felt vulnerable, as Treak had often said that on their way towards the wooded community of Tarsit, they were in constant danger, for these were not their lands. These were the lands of the Elf and Dwarf: races which had decided that the Gnomes would be hunted to their deaths. With Treak setting the pace, the four Gnomes started the long journey home. Sweat poured from the Gnomes' bodies. They had been running hard for the best part of an hour and Akkia in particular was beginning to feel the strain; he had let the others run on some distance.

"Treak!" shouted Crikken, who had kept looking back at the two younger Gnomes.

Treak though kept up his furious pace, not because he wanted to exhaust his fellow Gnomes, but because of his own weaknesses.

"Treak!" This time the loud shout from Crikken seemed to register with the Gnome. Treak slowed to a walk. He looked east towards the Great Eastern Divide, the mountain range which dominated the centre of the continent. He saw that some of the peaks had snow on them, a clear sign that winter was fast approaching. In front of him lay the fields of the farmsteads. Some had already been harvested, while others still held their bounty. The hedgerows were small, but provided channels of life for the smaller animals, which like the Gnomes, were in a constant struggle just to survive.

"Can we not eat first, Treak?" asked Crikken, his head shaking at the silent figure of the Gnome, who had turned to look at his three friends.

"Yes, we will eat. The Dwarfs still worry me though," came the distant reply.

"Those idiots will still be heading towards the

mountains. We need to keep eating. Relax, Treak, nothing around these fields but the crops of the farmers," said Crikken, who had already started to unpack some of the provisions he had carried for so long.

Kellek and Akkia followed suit. They had even got out their body wraps and laid them down on the damp ground.

"We do not have the time for this, but I will let it be this time, for Crikken seems to think the hunting party of Dwarfs is far away. You two, listen to me carefully. When we head north to our lands, I will wait for no one," Treak warned, his fingers clicking as he made the threats.

Meanwhile, some miles to the east, another situation was getting out of hand. The Dwarfs were beginning to panic, for a great noise was heard by them in the distance. The creatures had spotted the Dwarfs. The Elf who was running at the side of the Dwarfs veered away and turned back to run towards the army of creatures that were even now galloping as fast as they could in pursuit of the Dwarfs. Arrun soon had a clear view of what exactly he was up against. To his horror he saw that they were the Goblins of the northern wastelands. He wondered why so many had travelled this far south. He let fly three arrows within a split second, each travelling at tremendous speed towards the ones at the front. He stopped in his tracks as he saw the first Goblin die, its deformed shape sprawling to the ground, bringing others tumbling as it fell. The other two arrows hit their intended targets and more chaos ensued. The Elf turned again and sprinted away towards the west, quickly catching up with the slower race of Dwarfs. He came to the side of the leader of the Dwarfs.

"They are what I feared: Goblins!" he said quietly, making sure none of the others heard him.

"Then what are we to do, Elf?" asked the laboured Dwarf, his breath coming more quickly as the minutes went by.

"They will be amongst us within the next few minutes, I fear, for they run like I have never seen anything run before."

"Then we fight?" he asked again, his look of terror plain for the Elf to see.

"We have no choice, but do as I ask. We will not give them the pleasure of hunting us down like the Gnomes we hunt," said the Elf, who had already started to form a plan of counter attack.

Arrun ordered for the Dwarfs to split into three groups. One would travel with himself. The second would copy his movements while the third would continue on its way to Tarsit. They were instructed by the Elf to run like they had never run before. This they agreed with, their eyes showing the fear he had seen within the chieftains. The stampeding Goblins hurtled across the fields, the small hedgerows slowing them not in the slightest, being a mere three feet in height. Their naked forms devoid of hair, crudely made belts were all that they wore. These carried the many small pouches which in turn carried the weapons of the Goblin: small projectiles that when thrown by the Goblin in full gallop would kill an animal the size of a horse instantly. But what made these small creatures so dangerous was their lightning speed. They somehow had the ability to gallop in the same way as a horse, but many times faster, not for any great distance, but not many had the energy to outrun these killing machines.

The party of Dwarfs which the Elf had ordered to carry on towards the west now turned their heads as they heard the distant thundering of the galloping Goblins. The other two groups were now on either side of the advancing Goblins.

"Attack!" screamed the Elf, who had already let loose his first arrow, its intended Goblin dying instantly, causing the others to scream in panic and hatred of the Dwarfs they were so intent on killing. But the Goblins had not been simply galloping along, they had seen the distant group of Dwarfs and had sent a shower of missiles in their direction. Most fell harmlessly to the ground, but several cut their way through the outer clothing of the Dwarfs and entered the bodies of the dying Dwarfs. Arrun had now entered the fray without caring for his own life. The arrows screamed through the late afternoon air, killing mercilessly. The Dwarfs too had attacked with a fury that had made their race such a force upon Ursalane. Battle axes were drawn high as the two groups of Dwarfs charged into the hundred or so Goblins. Screams of death were joined by the screams of the attacking Dwarfs. But being so few in number, they did not really stop the Goblins from overpowering them.

One by one, each of the Dwarfs was either struck down with the fearsome eight sided spheres, or mauled and bitten to death. The Elf though was quite another matter for the Goblins. Whatever they tried, the Elf was always one step ahead. Dozens fell at the hands of the Elf, such was his speed and balance, but even Arrun realized that the numbers were just too great for him to conquer, so with three lightning strikes amidst the charging group at the rear, he disappeared as if by magic. He sprinted like he had never done before. The minutes passed and he was soon with the three remaining Dwarfs. They had the look of death etched into their faces.

"Run for Tarsit, it is your only hope," said the Elf, who had turned to watch the Goblins feasting upon the fallen Dwarfs.

With heavy hearts, the small group started to run in the direction of their home. The Elf was in the lead, looking for the easiest way, but there was no straight path amongst the fields. Hedgerow after hedgerow they jumped, their breathing laboured. One of the three remaining Dwarfs fell heavily; Arrun heard the grunt and turned to see the Dwarf he thought was known as Bark.

"Bark, a great loss you have suffered this sad day. None of my words may help, but keep them with you while you are running. You run so as to avenge the creatures you fought here today; you run for the sake of your families. Keep your thoughts open. May the house of my King look down on us today and grant us the hope that prevailed upon the Plains of Desire when another evil was defeated, for when an Elf is in need, hope always prevails," said the Elf, who had helped the fallen Dwarf to his feet.

"What trickery do you talk of, Elf? Have we not just seen the last of our hopes?"

Treak did not let his feelings be shown to his friends, but he wanted to be away from these lands. He longed for the volcanic peaks of his homeland, the warmth which was not to be found anywhere else upon Ursalane; he got to his feet and ordered Kellek and Crikken to pack up their belongings.

"Akkia has been gone too long," he said, clicking his fingers nervously. The hairs on the back of his head had started to irritate him; this was a sign of impending trouble, or so the Gnome had always assumed.

"But he has not been gone long, Treak," argued Crikken, who had enjoyed his wild berries and dried meat.

"The day is closing. I just want to be far away from the lands of the Dwarf and Elf before the Sun sets, that is all, Crikken," replied Treak calmly, though the same feelings did not apply to his insides. He had felt something. What? He did not yet know.

"I can remember when you and I got ourselves trapped within some of the bramble, just to the north of Wooded Hood. I wasn't nervous then, though I should have been," remembered Treak to himself.

"That was scary stuff, how many Dwarfs were looking for us again?" asked Crikken, who had overheard what Treak had said.

"I never bothered counting them, but after several days cooped up within that bramble, we were on the verge of going mad," added Treak, who had smiled at the memory.

"Kellek thinks we are joking, but it was no joke then. Our lives were in grave danger, not like today; this trip has been like taking honey from the bees," laughed Crikken, who had pushed the laughing Gnome away in jest.

Kellek liked to hear of the adventures these two veteran Gnomes had been through, though his laughter was shallow. He was missing his home. He now knew that he was not cut out to be a thieving Gnome. He looked at the two laughing Gnomes, pushing each other in a playful but rough way. They did not notice Akkia, the youngest of the Gnomes, bounding towards them from over the small hedgerow. He slid into the pair, knocking them to the ground. Treak and Crikken jumped to their feet and were about to reprimand the young Gnome, but they saw instantly that this had been no prank.

"From which direction?" asked Treak firmly, his eyes scanning the horizons for the Dwarfs he knew to be coming. Kellek was pointing in the direction of the Great Eastern Divide, his look of horror not seen by his friends. One Elf and three Dwarfs suddenly appeared, jumping the low hedgerow at some speed. It was obvious to Kellek that they had not known they were there. So once more on that day, Treak and Kellek had been sent flying onto the wet field. What followed was confusing for the four Gnomes, who had started to get their small bows out. If it was to be a fight to the death, so be it!

But Treak had been nearly knocked out. Crikken was at his side, his hands holding the arrow pointed at one of the Dwarfs, but the Dwarfs seemed to be looking past him, back from where they had just come. The Elf acted then with a speed of hand and foot that had the Gnomes looking at him in wonder, for he had taken his bow and put within it four arrows. He spoke quickly, but calmly.

"You should die here today and I should be the one who finishes your miserable existence upon these lands, but something even more repelling than yourselves is nearly upon us."

Treak spat in the direction of the Elf, his face twisted in hatred, as did the other three Gnomes, thinking amongst themselves that surely this must be the death of them.

"Spit once more in my direction and I will make your death as slow as I can make it. You have weapons of a sort, I see. I suggest you get them ready," warned Arrun, his voice as calm as ever. He had started to walk backwards, away from the hedgerow. Treak had listened carefully to what the Elf had said. He clicked his fingers urgently, and ordered the three Gnomes to prepare to fight whatever was chasing the Dwarfs and the Elf. He got to his feet, bringing out some arrows; he noted that his heart was beating like it had never beaten before.

The Elf looked at the bewildered Gnomes and wondered if they would survive the onslaught that was to come. At that precise moment he was not concerned for the loss of their lives, he just wanted to get back to the wooded community of Tarsit and raise the alarm. The long seconds turned into long minutes. Treak looked over at the three Dwarfs and saw a look of pure terror, and they had managed to retreat some one hundred paces. The distant rumble came to his ears as a warning. He clicked his fingers four times, and each of the Gnomes took up the strain on their small bows. But the Dwarfs had heard the noise also; they immediately started to run as fast as they could - away and into the west.

The Goblins appeared suddenly within the skies, their small hideous bodies silhouetted against the afternoon skies. The thundering noise as they landed though, made it quite clear to the watching Gnomes that these creatures were moving at some speed. The Elf had already let fly a dozen arrows, their screaming feathers hurtling into the attacking Goblins. The Gnomes followed suit; they were not nearly as quick as the Elf, but even so, their arrows killed at least five of the creatures they still did not know of. What happened next had the Gnomes gasping again, for the Elf had laid his bow down and had charged right into the twenty or so Goblins, with no sound coming from his mouth. He was like lightning, his swords dancing about the bodies of the Goblins, but more were jumping over the hedgerow. The Gnomes let fly with even more arrows, some missing the Elf by a whisker. They were still some distance away from the fighting creatures and Elf.

"Well?" asked Kellek, who had made his way quickly to the side of Treak, making sure none of the eight sided missiles hit him.

"Well what?" screamed Treak, who was running out of arrows.

"Will this be another one of your stories?"

Treak actually stopped himself from firing off yet another volley of arrows, and looked at the young Gnome with admiration.

"I think this just might end up as the story to end all stories. Now can we get ourselves organized," he shouted. " Crikken will find the bramble and cut his way into the dome, we will follow in a short while, Akkia!"

"What?" asked the youngest of the Gnomes, his yellow face streaming with perspiration.

"Go with Crikken. Kellek and I will join the Elf and save his life this day."

Nothing more was said, the two Gnomes had already sprinted off into the distance. Treak handed Kellek his bow and the four arrows he had left.

"Cover me. When you have no more arrows, take to the bramble, even if you see me and the Elf slain," ordered the Gnome, who had pulled out two weapons, a sword and a small dagger. He blessed his life and was gone. Kellek let fire with a passion, killing several Goblins even before Treak had entered the fray. The Goblins were in somewhat of a panic; they had even started fighting against each other. Arrun was amongst the pack of Goblins, dodging their frantic attempts to get hold of the evasive Elf, but then something happened to the Elf that he had not counted on. The green fields had turned red with the blood of the

Goblins; in certain areas small pools had gathered. It was in one such pool of slimy Goblin blood that he slipped. The Elf's world suddenly came crashing down all around him. Five of the Goblins had seen the Elf tumble, their deep guttural screams piercing the late afternoon air. But such was their frenzy, they had not noticed the arrival of the Gnome, his attack saving the life of the Elf.

"This is not the day I wish to die, Elf," said the Gnome, who had killed the three Goblins that had very nearly killed the fallen Elf.

"The choice is not for you to make, Gnome," spat Arrun, who had risen to his feet. They stood amidst dozens of dead Goblins, their small misshapen bodies lifeless, their mouths wide open, showing row after row of the razor sharp teeth that made them quite capable of ripping to shreds any creature they chose.

"You owe me a life, Elf," stated Treak, who had already started to head in the direction of Tarsit.

Arrun looked firstly at the departing Gnome, and then towards the Great Eastern Divide, from where he knew that even more of these hideous creatures were on their way. He lightly jumped over some of the dead Goblins and ran after the Gnome.

"And you owe Tarsit and I, rather a lot of wood pearls, Gnome."

"I did not dispute that fact, Elf. I was merely pointing out to you that if it had not been for me and my friends, you would surely be amongst the dead bodies that litter the fields. Why are you bothering me? You should act with the dignity that upholds your bond to me." Several clicks had accompanied Treak's speech; he knew that amongst the race of Elves, a saved life was to be treasured. For the one who saved the life, untold treasures were his to have if he so chose.

"Be very careful, Gnome, for the creatures that you think dead, have many more following them. It will be sooner rather than later that I will repay your deed, then we will be equal. Then will be the time you will see what I think of the Gnomes of Gutox and their stealing ways."

"You say there are more? Why did you not say so before? Follow me, quickly now!" ordered Treak, who had shot the Elf a look of disgust. Arrun followed the Gnome west, staying some distance behind. It was when the Gnome turned south that the Elf gasped out loud, for right in front of them was the bramble before which he had stood the day the Dwarf chieftain had called him over, asking him if he could hear anything from within the bramble. His thoughts went back to what he thought he had heard. It became even more clear when the Gnome disappeared within the bramble. Arrun dispelled his thoughts and ran as quickly as he could to where the Gnome had entered the bramble.

"Enter," gestured the Gnome, who had dropped his right arm in the direction of the Elf.

"This is a madness, the thorns will cut me until I bleed to death!" exclaimed the Elf, showing for the first time some of his fears.

"Quickly, before the Goblins you say are following, see the way I and my friends have entered this glorious bramble, which I have already blessed," urged Treak, his face brightened by the fact that the Elf was now entering their world." Stay close to me and watch if you must. This may explain a few things to you, mainly the reason why we have stayed undetected for so long."

"The tunnel, who has worked it into this shape?" asked the baffled Elf, who now knew what he had heard just the other day: the shallow breathing of four frightened Gnomes. He had stood within twenty feet of them.

"The Gnome is known as Crikken, he is masterful with the shears."

"I can see that, what are you doing now?" he asked, already knowing the answer.

"Obvious, even to an Elf, I would have thought. But what I am doing is just as important, for when those creatures enter the bramble, they will do so blind. No tunnel will aid them. That is what is needed for us to be able to leave in relative comfort, in the knowledge that whatever pursues us, does so not really knowing where we are," explained the Gnome, who had continued to remake the bramble. The Gnome seemed to take his time, the cut vines being arranged in such a way that even the Elf was amazed. An hour had elapsed since the bloody scenes upon the farmlands. The Sun was dipping quickly and with it, the last of the daylight.

"They will most surely find us!" exclaimed the Elf.

"Like you found us, Elf!" he replied coldly.

"I sensed you were within, but that does not count in the real world. I send you my apology."

"Just send us some of your Elf magic, that will do for starters," replied Treak, who had winked at the Elf and clicked his fingers several times.

Eventually, Treak remade the bramble in a way he had never done before. Even the other Gnomes could not see where they had entered, and Treak had also ordered his friends to start to dig the earth around the edge of the inner dome. Arrun the Elf sat alone, his face lowered to the thorny ground. He was collecting all his thoughts; these Gnomes had not tried to hurt him, which had troubled him, for he would quite gladly take their lives for what they had done. They had scurried around inside this bramble, making sure they were as safe as they could be. Out of the corner of his eye, he saw the tanned yellow boots that had made the Gnomes look somewhat childish, but the Elf noted now that most of what the Gnomes were wearing had a tanned yellowish colour except for the red waistcoat and jacket. Even their skin was yellow.

"Let us bless this bramble once again. Bless Crikken, for he most surely is the craftiest with the shears. But finally, let me bless the company of the Elf, for a life he owes me!" exclaimed Treak, who had sat away from the Elf.

"I will bless everything except for the being which would kill us while we sleep. He should never have been brought within the bramble," came the stone cold response.

"He is different from the rest, of this I am sure" He could quite easily have made his way home earlier, then what would have become of us?" asked Treak, who had lowered his voice. His hands had also clicked not quite as loudly. Something was on the fields, for all within the bramble had felt the ground rumble.

"They have others with them," said the Elf, not bothering to lift his face so that he could look upon the four thieves he had set out to kill just the other day.

"Then we must stay as silent as we can. The morning Sun will scatter our dark thoughts, then we will head away from here. Elf, you may leave and return to your home," said Treak, his face becoming harder to see. The Gnomes had by now slipped into their body wraps. The Elf looked on in surprise; he had only his travelling cloak, which he had fastened up to his neck. During the course of that night, the sounds of the Goblins could be heard all around the bramble. Arrun had heard the other creatures whose presence he had felt yesterday. This one seemed to speak fluently and with an authority that worried the Elf. He did not sleep that night as the four Gnomes did. He thought of Tarsit and the friends he had made, he thought of how he was going to get back the treasured wood pearls. But something had already been decided within his mind; he would not kill these Gnomes, he would not trick them. He would travel with them and confront whoever was their leader or King. He had wondered how the thieving race of Gnomes could have a king,but he had let this slip from his mind as the breaking of the new day was upon him. Treak was the first to wake; he looked at the Elf with a sly grin.

"I see you did not try and leave the safety of the bramble," said the Gnome.

"I rested and I thought of many things," replied the Elf quietly.

"Are they still roaming around the bramble? They will grow tired, just like all the Dwarfs do, even yourself, an Elf! Let us be, if no entrance can be seen, why make one?" he asked.

"They have others with them. They are altogether a different race. I must admit that I was worried during the night, trapped within this thorn ridden place," admitted the Elf, who had risen to his feet.

"You are an Elf of the forests?" Treak asked suddenly.

"And you a Gnome of the red mountains," came the quick response.

Treak had also risen to his feet, making sure at the same time he did not disturb the others, who were still fast asleep. He reached up into the canopy of the bramble and widened a small opening. Light came flooding into the dome of the bramble.

"Your name?" asked Treak, circling the Elf, his fingers silently rubbing against each other.

"Arrun."

"I am known as Treak. Over in the far corner is Crikken. He was the one who made the tunnel; he has a way with the bramble. Next to him is Kellek, not as experienced as Crikken and I, but he is learning." Treak paused before he pointed towards Akkia. "And here lies the youngest of our small band of travellers."

"Thieves!" interrupted the Elf.

"He has found the trip somewhat of a struggle," continued the Gnome, paying no attention to the Elf's remark. "I think this will be his last; he is not suited for the long treks we have to do. Why! We are already a day late, time is always against us when the summer is due."

"Did the young one choose to come on your thieving trip?" asked the Elf, who had resumed his sitting position.

"Nobody chooses. We are picked. Choice is not a part of the Gnome's life. The chieftains and the King decide who will do what. Is it not the same for the Elves?"

"On the whole, we choose to do whatever we want to do, for freedom of choice is the heartbeat of life. Be quiet!" exclaimed the Elf, who had heard footsteps outside the bramble. The deep guttural voice that followed confirmed the Elf's suspicions:

"They have entered the dragon weed. I sense the Elf. Find where they entered and follow. Kill the Dwarfs, but I want the Elf alive; my master will be glad of his fresh blood."

Arrun looked at Treak, a look of horror spreading across his face.

"They know then!" exclaimed Treak, who had awoken his three friends.

"They definitely know of my existence, this is true," replied Arrun.

"What are they, Elf?" asked the youngest of the Gnomes.

"A nightmare from my childhood, Akkia. They will not stop seeking us until we are found, this is one thing of which I am certain."

"They think we are Dwarfs!" said the leader of the Gnomes. He continued, his face becoming excited, "then we will be one step ahead for the time being. Crikken, head towards the north. I want to be well on the way before they find this dome."

"You know my name?" asked Akkia, who had walked over to the Elf.

"Treak told me," replied the Elf.

"What of you, Elf?" asked Crikken, who gave the Elf a menacing glance.

"For the moment, I choose to follow you, for you still carry items which belong to me."

"What the Elf is really saying, but does not want to admit, is that he owes us a life," taunted Treak, who had kept his voice as low as possible.

Outside the bramble in which they were hiding, camped within feet of the entrance Crikken had so skillfully made, over two thousand Goblins lay together in sleep. It must be said that this was the safest part of a Goblin's life, for this was when they allowed bodily contact. During the daylight hours though, any sudden contact would mean fighting, such was the way of the Goblin. Walking alongside the sleeping Goblins were the Brethren, five in all. They had lost well over three hundred Goblins so far and were not happy. They had spotted the Dwarfs and the Elf and seen in which direction they had run, but they had disappeared into thin air as soon as they had come to the bramble. One of the Brethren took out one of his pouches, emptied its contents upon the ground and spoke many words of magic, though only one was heard by the Elf.

The sudden illumination of several footprints going into the actual bramble had the Brethren shouting for the Goblins to wake.

"We have found stinking Elf and Dwarfs!" it had shouted.

Within the bramble Treak had gone into somewhat of a panic when he saw light up all the footprints they had made.

"But that is not fair. Have they a wizard with them? If they have, we are surely doomed," he said heatedly.

"No wizard is here, Treak. But there are ones with the simple knowledge of the use of magic. I sensed them yesterday. We must leave at once," added the Elf, who had packed away his travelling cloak; this would be a day of running, he knew.

"They are close, all of you, find them!" shouted the Brethren suddenly, his finger pointing towards the bramble.

Crikken had wasted no time as he hacked his way through the dense undergrowth, though he did give blessings with each mighty swathe of his shears. Kellek and Akkia followed, urging the older Gnome on with words of encouragement. Arrun the Elf though had stayed with the leader of the small group of Gnomes. Treak had spent long minutes within the dome of the bramble. He himself had started his own tunnel, though it had not got very far before he left it and concentrated on covering up the tunnel Crikken had hacked into.

"The Goblins will be with us within minutes, how long are you going to be?" asked Arrun, his ears picking up the crashing sounds of the first of the Goblins which had entered the bramble.

"Will this be the second time a Gnome has saved your life, Elf?" asked Treak, his tone of voice mocking the Elf.

"Be very careful, Treak, for we still do not know each other's ways, now hurry!"

As soon as the Elf had said this, a dozen Goblins came charging through the bramble into the dome, their screams piercing through the thin layer of bramble which separated them from the Elf and the Gnome. Arrun had his bow at the ready, one of his last arrows aimed at the closest of the Goblins.

But as he heard the Goblins scream when they saw the thin partition, he also heard the Gnome clicking his fingers.

"Run like the wind, for time has run out for us," said the Gnome who had disappeared down the thorn ridden passage.

"They will get more than a simple thorn in the side from this bramble," whispered the Elf, who had started to let loose his arrows. Six in all he had left; it took but two seconds to fire them, causing mayhem from within the dome of the bramble. When they looked to see who had shot at them, killing three, no one could be seen. The screams which were sent through the bramble sent shivers down the spines of the four Gnomes and Elf.

"I have become the hunted!" said the Elf as he caught up with the others.

"Then I hope you enjoy the experience, we have been the hunted for as long as I can remember. This is nothing new to us, Elf," snapped Crikken, who was still hacking his way through the bramble.

"Crikken, you are right, but let us try and get through this together. We need the Elf as much as he needs us," replied Treak, who had turned and given the Elf a look of hope.

Chapter Seven

The mountain pass for which the three Trolls were heading was dangerous country. One silly mistake and their lives would be at risk.. The pass was known to them as the Snake Bite , for as other running unit Trolls had said, the road would twist so tightly in amongst the mountains, that it reminded them of the grass snakes on the Plains of Desire. While you thought you had gone past the danger, the danger had always twisted back and caught the traveller off guard. The pass had a section which held no escape. Once committed to that route, nothing else could be done, other than going all the way back and the three Trolls knew that this was not an option. The trade route which stretched all the way from the east, Pavelem, to the far western shores of the forested home of the Elf, Follonday, was the busiest road on the continent. It was hailed as the greatest wonder of the world by the Dwarfs who had built it in less than ten summers. It had definitely helped in the making of at least a dozen new settlements along its course.

"The Snake Bite pass approaches, Henthorn," warned Bugram, who had quickly sketched the eastern view. The council may or may not find this useful. He drew what he was told to draw, but sketched places he liked the look of.

"Then put away your pencils and be on your guard, the road is treacherous here," ordered Henthorn, who had already withdrawn his mighty sword.

The three Trolls of the second running unit looked brutal as they started to trot into the pass. With their shields up around the left shoulder, the right hand grasping the biggest swords within the lands; their matted hair, a pure black; with the all white animal bones tied at the ends; their broad flat noses starting to flare as they picked up momentum; the blackness of the skin; rippling muscles aching to break loose from the skin which held them in place, going at the quickest pace they could, the Trolls thought quite rightly that if anyone was coming the other way, they would be the ones hiding, not them. They hurtled through the first section of the pass, undaunted by the sheer rock faces the Dwarfs had cut into all those years ago. Henthorn called for a rest.

"You're getting too old for this, Henthorn!" exclaimed his age old friend, Browfell, his face covered in sweat.

"Do not worry for me, Browfell. Worry for yourself. We approach the Snake Bite Pass. Bugram, you scout ahead, see if there are any signs of Dwarf," ordered Henthorn, who had shot Browfell a rueful glance.

"Let us just enter this place. Three Trolls running through will not be stopped by a hundred Dwarfs; you worry too much," scoffed Browfell, who had walked some distance within the said pass.

"Do you know how many we have lost within this evil Dwarf place? Too many! I am making sure we are not walking or running to our deaths, old friend," replied Henthorn, who had remained standing where he had stopped. Browfell felt as if his old friend was being too cautious but did not pursue his taunting of the Troll.

"I hear you loud and clear. Well hurry, Bugram. We have not got the whole of the day to spend within a land created by the Dwarf!" he said, breaking into a grin.

Bugram made his way carefully into the Snake Bite Pass and was soon lost from view, such was the way the Dwarfs had wound their way through the mountain. An hour had passed before the Troll returned.

"Nothing within the pass, not even high up as I feared there had to be. It is still a frightening place to walk, there are skeletons littering the pass in places. I am glad we run through it during the day, for I would surely fear for my very soul within the darkness of the night," explained Bugram, his hand wiping nothing away from his forehead but fear.

"Skeletons, you say?" asked Browfell.

"They would be the dead of Yea-Bor. Come! We run until we see the Plains of Desire. Run hard!" he warned.

The mountain pass had taken the Dwarfs many years to complete. Within the pass itself, the sheer rock face of the mountain rose hundreds of feet into the air, its width being only a few feet, wide enough though to carry the wagon loads of trade which passed through it on a daily journey that would take a couple of hours. Most of the trade these days was solely between the two races of the Dwarfs and the Elves. The three Trolls started off at a brisk walk, wary however of the threat of the Dwarfs they would surely come across within the pass. Henthorn was the one who always set the pace, so when he suddenly broke into a sprint, the other two followed, not questioning their captain's decision. Their heartbeats had quickened somewhat once they had been running for only a few minutes. They all knew that there was no turning back now. Three huge Trolls running faster than any horse was a fearsome sight, their dark tanned skin glistening with perspiration running down their muscular arms. Braided trestles of hair, the animal bones bouncing about their faces seemed to give the three Trolls energy not found amongst any of the other races. Their stamina was legendary.

"Unleash your swords and prepare your shields; I sense danger now," shouted Henthorn, who had effortlessly done what he had just told the other two to do. None of the electrifying speed had been lost because of this. The bends twisted tightly in places. Henthorn actually used the sides of the mountain to help himself around the tightest of them, his bare arm rubbing against the cold of the rock face.

The group of Dwarfs which had travelled from the

forests of Follonday was in good heart. The wagons the Dwarfs had filled with the wines and fruits of the forest were going to be their winter's supply. The ever trustworthy mountain ponies were pulling sixteen wagons in total. An animal which suited the Dwarfs' way of life, the Dwarfs thought so much of the animal that it was regarded as sacred. None could hurt the animal; the sentence for those who did was death. The convoy of wagons had entered the mountain pass with the dozens of Dwarfs singing heartily, for they were happy to be off the Plains of Desire. This was their land; their forefathers had toiled for many years building this pass and the last thing on the singing Dwarfs' minds that afternoon was the sight of three enormous Trolls heading straight for them.

The singing died away almost immediately. The stunned Dwarfs could do nothing as the roaring enemy charged at them. Henthorn had no real desire to fight the Dwarfs. His mission was to go scouting the southern grasslands of the Plains of Desire. He shouted back at his two friends,

"Run hard and avoid contact with them. May we get through this in one piece!"

The main problem for the three Trolls was the fact that the Dwarfs had started to panic. Two of the wagons had crashed into the sides of the mountain, blocking their way, plus three of the Dwarfs had drawn their battle axes, arcing them two and fro in front of them. One hundred paces stood between the two rival races, but such was the speed of the Trolls, they had passed the large convoy in a matter of minutes, but not without incident. Henthorn had been the first to encounter the horrified Dwarfs. He had easily knocked aside the leading Dwarf, sending him crashing into the hard rock face, loud shouts echoing along the Snake Bite Pass. Henthorn then jumped onto the loaded wagon which had crashed into the rock face. He turned and beckoned Bugram and Browfell to follow, making sure at the same time that his shield was protecting his right side. The stunned Dwarfs had neither the time nor the skill to deal with three of the best Troll warriors that had ever lived. Even as the Trolls were jumping from wagon to wagon, the Dwarfs simply watched in horror.

"Kill them!" shouted the Dwarf who had been knocked into the rock face, his pride severely dented.

"They have gone!" exclaimed a Dwarf, who had rushed to the side of the fallen Dwarf.

"Then what are you doing here? I want them dead!" screamed the Dwarf, who had managed to pull himself up, but to his amazement none of the Dwarfs had bothered to follow the three Trolls.

"They were the ones from the running units. Let us be happy they decided we were not a threat, otherwise we would surely be lying in red pools of blood. We are not warriors," said one who had come to the Dwarf's aid.

"They are lucky on this day then, but let me tell you one thing: if I ever set eyes on the one who sent me flying, I will chop off his head without a second thought," he warned, rubbing his hands up and down his clothes, trying to remove the dirt he'd picked up from the wet floor.

Some hours later and the convoy of Dwarfs was on their way again, though no singing would emanate from their vocal chords for the rest of their long journey. The three Trolls on the other hand were reaching the end of the dreaded pass, their faces split with big grins. Sweat was pouring from their faces, but they were happy.

"The Dwarfs seemed a little confused, Henthorn," laughed Browfell.

"They are so wrapped up in their self-importance, they forget sometimes how puny they are. None of them even tried to stop us!" he said in wonder.

"Or chase after us; we are monsters from the bleak mountains, wild and unforgiving. We would wring their sorry necks until they saw no more," added Brugram, his voice raised into a pitch like that found within the race of Gnomes.

Loud laughter followed. All the Trolls knew of the reputation they had within the lands of the Dwarf. They thought of the Troll as merely a wild animal.

"There," said Henthorn, his finger pointing to the west. "The mighty Plains of Desire! Let us feel the open lands beneath our feet."

Browfell and Brugram looked at the green desert that lay before them, for as far as the eye could see, there was nothing but the grasses of the plains..These were the lands of the wild horses; thousands galloped freely here. One river could be made out in the north, it being but a thin slither from where the three Trolls stood.

"The River of the Elf is two days away. From there, we travel east towards the badlands. Let us make haste while the day is still yet young," suggested Henthorn, who had sheathed his mighty sword and strapped his shield upon his back. Just as they were preparing to leave the trade route, something caught Henthorn's attention out of the corner of his right eye. Far in the distance to the north, a thin black line of smoke had begun to wind its way up towards the heavy grey skies.

"Browfell, what do you make of that?" he asked as he pointed towards the distant trail of smoke. Browfell ran down the side of the steep slope and cupped his hands around his forehead. Within moments he was back before Henthorn.

"Campfires upon the plains are indeed a rare sight. It is too far away for me to see."

"We approach with caution; remember that there are creatures of a foul nature abroad," warned Henthorn.

The side of the mountain along which lay the trade route, was not one of great size; its slopes rolled away and onto the plains. No trees grew here, just the odd shrub and on the Plains of Desire, nothing grew but the grasses. Henthorn felt better once he felt the flat lands of the Plains of Desire beneath his feet. Now they could stretch out their legs and run hard. By the time the darkness of the night was upon them, they had travelled a great distance. Their camp that first night upon the Plains of Desire was a cold affair; Henthorn had not allpwed any form of fires. Lying upon their backs, squeezed up together for warmth, they ate some of the sparse provisions they had brought with them and drank some of the whiskey, which helped them through the cold hours of the night. Each took it in turns to keep watch, but as Henthorn had said, they would be quite safe on this night.

Morning came with the grey skies threatening rain. Luck had been on their side the previous night for it had remained dry. However one thing had changed from the previous day: a wicked wind had sprang up from the west, strong gusts flapping the tops of the grasses every few seconds.

"The smoke is not visible, Henthorn. Are we still set on that course?" asked Browfell, whose very bones felt as if they had been chilled.

"We will travel north, Browfell. We will see if there are any signs left of the fire; it may hold some answers to the questions we are asking," replied Henthorn, who had stretched his arms high above his head.

"Running will be hard with the wind gusting as it is," remarked Bugram, who had also started to stretch his limbs.

Even as the Troll remarked on the strength of the wind, a gust of wind whipped across them, making Henthorn lose his footing. He signalled for them to start their journey and within the hour they were well into their stride. The wind was hampering them, causing them to lose some of the rhythm on which they so relied.. It was after they had been running for the best part of the morning that Henthorn spotted the smoldering pile of dead horses. Hundreds lay there. Some of them had had their legs hacked off; others had no heads. The three Trolls stopped running and circled the horses, unable to speak of what they were seeing, such was the shock of it.

"Evil walks upon the Plains of Desire," said Henthorn quietly.

"Shall I record this?" asked Bugram, who had already started to sketch that which was before him.

"I do not know," replied Henthorn.

"But the council should see this," said Browfell, who had walked off towards the north, his eyes looking in the direction of the mountain range that was his home, Yea-Bor.

"Then draw quickly, Bugram, for we have to tell the council of what has happened here. Evil walks upon the plains, the Trolls must act," replied Henthorn, who had withdrawn his sword. He had sensed something, something close at hand, a sixth sense some had called it. But the mighty Troll had dismissed this talk, saying that he merely sensed danger before others did so. The hairs on the back of his neck stuck out; his heart had started to beat a little more quickly. Henthorn walked around the pile of horses, somehow knowing that the sight that he was about to see would change his life forever. Browfell and Bugram had not noticed that Henthorn had disappeared to the other side of the smoldering pile of stricken horses.

Bugram had nearly finished drawing the awful sight of

the decapitated animals. He looked at the way they had been cut to pieces and felt a sorrow enter his being. *What could do a thing like this?* he thought as he wiped away a tear.

Henthorn though had just seen the creatures that had probably butchered the horses. He watched as the creatures started to rise from the grasses of the Plains of Desire. They were only a few hundred feet away. All in all, he counted two to three thousand at least. They were getting noisy as well, deep snarls and shouts he could not understand. He turned and ran back around the pile of horses, ordering the other two Trolls to run at once.

"What have you seen, Henthorn?" asked Browfell, a worried look spreading across his face.

"Goblins!" he replied instantly.

"Have they seen you?" asked Bugram, who had rolled up the parchment on which he had just drawn.

"No, but believe me, we do not want them to," replied Henthorn, who had returned to the standing figure of Bugram.

"But the council sent us to locate these creatures. I will draw them as quickly as I can. You two head off north, I will follow soon," replied Bugram, who had already withdrawn another rolled up parchment. He then disappeared from view.

"We will wait," said Henthorn, his head shaking in frustration, for he knew time was all they had now.

Bugram had dived into the tall grasses which were still being blown erratically by the strong gusts of wind from the west, the very same grasses amongst which the Goblins and Hobgoblins had rested. Amongst them were several of the Brethren and they were having some trouble keeping order. Small fights were always breaking out between the small Goblins. They had nothing but hatred within their beings and thought nothing of murdering one of their own; this is what the Brethren had to control. It was still a long way to the wooded settlement of Tarsit. The wizards had ordered them to teach the Goblins to fight side by side. The Brethren had killed many of the Goblins, but the one thing the small creatures did not fear was death; they seemed to relish it. But with the help of the wizards' strong spells, the Goblins seemed to be focused on the task they had been set. The horses had been hunted down for two days, the Goblins tearing them to pieces as the animals had run out of stamina. The Brethren had ordered the Goblins to fetch all the dead horses they had hunted down and burn them. The Hobgoblins had helped with this and had feasted on the horse flesh. The Brethren were pleased with this team work and had allowed them to rest for a few hours. Little did they know that they were being spied on.

Bugram drew quickly; he shook his head as he realized that all of the hideous creatures were naked except for the various belts which carried the weapons of destruction. He took more time on the clothed ones, drawing in detail the robes and the pouches that hung from within. However, the faces were hidden. Happy he had completed his task, he made his way slowly through the grasses. The screams and shouts didn't bother him, such was his determination to crawl undetected away from the army of Goblins and Hobgoblins. But his luck was just about to run out; the ever watchful Brethren had spotted the Troll's back as he rose to meet his friends. They had such powerful eyesight, that they could look through the smoldering pile of horses and still make out what was on the other side. Their screams seared through the air and reached Henthorn's ears as a dire warning. He knew immediately that something was wrong. He looked as Bugram rose from the grasses.

"You have been seen!" exclaimed Henthorn.

"Then we must hurry," came the calm response.

"Run like you have never run before, for they will hunt us down like they hunted down these poor horses," Henthorn ordered, who had already started on his way north.

The Brethren had acted almost immediately. They summoned thirty of the small Goblins to hunt down the ones they had seen. The Brethren though did not pursue the said Trolls. They had neither the wish nor the time to hunt them down; they were heading south as quickly as they could.

Henthorn and the two other Trolls had veered east towards the edge of the Plains of Desire. Here they sought cover, but none was to be found. The lands here were devoid of any trees, only small shrubs survived the bitter west winds. Even these found it hard, their shapes distorted heavily by the wind. With the hour passing, the screams of the Goblins could now be heard quite clearly.

"Get ready you two, for our time has run out," shouted the Troll, who had removed his round shield.

Henthorn then veered suddenly to his left, pulling out his bow and several arrows. Browfell and Bugram carried on running northwards, their heads turning to see what Henthorn was doing. The Goblins screamed as they saw the lone Troll running towards them. They started then to throw the eight sided spheres which whistled through the air. Three of them screamed into the shield of Henthorn. He though had unleashed two arrows from his bow, one of them missing the hunting pack altogether, the other piercing the throat of one screaming Goblin, sending the small creature tumbling to its death. With a sudden burst of energy Henthorn then sprinted back towards the other two Trolls.

"Browfell!" exclaimed Henthorn.

Browfell then realised what Henthorn wanted of him. He veered away suddenly, doing as Henthorn had done. He however missed the Goblins altogether. Next it was the turn of the youngest amongst them. Bugram looked at the tiny creatures that were closing in on them and screamed as he let fly with several arrows, none going anywhere near the Goblins They however had struck him twice on the left thigh, his screams of agony making the other two Trolls run to his side. The eight sided spheres were flying all around them; their time had apparently run out. But as Henthorn had attacked again and had managed to kill yet another Goblin, he realised their only chance was to head for the rocky plateau that lay to the east. Here the ground was littered with boulders which had found their way from the mountains over the years, some being the size of one of the creatures that were following them.

"We head to the rocks. Drop all that you can, even your swords. We have only one chance. Yea-Bor is but three hours away, do it now!" ordered Henthorn in such a manner that the two Trolls did what was told of them. With all the weight they had been carrying gone, the three Trolls seemed to make some distance between themselves and the screaming Goblins. Another hour passed. The three Trolls had never run like this before. Their hearts were pounding with the exertion of running at such a speed for so long. Sweat was pouring from their bodies; stitches had come and gone. The pain though was constant. Henthorn could plainly see the city of the Trolls on the distant horizon. His hopes were cruelly dashed however as the screaming Goblins were suddenly running alongside them, their four limbs galloping like that of the horses they had butchered earlier. Henthorn looked at the hatred within the eyes of the creatures that were hunting him and knew then that he and the other two Trolls would never reach the safety of Yea-Bor.

Chapter Eight

Sarratt the wizard had quickly left the Witches Watch, collecting the various items he needed for such a long journey. He collected a pony from the stables and loaded the animal with provisions. He would not use the caves that cut through the mountains to the north of the Watch. Instead he would head west and towards the lands of the clerics, a race of humans dedicated to the art of healing. The Rainbow Falls were a magical place for the wizard; he had spent long periods of time within this land, learning his art of magic, the spoken word. The falls themselves were huge and stretched for miles. Mighty conifer trees abounded. The wizard had named this the Rainbow Wood. He knew that in time, everyone who visited the clerics would ask of the wood. They in turn had promised the wizard that they would call the wood what the wizard had suggested. Though Sarratt was in a big hurry he lingered besides the magnificent falls, the distant roaring of crashing water having a calming effect on his mind.

One week he had spent travelling through this land, though he never visited the clerics. So with one final look at the eternal rainbows, which looped one after another for the whole stretch of the waterfalls, he made his way then northwards and towards the mountain pass the Dwarfs had so skillfully laid. Sarratt knew that he would probably meet the odd Elf and Dwarf along the way, so he had chosen to wear the robes of the Watch. This would enable him to travel without hindrance. His path though veered slightly eastwards once he had climbed several hundred feet. He knew that the Troll and Dwarf armies where fighting within the Golden Valley. Curious as he was, he headed eastwards for two days, not resting at all during this time. It was when he saw the flags of the Troll king fluttering in the breeze that he cursed out loud. His hands moved upwards and pointed towards the King's tent, albeit a mere speck in the distance, then the wizard spoke softly.

"Of all the ages where peace finds a way, a Troll must listen to the few who know the consequences of war, be it a stubborn Troll king in this instance. Do you not gauge the strength of the Dwarfs? Do not delude yourself that you are acting like a king, when in truth you are wasting your time here upon the slopes of the Golden Valley. If I had more time, my friend, I would come to see you. But it is the Elves who I must visit now. Find peace within yourself, Thengost. Act like you are the king, change your ways before it is too late." As the wizard finished what he was saying he again spoke a single word which had many hidden words within it; the spell flew towards the King's tent.

Three days later saw the wizard enter the mountain pass, or as others had named the land, Snakes Pass and the Devil Tail Pass. This made the wizard smile as he wandered through the mountain pass. He encountered only the one convoy of Dwarfs. They spoke of being attacked by the monstrous Trolls of the north. Sarratt promised them he would try and see what the Troll council had to say about the matter. They parted company, with the Dwarfs shouting their anger at the wizards and how they always seemed to take the side of the Trolls. This had brought Sarratt even more laughter. Shaking his head, he left them as quickly as he had met them.

But his smile was shattered as he looked upon the Plains of Desire that morning, for even though he did not see anything, he sensed at once that evil was upon the land therein.. He turned to the pony and spoke with him.

"I promised you that I would find a suitable name for you, for we were going to spend a long time within each other's company. But time has suddenly caught up with the races of Ursalane and I will not put you through the danger that lies ahead. You I will name Rainbow," said the wizard as he touched the pony on the nose.

"Now leave. I travel onto the Plains of Desire to seek out another of your race. Go back to the Witches Watch and seek out the Watch Wizard. Tell him everything I am about to tell you," said the Wizard, who had rubbed the pony on the nose. He simply nodded his head and turned. The pony disappeared from the wizard's view within minutes. He had also reassured the pony that he would not be bothered by any other race or animal. Sarratt then made his way quickly onto the edge of the Plains of Desire. He had noted the change in the weather also, and the strong winds had started to whip across the green desert. The wizard strode onto the Plains of Desire, the Great Eastern Divide behind him. He clutched his black staff in his hands; the staff he had personally cut off a wood pearl tree, its gnarled end resembling a dragon's claw, and knelt upon the lifeless grasslands. He emptied his thoughts, his staff entering the Plains of Desire. He could sense them, thousands of them. He called for them, his chanting travelling down the staff and into the grasslands. The one he sought however was fighting against the spells the wizard was sending. Sarratt thought of how strong of mind this one individual must be. For two whole days the wizard fought with the legend of the Plains of Desire, sensing how the stallion valued the freedom of his race. "I seek your leader, your king, your stallion. I have great need of him," he said in the language of the horse. Three more hours passed by, but the wizard was determined to break the mighty black stallion, the leader of such a proud race. Suddenly the earth started to tremble; he could feel it through his staff. They were coming, thousands of them. The wizard's whole being could now feel the approach, and he looked towards the west and saw them: an army of horses, wild and free. Then they were past him, thundering around the wizard. He remained kneeling, waiting for them to meet with him.

The commotion had died down somewhat. The horses had formed a close circle around the wizard. It must be said though that this was a huge circle in depth. In places, they stood three to four hundred, each happy to be standing within the company of one which held the power to speak with them. From the middle of the horses came a black stallion, its mane nearly touching the grasses of the plains. Sarratt looked upon the mighty horse and admired the strength that the animal possessed.

"I seek your help, Stormbreaker. Will you carry me north?" asked the wizard, though no spoken words were said. Stormbreaker simply nodded his head. The other horses then started to retreat backwards, the circle becoming ever wider.

"Send your kind as far south as possible. An evil has come onto these plains that will threaten your very existence. The southern farmlands will be safe, for the time being.

Stormbreaker then reared up onto his hind legs and neighed for some time. The message had been given; the wild horses stampeded away from the watching wizard.

"You will at all times be able to communicate with me. Do not be afraid, for I will protect you with my life. Come, let us ride as one," said the wizard who had mounted the mighty black stallion. The wind was still whipping across the plains, bringing with it a foul stench, one which the wizard had smelled before within the badlands, in a place which was known as the Devils' Gorge. This place was, a deep, open wound upon the land, a land where the Goblins, Hobgoblins and Ogres lived. What brings them this far south? asked the wizard within his mind, at the same time urging Stormbreaker to break into a gallop. Within the hour, Sarratt suddenly turned his gaze west. On the far horizon he saw the black shapes running south, some taller than others. They were running hard. Part of the wizard was drawn to them, but something else had caught his eye, further to the north. Without hesitation he immediately asked the horse to hurry onwards. Stormbreaker neighed loudly as he sped at a speed no other horse had ever reached before. At times, the horse's hooves did not touch the plains for long seconds. This was not due to the speed of the horse, but because of the spoken word of magic the wizard had whispered. From a distance they were but a blur; within minutes they had reached the murdered pile of horses. Stormbreaker thudded his hooves in anger, his thoughts going into the wizard's.

"Why and how could such a terrible thing happen,my kind wizard?"

"There are creatures abroad that do not belong here; they have no respect for the living. I truly feel sorrow for you on this sad day," came the quiet response.

As the wizard dismounted from the horse, he again spoke a word of magic. He felt the power and the madness surge from his very being. The pile of dead horses suddenly caught fire, the flames reaching high into the windy skies, but there was no smoke to be seen, such was the heat of the flames. Within minutes there was but a small pile of ashes. The wizard then knelt down at the murderous scene and scooped up the ashes with his right hand. He stood tall and scattered them onto the Plains of Desire.

"Gallop freely upon these grasslands. Your souls will live on and you will not be forgotten."

Stormbreaker nodded his head and neighed. The black stallion wanted away from this place; his hooves where stamping down impatiently.

"Let us ride north. To Yea-Bor I must travel," said the wizard, who had once more mounted the horse. But again his attention was drawn to the dead bodies of the Goblins that had been hidden by the long grasses of the plains. He saw the arrows protruding and realised that they were those of the Trolls. He slapped the horse's rump and together they raced northwards, the wind having no effect on their progress. Once more the black stallion lifted from the Plains of Desire, Sarratt leant forward, his long black hair billowing behind him, but his eyes were darting to the left and to the right, for he knew that to be caught off guard could cost them dearly. He saw on the distant horizon the black outline of the Troll homelands, Yea-Bor, but something else attracted his attention: to the right of them, a small glint of light had turned the wizard's gaze downwards. The objects that lay on the Plains of Desire made the wizard hurry even more.

"Do not be afraid, Stormbreaker. You will not come to any harm, just do as I say," whispered the wizard, who once more spoke the word of magic that lifted the horse's hooves off the grasslands.

Henthorn was near to collapse. Bugram had slowed to a limping trot. The Goblins which numbered thirty at least had run on for some one hundred paces. Here they turned, facing the three shocked Trolls. There was nowhere for them to run.

"We fight with our daggers," shouted Henthorn, who was bending over in agony.

"I have nothing. We are surely doomed to die here!" exclaimed the wounded Bugram.

"Here, I have another dagger. They do not frighten me," said Browfell, who had handed Bugram one of his daggers.

The Goblins stood in a line, low to the floor. Their arms could easily be mistaken for legs, such was their shape, but these forearms were powerful. A flick of the wrist could send one of the eight sided missiles hurtling through the air. The grunting screams pierced through the wind, which, if anything, had picked up. Suddenly two of the Goblins attacked the three Trolls. Galloping towards the startled Trolls, they were soon upon them. But it was the wounded Bugram who reacted first. He met the screams of the Goblins with his own, his yells of hatred carrying him into the two Goblins with a sickening crunch. This sent one of the Goblins into the path of Henthorn, who immediately dived onto the slime- ridden body of the evil creature, plunging his two daggers into its head; it died instantly. Bugram though had been nearly knocked unconscious. The remaining Goblin was closing in on the stricken Troll, bearing its razor sharp teeth, snarling like a wild animal.

"No!" screamed Henthorn, as he saw what was about to happen to the fallen Troll. Even as he started to run to him, he saw a black flash go past the two figures. He thought he saw blackness as well, a thin black blur which passed through the figure of the Goblin. Henthorn watched as the Goblin fell onto the barren rocks in two pieces, its vile blood spurting high into the air.

Stormbreaker came to a sliding halt upon the rocky surface, its nostrils flaring wildly. But the animal felt no fear as it faced the creatures which had been responsible for the butchering of his kind.

Sarratt leapt from the horse, his hooded cloak hiding his features from all who looked upon him. Ancient words were forming in his mind, words from another age, dangerous words that had the capacity to capture the one who was spoken to, sending him down into an abyss of evil.

The Goblins screamed as one as they charged at the two figures of the horse and the wizard.

"Go back to the depths of the netherworld where you belong, into the crack of blackness that gave birth to you. You do not belong among the living, "said the wizard, who had started to walk towards the charging Goblins. He let the ancient words come from the depths of his mind. He knew not how they had come to him, but let them form on his lips. He knew them to be that of the ancient Elf tongue that was not spoken anymore, but did not fully understand the content of the spell. But as he let them forth, an energy of immense power came forth. The rocks beneath the wizard's feet actually cracked open. The ground shook violently as if a thunderstorm had suddenly started. A wave of light sped towards the Goblins, engulfing them in a torturous glow. The crack opened wider, the noise of the splintering rock deafening to the stunned Trolls, who had retreated somewhat from the black figure that had showed them a power they had not thought possible.

The Goblins disappeared into the crack and were never seen again, their screams of hatred dying slowly away. The black robed figure fell onto one knee, his body hunched over in apparent pain.

"Who are you?" asked Henthorn, his voice raised so that the figure could hear him.

The wizard had not the energy left to answer the Troll.

"Where are you from?" asked the Troll, who had remained some distance away from the kneeling figure.

After some minutes, Sarratt regained some of his thoughts. He had nearly fallen into the black abyss with the screaming creatures, the power of the words he had spoken had been the most evil he had used. But something attracted him to them. Was this the thin line the Watch Wizard had spoken of? To falter just a little from the white side and see what treasures could be had with so much power? No one had ever been able to control the selfwill; those who had tried had fallen into the abyss of hell. He rose and turned to look upon the three Trolls. He thought of the way they feared him.He pulled his black hood tightly around his head, which was still pounding. He walked slowly to Stormbreaker and patted the great black stallion softly on his nose, reassuring the horse that all was well. The wizard then brought forth from the back of the horse a large cloth bag which clanked noisily as he carried it.

"These must be yours," said the wizard softly, as he lay down the bag.

Henthorn bent down and felt inside the bag, finding his sword. He emptied the contents upon the ground, shaking his head in wonder.

"We owe you our lives, hooded one," he said.

"Take me to the council chambers and I will forgo your debt to me," replied the wizard, who still had the hood wrapped tightly about his head.

Browfell came forwards with his arm supporting the limp body of Bugram. His face was stretched with a fear, his eyes were bulging.

"But there are hundreds of the creatures behind us. We will die upon these rocks, Yea-Bor will be but a memory for me."

"They are heading south. Their destination is still a mystery to me, as is the appearance of them within the grasslands of the Plains of Desire. You will be within your city this evening. Let me see to the wounded Troll," replied the wizard, who took Bugram in his arms and tried to lay a soft comforting spell over his being. But the wizard found to his dismay that he was far too weak to cast any spells, so he and Henthorn laid the stricken Troll over the flanks of the horse.

"If you are seeking the King, your journey is but a wasted one. He is failing us within the Golden Valley; he is but a shadow of a king," said Henthorn, who still did not know the identity of the the robed figure..

Sarratt then removed his hood and looked upon the two standing Trolls. His eyes were but mere slits. His featureless face said nothing of what he was thinking.

"Your King will return to his lands a different Troll. You above all, Henthorn, should remember what the council did to your King."

"Behold! It is the wizard known as Sarratt! But you are but young in the art of wizardry?"

"Have I then grown older within your eyes, Henthorn?" he asked sternly.

"Your face remains in shadow. I cannot see what my memory remembers, but it is a joy to realise that it is you who stands before us now, for I feared that you represented only death. I sensed no goodness, not until you removed your hood," came the joyous reply.

"Then let us hurry onwards to Yea-Bor. The council will have to be summoned, for if there are more of the Goblins abroad to the west, then the running units will have to act quickly."

With the wounded Troll slipping into a painful sleep,

the wizard and the two Trolls made steady progress towards the walled city of Yea-Bor.

Yea-Bor stood on top of an outcrop of granite rock, the jagged edges of the granite providing the whole of the city with a natural defense. It stretched for miles, its outline clearly seen from miles away. No trees grew here, not even the smallest shrub or bush. To the south and west were the Plains of Desire, a green desert that stretched for hundreds of miles. To the east and north lay the mountains of the Great Eastern Divide. Winters were long here and the Trolls of Yea-Bor relied upon the Golden Valley for the harvests that kept the hundreds of thousands of Trolls alive during the fierce winters. Massive stone towers and a wall had been built long ago on the edges of the city. This was known as the outer wall, reaching as high as thirty feet in places. The only way inside was through the secret stone doorways which could only be opened from within. Beyond the outer wall lay fields of earth: red and brown soil which the Trolls had carried from the Golden Valley. This had taken many years, but such was the importance of this soil to the Trolls that the effort had seemed worthwhile, for they grew nothing else but the potato within these fields. A further ten miles within stood the midder wall. This was not as high as the outer wall, standing fifteen feet at its highest. This was built in the event of an enemy breaching the outer wall and had large ornate wooden doorways that were kept open during peaceful times. Numerous towers were built around the midder wall, more as an aesthetic than a proper defense system, for only one Troll could squeeze into a turret at any one time. Beyond this wall stood a further three miles of the potato farms. It was beyond these that lay the actual city of the Trolls. There stood a magnificent twelve foot wall, carved with the army of the running units, each stone carving facing outwards, their swords drawn ready to defend the city. Within this wall were built the only two doorways: the silver doors that faced the Elves and the golden ones which paid homage to the Golden Valley. Each had cost the race of the Trolls many thousands of lives as they fought for the right to mine within the Valley of the Golden River. Finally, within the inner wall, stood the city of the Trolls, made up of thousands of single storey buildings, with only the watch tower standing right at the centre of the ringed city, for most of the buildings had lower levels which housed the families. This had been done because of the constant warmth the lower chambers gave. The great debating chamber was several floors beneath the cobbled flooring of the streets of Yea-Bor, situated under the watch tower.

The stone outer wall loomed into view. Several members of a running unit had come out of one of the secret doorways to help with the wounded Troll.

"These are strange days!" exclaimed one of the approaching Trolls; he had noted that a wizard was amongst the small group of Trolls.

"Goblins are upon the Plains of Desire. Go quickly and seek Denjom, he will do the rest," ordered Henthorn, who had helped Browfell bring Bugram down from the horse.

"But he could be anywhere!" complained the Troll in disbelief. After all, the city of the Trolls was a massive city, its streets winding this way and that. Even some of the older Trolls had got lost after taking a wrong turn.

"Look at me," snapped Henthorn in disgust. Only then did the Troll realise to whom he was talking.

"I will find him as quickly as I can, Henthorn. Forgive my rudeness," he replied, bowing low to the floor as he turned and sprinted back through the outer wall doorway.

"You three will tend to Bugram. He was wounded upon the plains. Take him to see the healers, they should be able to sort out his leg," ordered the Troll, whose tiredness had somehow disappeared. He beckoned the others to him.

"Take this horse to the stables. Make sure he is well looked after, he belongs to the wizard."

"Stormbreaker will wait upon the Plains of Desire. A stable is no place for such an animal," interrupted the wizard, who had moved over to the waiting horse. He once more asked the horse if he may wait for him. He would call him within the week. The horse nodded its head and neighed softly, rubbing against the right shoulder of the wizard. Then he was gone, galloping off towards the south.

"So be it, Wizard! Will you then please be my guest while you are within my city?"

"I would be pleased if I could have a bed for a couple of nights, but do not let too many know of my return. I will make myself known once the council have discussed what you and the other two have seen on the Plains of

Desire," replied Sarratt, who had offered his left hand for the Troll to hold. This Henthorn did; the contact with the wizard was a shock for the Troll, for touching the skin of the wizard was like touching a block of ice.

"You need a roaring fire to sit before!" he exclaimed as he led the wizard to his home.

As the wizard scratched his chin and stared into the roaring fire, he thought of where he was meant to be going. Little did the Trolls know of the plans the Elf king was making with the Dwarf lord of Pavelem. It seemed to him then that he was amongst a race that was bearing the hostilities of so many. He wondered, as the flames licked against the chimney breast, if they would survive this coming winter. Sorrow crept into his being, finding its way into the very soul of the wizard.

"Here, drink this," offered Henthorn, who had handed the wizard a tankard of hot whiskey ale.

"Oh! Many thanks, Henthorn. Is there any news of the council?" he asked as he sipped at the strong smelling drink.

"I will go and find out what is happening. Enjoy your ale, for it will warm places you never even thought you had," joked the Troll as he departed up the stone stairway and up through the hatch in the ceiling.

Sarratt smiled at the Troll. He did drink the strong whiskey ale, but his hands were still freezing, for it was not the weather which had turned his hands cold, it was the use of the spell of the ancient Elves. He knew that within a day or two he would once more feel heat from his fingers, so he had simply pushed the pain to the back of his mind. It was all part of being a wizard, he had thought.

Three hours later and the wizard was escorted down the spiral stairways of the debating chamber. Henthorn led the way, a burning torch in his right hand. The deeper they went, the warmer it became. Eventually they entered the chamber, a massive room considering it had been dug out of the granite rock by the Trolls. In length it was two hundred paces, its width fifty at least. The table which stood in the middle was one hundred and twenty paces in length and ten paces in width. It had been carved from a tree from the Elves, when the two races had been trading with one another. However, that had been a century in passing. To the left of the table, as Sarratt came down the last few steps of the spiral stairway, there started a wall painting that stretched all the way down the length of the debating chamber. The artists which had painted these works of art had taken the scenes from the many battles the Trolls had had with the other races. Some of them looked so real one could almost feel he was there. At the very end of the debating chamber was yet another chamber, this being a fraction of the size of the great hall. It contained thousands of maps and drawings; in times of war it was in constant use.

"If you really want to stay within the map chamber until you are called, then so be it. I however think it would be wiser if you were here at the start of the debate," suggested Henthorn, who had unlocked the smaller chamber.

"The council will not like debating its business in the company of a wizard, this you know well, for the last time I was present at the beginning, the debate did not get under way until Denjom had ordered all the chamber to keep their own counsel. We have not the time for such trivial things. Tell them, Henthorn, of what you have seen. Make it clear that there will be more Goblins coming from the west. Of this I am quite certain," replied the wizard as he slipped into the darkened room. He wandered over to the war table. Various maps had been laid out upon it. He ran his finger over the Plains of Desire.

"I hope this is but a few who have strayed from their vile homelands," said the wizard quietly.

One hundred Trolls sat around the long table, each having something to say about the rumours from the west. At the head of the table sat Denjom, head of the Troll council. He was quiet, contemplating the news he had been given by the Troll who was standing behind him. Eventually, when the council had quietened down, he rose, his huge frame towering over the table. He spoke just a few words.

"Let the debate begin."

Denjom then made way for the Troll who was standing behind him. Henthorn walked forwards until he too was standing at the head of the table; his face was etched with worry.

"Council of the debating chamber, let me if you will, tell you of the journey I have just made."

A rumble from the lower end of the chamber made its

way up the table, with each of the members having to verbally agree to let the Troll running unit warrior speak within the ancient chamber.

"I will begin with news of the King. He spends his days watching the battles upon the Golden Valley. He is vastly overweight and offers no direction for the council. He says he will do as he likes; it was a sorry sight to behold. May the council carry out the penalty for a lost King."

The seated chamber erupted with a fury. Shouts of anger rang out. Some of the Trolls actually threw their filled tankards into the stone walls, such was their disgust. But the wizard who had remained within the small room heard everything and knew that the King of the Trolls had much to offer. The council though were already acting on what the Troll had said. They had the power to strip the King of the throne. Several Trolls were even now spelling out to the head of the council their rights in the matter, but Denjom waved them all away and shook his head at Henthorn.

"Why whip them up like this, Henthorn? The King is still the King until he stands before this council. Tell them of what you have seen and forget about these politics," said the Troll quietly, his hand reaching out to touch Henthorn on the forehead.

Henthorn was about to tell the council that his travels had taken him onto the Plains of Desire. He even had in his grasp the drawings Bugram had sketched, but something caught his attention right at the other end of the chamber. A shadowy figure had suddenly appeared.

He looked to the head of the debating council and told him of what he had seen. Henthorn peered past the sitting assembly and also saw the approaching figure. This was no Troll that walked within the Trolls' chamber.

"Stranger who dares to tread within this sacred chamber, declare your intentions before you are dealt with," ordered Denjom, pointing to the robed figure.

"Trolls of Yea-Bor, I have a message from the one. Listen carefully, for your very existence depends on your answers," came the rasping reply.

Three of the seated Trolls acted immediately. They rose as one, withdrawing their swords as a sign of intended aggression. Prestersfordle looked at the three Trolls with a look of pure hatred. His face was hidden within the shadows of his black hood. If the three Trolls had seen the face, then they might have thought twice about the actions they were performimg. The robed wizard spoke words of evil under his breath, long sentences that ignited the air around him with static electricity. At that precise moment, every Troll within the debating chamber felt the hairs on the back of their necks stand up. The three Trolls stepped closer to the wizard. Shouts of outrage from the other seated Trolls caused them to feel confident in what they were doing, but as Prestersfordle spoke again, the chamber fell quiet; the stunned Trolls could only look on in horror at what they were witnessing. The first of the three Trolls died instantly, his body torn apart by the unseen evil which had been let loose within the chamber. The second tried to charge at the wizard, but he too received the same fate as the first. Last of all was the third. Prestersfordle pointed his gnarled finger at the charging Troll. The sword fell with a clang onto the cold slabs. The body of the Troll was then lifted into the air as if he weighed less than a feather of the Golden Valley eagle and floated helplessly above the watching assembly of Trolls. The wizard walked underneath and made his way to the head of the debating table.

"See how weak you are. I could wipe out this chamber within a few minutes. Tell your Trolls to remain seated. If they attempt to fight me, they will suffer what he is going through," warned the wizard, who had turned to see the floating Troll scream in agony. He was being stretched by an unseen force. Eventually, when his limbs could not take anymore, cracking noises resounded around the chamber. Then his body separated, sending out a shower of blood and guts directly onto the debating table. Gasps of shock and outrage rang out as they watched one of their own die in such a needless way.

"What do you want of us, evil one?" asked Denjom, his hand gripping the hilt of his sword. He did not fear death and only held back from attacking this dark figure for the safety of the others.

Meanwhile from within the small room at the end of the debating chamber, Sarratt had sensed the presence of the other wizard immediately. He recoiled his body and stooped low to the floor. Spells had come to his mind: spells of protection. He knew he was still too weak to challenge the wizard, so he stayed in that position readying himself for his coming.

Prestersfordle though had not felt the presence of Sarratt. His mind was concentrating solely on the assembled Trolls. Even though he was safe enough, one mistake could cost him his life.

"My master desires that you, the council, send fifty running units to the Keep of Helgost."

Denjom looked at the wizard in amazement. How could he respond to such a request?

"If you do not do this, a winter will fall on Yea-Bor that will end your days upon this earth," rasped the wizard who had jumped on to the table.

"These Trolls you ask for! Are they to be killed within the lands of the shadow?" asked Denjom, his thoughts dark as he thought of the place where the most evil Troll had lived. So evil he had been that no living Troll had ever set foot within the dreaded Keep.

"It is a small price you pay for life. You have but one cycle of the moon. If his wishes are not met, then this city will fall," replied Prestersfordle, who had walked closer to the head of the debating chamber. As he strode forwards he took from his cloak a bloodied head of a Troll. Denjom withdrew his sword as the wizard brought the head into full view. He lifted his sword high above his head in defiance. Other Trolls did the same. The low rumblings from the bottom of the debating chamber were rising as they realised yet another of their kin had been slaughtered by this wizard. The wizard though had expected worse. He threw the decapitated head at the figure who stood before him. Such was the force of the impact that Denjom was lifted off the ground and flung against the far wall, missing the door to the map room by inches. Henthorn roared at the black robed figure and charged, but the wizard had already spoken a simple word of magic. Henthorn was lucky to survive as he too was smashed into the stone walls of the debating chamber. Prestersfordle then spoke quickly as several other members of the Troll council attacked. His whole being faded as the Trolls lunged for him, but as the wizard was departing, he sensed the other wizard and felt a power there that he had not felt before. His mind tried to seek out the identity of the other wizard, but he had already left the city of the Trolls. As he landed upon the Plains of Desire, he thought of the magic he had felt for that briefest of moments and shivered. His master was not the only one then, he thought, as he walked away into the west.

Back within the debating chamber, the atmosphere was hectic. Shouts of fury had risen up to such a noise that even Sarratt covered his ears from within the map room. Suddenly the door opened and there stood a Troll Sarratt knew well. He looked at the head of the council with pity; blood was flowing freely from the gash on the side of his head.

"The age of the Trolls is coming to an end, Wizard," he said flatly.

Sarratt rose to his feet and uttered a simple healing

spell that would help the stricken Troll mend quickly from his wounds. He put his hand on the Troll's forehead and spoke quickly, the pain of the simple spell nearly

"Remember this, head of the council. As I live and breathe, the race of the Trolls will prevail. As a race, you have much to offer. From where this wizard came, I do not know, but I felt the power he possessed. I was unable to confront him. Understand me when I say that when I use the magic, I have to rest for many hours. Go and tell them that Yea-Bor will not fall. Give them the hope they deserve."

"How can the race of Trolls have hope when the King idles his days away? We have no hope left. The Dwarfs of Pavelem will not listen to the caution of the wizards much longer. The Elves no longer recognise us as a race. We are here only because of the wizards of Wizards Watch. Even the Gnomes of Gutox stay away, Wizard! Hope vanished the moment that monster walked within the debating chamber," said the despondent figure of the Troll.

"Hope will see you through the darkest of the coming months. Recall the council of the Trolls. It is time I spoke with them," replied the young wizard, who had patted the Troll upon the shoulder. As he was saying this however, he too thought of what was amassing against the Trolls and his mood saddened. Time was against him, as was the little hope the head of the council had left to hold onto.

Chapter Nine

Treak heard the creatures enter the tunnel and shouted for Crikken to make haste. The latter nodded his head without saying anything. He could see the edge of the bramble and swathed his way through its twisted branches, not bothering to be precise with his swings. He suddenly found himself within a field, its crop already harvested. In the distance there was a hedgerow, then another field and so on into the distance.

"Run!" screamed Treak.

The four Gnomes and the Elf ran as fast as they could. Arrun though found that he had to slow down and wait for the Gnomes to catch up. He helped each one of them over the hedge, the height of it being only a few feet. Even so, the Gnomes would have struggled with the ditch that ran alongside.

"See, Crikken, the Elf waits for us, he offers us his hand. This is what I expect of the fairer race," said the overjoyed Gnome.

"Then why do the ones upon the horses hunt us down for the mere merriment it brings them? They are different from us, Treak. This one is with us for we carry some of his treasure," came the maddened response.

The bramble they had only moments before departed, seemed to explode from within; hideous shapes jumped from it, screaming.

"The bramble, I see, has taken a bite at them!" exclaimed Kellek, a wry smile spreading across his face.

"We must keep on running," urged the Elf.

"He is right. East we travel. The slopes of the Great Eastern Divide will hopefully offer us some hope," said the leader of the Gnomes.

The Goblins were quick though. Two had already caught up with the ones they were so desperate to slaughter, their squat rounded bodies hurtling across the farmers' fields, the hedgerows being ignored completely as they bounded over them in a single leap. Snarling, they closed in on the last of the hunted group. Crikken was unaware that the two Goblins had been so quick. He screamed out loudly as one of them scratched his side with one of its front legs. He looked down at the rows of razor sharp teeth and bulging eyes and saw within the stare a hatred he had never seen before. Arrun had seen the two approach them and had veered sharply to his right, at the same time signaling to Treak to carry onwards towards the mountains. He then started to run as fast as he could, withdrawing as he ran his two small daggers. Crikken merely saw a green flash go past him, but the two Goblins had seen more than that. They had witnessed the full fury of an Elf. Even they who relished the thought of death, shivered as they were cut down within inches of their first kill. Their bodies rolled helplessly for some fifteen paces. Arrun laid his two daggers horizontal to the green grasses and cleaned them as he ran. It had taken but a few seconds, but the memory of that kill would stay with Crikken for the rest of his life. Up until then, he had never thought that an Elf would waste its breath on a Gnome.

"We go to the place I know as Wooded Hood. We need to see to the injured Gnome here, he is bleeding quite profusely," ordered the Elf, who had taken the lead, his two daggers back within their resting place.

"But Wooded Hood is full of Dwarfs!" exclaimed Treak, spitting in front of the elf.

"Then die amongst these fields, Gnome," came the harsh reply.

The Goblins who had fallen at the hands of the Elf were indeed quite dead, but several others had screamed from within the bramble. Bursting forth into the field, their eyes locked instantly upon the distant bodies of their own, just about visible above the hedge. Then they caught a glimpse of the small group, heading north. With another scream of hatred, they started to gallop after them, hurdling the hedgerow with ease. Crikken was struggling to keep up with the rest. His side was burning with pain; each step was excruciating. He called to Treak,

"Leave me here, I will fight the monsters for as long as I can."

"Give your wood pearls to the Elf then. May every Gnome bless your life," agreed Treak instantly, his fingers telling the Elf to get the wood pearls from the back of the stricken Gnome.

"You will last but a few seconds, Gnome. Your body will be torn apart as if it were a tender piece of chicken. You should be ashamed of your actions, Gnome," said the Elf, pointing in disgust towards the figure of Treak.

"It is the way of the battle, Elf. You would not understand," replied Treak in self- defence.

"He comes with us to Wooded Hood, you two! Help Crikken or face the wrath of an Elf," warned Arrun, who had spotted the livestock in the adjoining field. He went to Crikken and took the two sacks from him. Crikken could not help but spit at the Elf, his eyes still showing hatred for him..

"Do not worry, Gnome. I will give you these back when you are feeling better. Now let us hurry or we will all fall."

The Elf urged them all on, guiding them into the heavily stocked field. Here were cattle and ponies, pigs and chickens, plus the local delicacy of wild deer. Soon they were amongst the grazing animals. The four Gnomes were petrified. So would the animals have been, but for the calming sound of the Elf humming different tunes under his breath. None stirred as they walked through to the far side. Here they climbed over the wooden fence and vanished into the dense woodland that would lead them to the heavily populated area known as Wooded Hood, a trading post that had grown over the years, feeding the trade routes between Follonday and Pavelem. The Dwarfs who lived here were a happy race. They had long since forgotten about Pavelem, forgotten about the harsh lives they had once had to endure under the Kingship of Forgehammer, a Dwarf of legend, a Dwarf who was feared throughout the city of Pavelem.

The Goblins meanwhile had entered the field where the livestock was kept. All of them sensed the hideous small creatures and somehow knew that evil had entered their field. The Goblins seemed to dwell within the field. They smelled the warm flesh, they wanted to feast upon the animals. Such was their hunger for death they did slaughter several of the terrified beasts, feasting until they were full. With bloodied faces, they moved off into the woodland at a much slower rate, their small minds contented with what they had done.

"Are they behind us, Elf?" asked Treak in a distressed voice, worried that Crikken might be the death of them all.

"They seem to be feeding," was the simple reply, his thoughts heavy with the knowledge that Crikken had been quite happy to sacrifice himself for the sake of the others.

"Elf," said the leader of the small band of Gnomes, his eyes mere slits as he looked at Arrun.

"What?" he asked sharply.

"Understanding our ways is most important for you,

otherwise you might think we are no better than what hunts us."

"You all spit at me still."

"Nothing personal."

"Wooded Hood is still some way off. If we are to find our way through this woodland while there is still daylight around us, we should set our pace now and keep it up. As you well know, Treak, you are in the lands of the Dwarf. Even though these are moderate in their views, they would not think twice about killing you," replied the Elf, ignoring what the Gnome was trying to explain to him.

High above the woodland, the skies had begun to darken. Raindrops had started to fall. The wind whipped across the tops of the trees, taking with it thousands of leaves. Howling screams whistled through the tree tops. Many of the smaller animals of the wood scurried into their homes. Tonight, as they knew, was going to be a howler. The five companions still had several miles to travel until they reached the outskirts of the trade town. The main trade route lay well to the north. No roads had been laid this far south, though rough lanes had been cut through the wood, enabling the inhabitants of Wooded Hood to farm the southern fields.

"That wind sounds like an evil one," stated the youngest of the Gnomes.

"It comes from the west, Akkia. It is the tree tops that make it sound worse than it is. I have felt the odd drop of rain, but rest assured that outside of the wood, it is torrential in its downpour. See, there in the distance, can you see the rain coming down?" he asked as they walked towards the sight that would stay with the young Gnome for the rest of his life, for it was as if the sky had started to rain in that place only. The last glimmers of the setting sun had given the rain a gleam, so with the rain also came a light.

"It is a wondrous sight," gasped the Gnome.

"We Elves regard this as the light of Esslestar, for he looks upon every woodland within these lands. Come, before the rain starts to drop off the branches. We will be there soon," he promised.

The four Gnomes had only looked upon Wooded Hood once before and were once more amazed at what they saw. Suddenly dozens of stone buildings came into view. Some were as high as the treetops, while others were only a single storey. Each was painted white, with small wooden doors and very small wooden shuttered windows. No lights could be seen from the dwellings of the Dwarfs; this made the four Gnomes sigh with relief. Arrun led them around the first set of buildings and they moved northwards for another hour. The storm of that evening was growing; great booms of thunder could be heard coming from the west.

"We are here," said the Elf quietly as he walked up to a large stone building.

"This place stinks!" exclaimed Kellek, who disliked the race of the Dwarfs with a passion. He spat at the whitewashed building.

"Is it safe?" asked Treak, ignoring the comments of Kellek, spitting all the same though.

"Is anywhere safe?"

"You know what I mean," replied the Gnome, who had clicked his fingers in frustration. He was not used to following anyone; he was a leader after all.

"Let us find out. Be quiet though, we might disturb the rats," mocked the Elf, a wry smile spreading across his lean features.

The room they stepped into was dark Arrun though headed into the darkness as if it was during the day. He made his way to the centre of the room and waved the others to follow, but the four Gnomes remained at the doorway, wary of the darkness from within. Arrun brought forth from his cloak a crystal; it glowed faintly within his grasp.

"Enter, as you will be quite safe here. I need to see to the one who you would have left to the mercy of those monsters."

Treak, Kellek and Akkia then looked behind them. Crikken was standing there, looking past them. He walked into the Dwarfs' building without saying a word to his friends; he was close to passing out. That first night was one where the Elf tended to the wounded Gnome. He brought forth a leaf from his cloak and spat on it. Next he massaged it into the wounds. There were many; the Goblin had dug its claws deep into the side of the Gnome. Arrun then spat directly onto the wounds, blowing as he did so. A white foam started to froth amongst them.

Crikken screamed out in agony, trying to hold his side, but Arrun grasped the Gnome's hand and held it away from the bloody mess. Long minutes passed and still the Gnome screamed. Treak had come to his side.

"See! You also spit at us. Does that mean you are like us, Elf?

Elf magic is the one thing I never thought I would see. Your mythology is true then?" he asked in wonder.

"We can heal, this is true. But we need the help of the forest. I applied a leaf from the forest of the Elves. It is called simply green leaf, though you must know where to look within the forest. Calm down, Crikken. The pain no longer surges through your being, for now you are safe. Relax your mind and think only of things that bring you pleasure."

It was indeed true; the pain had receded from the Gnome's body. But Crikken could not bring his mind to think of his homeland, he saw only the Goblins that had tried to kill him. He closed his eyes and drifted in and out of sleep, tossing and turning as if he were in a fever.

"Is he going to live?" asked Akkia, who had come to sit by Crikken's side.

"He will live," replied the Elf. "and I spit for his recovery, not out of hatred!"

"Then we must leave him here," stated Treak, who had already begun to pack his belongings.

"For three days we will have to wait here, and then Crikken will be well enough to carry on," said Arrun, his angry face turning away from the Gnomes' leader.

"But it is the way of the Gnomes. We wait for no one; every Gnome understands this. There are no hard feelings towards Crikken. If he makes his way back to Gutox, we will be the first to celebrate. Do not stand in the way of our customs," warned Treak, clicking his fingers to the other two Gnomes.

"Then if I see you again, I won't. The roads are treacherous within this region. Not only are there Goblins hunting you, you have the Dwarfs. As you well know, they will strike first, then ask questions. But apart from this, there are the mountain bandits. These will trap you like the poor deer that get snared in their crude traps. You may think you know the way out of Wooded Hood, but one wrong turn and that will be the end of you. I myself choose to stay here until Crikken is well. You do as you like, Gnome, but think of the two younger Gnomes you take to their deaths," replied Arrun, who had walked over to the doorway. He opened it slightly, peering into the stormy night. The wind whistled through into the room.

Treak remained where he had packed his bag. His two sacks of wood pearls lay on the floor before him. The Elf had sown a seed of doubt into his normally rigid outlook on destiny. He thought of their chances of finding their way out of the wood, thought of the bandits with their traps, but most of all he thought of the Goblins he had seen attack Crikken. If it had not been for the lightning speed of the Elf, he would surely have died a horrible death. He looked then to Akkia and Kellek. They had not moved. This place seemed safe enough, he thought. He then walked to the Elf.

"Then I will discard the ways of the Gnomes. I will do as you say. I will choose to stay within your company, but tell me why you are staying with us. You have enough fighting ability to take the wood pearls from us and return to Tarsit a hero!"

Arrun returned to the side of the stricken Gnome. He knelt down and felt at the wound, happy that it was healing. He sat with his back against the stone wall.

"I thought of doing that, Gnome. I thought of the deaths of you and your thieving friends, but the sight of the Goblins made me think only of them. You are indeed lucky, but feel safe in the knowledge that those thoughts are no longer with me. I will stay with you as a friend and I will try to understand your ways. Now, enough of this talk, Treak, and enough of your clicking fingers. Let us eat," said the Elf, who had laid a hand upon the wound of Crikken.

When the simple foods had been eaten, the Gnomes prepared themselves for the sleep for which they were longing. Each of them slipped within their body wraps and were soon fast asleep. The soft light of the Elf's crystal dimmed until no light shone from its tip. Arrun though did not sleep that night; his senses were alert for any signs of danger. He did however let his mind take him to the forests of Follonday… he walked amongst the magnificent trees, looked upon the giant waterfalls which cascaded throughout the lands, smelled the scented flowers and knelt amongst his favourite: a lush carpet of snow drops. Arrun did this many times, for his heart always yearned to be within his lands, but as he had chosen to leave his birthplace he was able to cope with his homesickness.

Morning came and the small party were relieved that Crikken was awake and chatting to Treak; they seemed in deep conversation.

"You understand why I wanted to carry on?" asked Treak, his hand touching Crikken's shoulder.

"I am surprised that you and the others are here; the Elf must be the cause," stated Crikken flatly without emotion.

"He says things to me that tell me that he is right and I am wrong. There is no arguing with him, once he says what he thinks. It works its way at an alarming rate into my mind and I start to think how stupid I was before he said it."

"It is true what you say, Treak. He knows what is right, it is as simple as that. He is magical," added Crikken, who smiled as he spoke. He almost broke out laughing.

"He is the first Elf we have met, so how can we judge him?" asked Treak, who liked it when he could talk the way he wanted. Crikken had been his closest friend for the past ten years. He suddenly realised that if he had indeed left him, he would not have seen him again. This had a profound effect upon the Gnome, not visible to his closest friend who was still chuckling to himself, but within his mind.

"I have already decided I was wrong in my judgment

of the Elf, but one good Elf does not make a good race," replied Crikken.

"I am going to see if any of the local Dwarfs have had any trouble with the Goblins. I will also see if I can get us something to eat. Do not leave this building, you are quite safe here," said the Elf as he disappeared out of the wooden doorway.

"How can we trust this Elf?" asked Akkia in surprise.

"Because we can," answered Treak confidently.

"The Elf known as Arrun is strange, mainly for his actions up to this day. Maybe it is because there are Goblins roaming the lands, maybe it is the wood pearls, but I trust him with my life," added Crikken, who was rubbing his skin where the wounds had been.

"The Elf said that he chose to travel with us. What do we do if he suddenly decides to take what he thinks is his, what then?" asked Kellek, who still mistrusted the Elf.

"I for one hope he will choose to come back with us to Gutox. The wood pearls will be out of his reach then, we will decide if he can have any," said Treak, who had not clicked his fingers since waking.

Two long hours passed and the Elf had still not returned. The four Gnomes had busied themselves with taking out the wood pearls and shining them. The one thing the wood pearls needed was to be cared for. They became ruined if they were allowed to become damp while carried within the sacks. A fungus would grow and the seeds would soften and turn into a mulch. When this happened they became useless as the fuel for which they were mostly sought.

"Can you see any of the slime on the pearls?" asked Treak. The three friends shook their heads. This was a special occasion for the Gnomes, for these wood pearls would generate great wealth for their homeland. The Trolls of Yea-Bor would pay them handsomely for this amount of wood pearls.

It was while they were putting back the wood pearls that the door swung open. Arrun came bounding into the room, and his face was ashen with shock. He went past the sitting Gnomes and headed for the shuttered windows. He prised them open an inch; he still did not say a word to the open-mouthed Gnomes. Treak would normally have been clicking his fingers in annoyance at the actions of the Elf, but instead he just watched and waited for the Elf to tell them what was bothering him. Finally the Elf turned and looked at the four Gnomes; he had tears running down his face.

"What has happened, Elf?" asked Crikken, who had risen to his feet.

"Something of such evil has taken place here that I am struggling to come to terms with this madness," replied Arrun, his tear stained face full of sorrow.

"What evil?" asked Treak, his fingers not clicking the once.

"An evil which has come from the bowels of Ursalane; the Goblins and Hobgoblins have ruined Wooded Hood, not one living Dwarf have I seen."

"They have all left the wood then?" asked Akkia, not understanding fully what the Elf had said.

"I wish they had. No, Akkia. Out there is a sight that no one should have to witness. There are mutilated bodies strewn across every byway. In every dwelling I entered I saw death. A massacre has taken place here that is all evil; we are in grave danger," he said as he once more peered through the window.

Wooded Hood was built up of stone buildings, stone structures that had been carefully built so as to live hand in hand with the trees. Some of the buildings had virtually no foundations as the Dwarfs did not want to disturb the roots of the majestic trees. The actual trade route was to the north of the wood, but the problem the Dwarfs had been faced with was that all the surrounding lands had been watery flatlands. The great Elven river Alluvia wound its way just to the north as well, thus making the Dwarfs decide that the ancient woodland would make the most stable footing for a settlement. Over the years the settled Dwarfs had even taken to fishing the great river. Many boats had been built to fish the well-stocked river. It has to be noted though that the Dwarfs had taken many years to get permission from the King of the Elves. In the end, Esslestar had granted them a season in which they could fish his river. So it was that Dwarfs were normally found on the rocks of the land, fishing as if they had been born to do so; this was the main characteristic that set the Dwarfs of Wooded Hood apart from their distant cousins.

Suddenly, noises could be heard outside, low guttural

sounds. Lots of scraping too could be heard. Arrun put his slender fingers to his lips. He walked swiftly to the doorway, which was ajar. As quietly as he could he closed the door. He then started to bolt it. Treak realised instantly what was happening and came to the side of the Elf. He helped Arrun lift a heavy table and put it in front of the door.

"They are all around us," exclaimed Arrun.

The sudden crash against the door brought everyone present to a state of high awareness. The door had not budged, but how long it would keep at bay the evil that crashed against it, they did not know. Arrun told them to follow him. He led the way up the narrow staircase, looked into three rooms and decided to climb the final set of stairs that would lead him to the attic room of the building. This had no windows, but instead, a wooden hatch that opened onto the flat roof of the building. Once everyone was on the roof, the Elf withdrew his sword and slid it in in such a way that the hatch would be impossible to open.

"You leave behind a precious item, Arrun," said Treak in amazement.

"I am more precious than any sword, Treak. We have only one chance to escape, I fear. See the way the trees lean towards us? They are happy to be of assistance. Have you ever walked on the top of a woodland?"

"Never, but I will relish the experience, for we are happy to be amongst the high bramble of the lower slopes of the Great Eastern Divide. We will follow you, Elf," replied Treak silently.

The screams that entered the stone building told the four Gnomes and Elf that it was time to climb within the treetops of the wood. But as Arrun guided them one by one onto the first branch, a Goblin appeared on the roof, its grotesque rounded figure heading straight for the Elf. Arrun though showed yet again his frightening speed in conflict: as the Goblin opened its jaws to rip into the Elf, Arrun brought forth two daggers and crisscrossed the face of the Goblin, opening up the head as if it were a ripe plum. It plummeted off the edge of the roof and died as it struck the floor. But it was not the only Goblin that had climbed the stairs; three more came instantly for the Elf. The four Gnomes had travelled some distance within the treetops, finding the branches similar to the higher bramble they so loved to climb, but they did stop and look back towards the stone building. They saw again the lightning speeds of the Elf. Arrun had remained, crouched on one knee, waiting for the Goblins to attack. When they did so, he twisted upwards and lifted off the roof a few inches. This gave him the momentum he desired; the snarling Goblins rushed as one, but each was slain before they could scream their hatred of the Elf. More had climbed the stairs. Arrun thought how easy it was to kill these creatures, but he had sensed something else enter the building, for even the Goblins cowered as whatever it was climbed the stairs.

The Brethren came onto the roof and knocked away a Goblin, whose body rolled off and plummeted to its death. From within the shadow of its hood, the creation of the three wizards contemplated the Elf, its broken speech cracking the air as it spoke.

"Elf being, you die!"

"Who are you?" asked the Elf, showing no signs of being scared of the Brethren.

But instead of answering Arrun, the Brethren opened its cloak, revealing many pouches of different colours. This was when the Elf realised he may be in danger. He knew of the ways of the black art of magic and recognised the pouches which usually contained dust of a magic nature. These ranged from a simple sleeping dust to a dust which could blind you instantly. But even as the Brethren moved closer to Arrun, the Elf did not retreat, for it had been said down the ages that no magic could be inflicted upon the fair race. The black pouch was suddenly within the grasp of the Brethren. Low mutterings entered the air around the Elf. Arrun gripped his daggers tightly, waiting for his moment. As the Brethren emptied the dust into the air, it spoke quickly: a language the Elf did not understand. The dust surrounded the body of the Elf completely. It was now that the Brethren withdrew its long curved sword. As it lifted it high into the morning air, the Brethren took one step closer to the Elf it thought it had immobilized; but the spell and the dust had had no effect upon the Elf. Arrun struck the Brethren underneath its right armpit. He felt the dagger enter the body of the cloaked stranger, felt the stench of the breath as the Brethren let out a scream of agony, watched as the body crumpled onto the flat roof of the building. When the Brethren felt the open wound, it looked up to see that the Elf had gone into the tree tops. Another pouch was opened and more words of another age were spoken.

"Quickly, for we will surely be hunted down. We are in grave danger, let me show the way," said the Elf as he bounded over the slender branches of the ancient Oak: the tree the Elves adored the most. The four Gnomes followed silently and in fear, for this was the first time they had seen Arrun frightened. The voice that caught up with them was so deep, it actually shook the tree through which they were treading.

"Run Elf! Run in death. I will hunt you down and skewer you to the tree you so adore."

By the time Arrun had found his way to the outskirts of the wood, they could hear the pack of Goblins in the distance, screaming loudly into the air. Another voice could also be heard; this was the sound that had the Gnomes looking back in fear, for it seemed to travel through the wood and keep all of its vocal clarity.

"We have no more trees, I'm afraid. We head for the river; that is our only hope," said the Elf as he jumped lightly down onto the floor of the wood. The Gnomes also jumped from the tree with ease. They looked to the Elf for his decision. Their lives had become so dependent on what the Elf did and said. Even Treak who thought himself to be a true leader was happy to lay the responsibility with the Elf. For long periods they ran, eventually breaking out of the wood and into the brightness of the midday sun, which was low in the western skies. Dark storm clouds seemed to be amassing to the north. Arrun noted instantly that the blackness of the clouds seemed unreal. He did not mention his observations to the four Gnomes, but told them to keep up the torturous pace he had set. In the distance the fields seemed to dip swiftly away.

"Alluvia!" exclaimed Arrun.

"We hate the water, Elf!" moaned Crikken.

"One of the four great rivers that give Follonday so much, I am gladdened to be seeing the waters that will end up feeding the trees of our forest."

"Where are you going, Arrun?" asked Treak tentatively.

"We are crossing the Alluvia. Now let us hope the current is not too strong. Many boats we will find on the shore of the river. Do not worry about the river. Remember that you are within the company of an Elf; the river will do us no harm," encouraged Arrun, looking back towards the devastated woodland of Wooded Hood. They had covered half a mile through the sodden fields. The screams that exploded behind them had them turning around to see how many Goblins were chasing them, but they could only see the tops of the trees as they had started to drop down towards the magnificent river, which they could now see in the distance. It was still at least a quarter of a mile off and the earth beneath their feet was becoming even wetter.

The Brethren strode out of the wood, its cloak billowing behind its body. The hood however remained secured around the head. The voice resonated through the air, ordering the dozens of Goblins to hunt down the fleeing Elf and what it thought were Dwarfs. It still did not realise that what it hunted were the Gnomes who had stolen that which its master so required: the wood pearls. If it had known this, then every spare Goblin and Hobgoblin would be charging towards the fleeing group, not a mere two dozen. As the evil being sank into the sodden fields, it rubbed its chest where the Elf had struck it.

"When we meet again, Elf, you will die a death you never thought possible." Its fists clenching into a ball, it turned away from the river and decided that the Goblins could not fail in capturing the Elf. The Dwarfs would die as it had ordered, but the Elf had to be brought to him alive. It now moved in a south westerly direction. Its main army of Brethren, Goblins and Hobgoblins was at present surrounding the woodland settlement of Tarsit. Here they would capture prisoners for the three wizards and seek out the golden wood pearls. Like a black shadow, the Brethren moved swiftly into the western horizons.

Present Day

The darkness of the night had crept into the interior of the Range Rover. The black storm clouds that had come from the west, had started to rumble with thunder. Every now and then the skies would light up with a flash of lightning. Each time this happened the seasoned reporter would glance in the direction of the young man, but he still had not even caught the merest glimpse of his face. He wanted to ask so many questions, but realised that he was here to listen only.

"I need the toilet. Will you excuse me for a few minutes?" asked Miller, his hands tapping upon the steering wheel. "And I need to phone my wife."

"I will wait, Peter Miller," replied the soft voice.

It was only when the man from London entered the main service area did he realise what a stupid mistake he had just made. He had left a mere youth in his car: a youth he had never met before. He turned and walked back towards the automatic doors. They opened and he stood within the opening, looking to see if his car was still there. It was. His thoughts were bad as he looked at the motionless figure sitting inside his car. To get into someone's mind, one had to get trust before anything else, and he had just failed.

As nature beckoned him to the gents, he scratched his balding head. One phone call he would make. Having washed his hands as he always did, he made his way to the restaurant, ordered two coffees to take away and sat down at the nearest table.

"Sally, Peter Miller here. Put me through to the producer please."

"He's in a meeting, Peter. Is it important?" asked Sally, who did not relish the thought of interrupting her boss.

"For fuck's sake! Important! If it wasn't fucking important I wouldn't be fucking calling you, you stupid bitch!" screamed Miller down the phone. He almost immediately caught his breath. This wasn't him speaking that way, was it?

"I beg your pardon. I will let him know, Peter, but he might be sometime. He is with the new MOT minister, grilling him about the new expansion plans on the motorways."

"Fucking hell! So fucking useless!" screamed Miller, putting the cellular back inside his jacket pocket. He reached for the coffee and made his way back to his car. The rain was torrential; he could feel the its coldness as it started to run down his neck. He shivered, hunching his back and running the last few yards, swearing silent obscenities all the way.

"Here, I've bought us a coffee," offered Miller, who put the steaming plastic cups into the drink holders.

"No, I do not drink coffee. But thank you all the same, Peter Miller" said the figure quietly.

"Don't fucking have one then."

"I won't."

"Who the fuck are you?" asked Miller, sipping at the awful- tasting coffee.

"Well, one thing I am not and that is a thief!" replied the figure.

"Where the fuck are you from?" Miller asked more insistently.

"All will be revealed to you in the coming of time. But first I must tell you what I consider important," replied the figure, whose finger was pointing to where the cellular had been earlier.

"But why the fucking hell did you choose me?"

"Please do not lie to me, Peter Miller. You did not phone your wife. Give it to me please."

Peter Miller felt that he had been caught like a naughty school boy. He handed over his phone without any objections. The phone was switched off and flung into the back seat.

"Fuck!"

"Now I will continue with the history lesson that will help you better understand the present and the future."

"Wait a fucking second!" exclaimed Miller, who had

turned all of his body in the direction of the seated figure.

"Yes?" asked the soft voice.

"You're telling me that this is fucking true, and then what the fuck are you? Who the fuck are you? Show your fucking face at least, for until you do, my thoughts will be distracted from this fucking tale you are trying to tell me," cried the reporter.

The hooded figure then turned his head and looked at the middle aged reporter. He let his hood fall down around his shoulders, revealing a shock of pure white blonde hair. The eyebrows were arched femininely; his ears seemed to be pinned back tightly against his head. Miller looked at the highly defined cheekbones, noting quickly that the lips were the thinnest lips he had ever seen. The bleached blonde stranger then gave the reporter a smile that seemed to light the darkest corners of the reporter's mind and heart.

"Fucking Hell!"

"It is true what I say, Peter Miller. Now if I may, I will try and tell you as much as I can before it is time for me to leave," said the figure as he pulled up his hood again. Miller felt light-headed as he leant back in his seat. He had lost count of the number of times he had sworn. He closed his eyes and waited for the story to begin again, this time though he would listen to every word as if it were the first voice he had ever heard.

Chapter Ten

Sarratt stood before the assembled Trolls and felt a lump within his throat. He sensed the fear that swelled amongst them: a wave of terror that none of them knew how to stop. He also saw hatred within the terror. He knew he would have to make them feel that he was not here because of the previous wizard. He coughed as he tried to bring up the sadness from his soul.

"An evil has walked amongst the Trolls. A wizard of whom I have no recollection entered the debating chamber. I am here by chance, but I will surely act on what you were ordered to do. I will travel to Follonday, as I was intending to do, before I came across the three Trolls who stand behind me. There I will ask the King to act on the evil that grows from his northern borders."

"The Elves are not interested in the Trolls," said a Troll, who was sitting close to the wizard.

"They stopped trading with Yea-Bor some years ago, they will not assist us," said another.

"Rumours are spreading that they intend to join the Dwarfs within the Golden Valley," shouted yet another; his eyes actually filled with tears of despair.

"From the east we are faced with a war against the Dwarfs and Elves, a battle which we would be hard pushed to win. Plus now we have an unknown attacker from the west. This is it. We cannot hope to fight all three at the same time. The wizard will not achieve anything with the Elves, for as he knows, his magic is useless against the fairer race. We are doomed," shouted a Troll from the end of the debating chamber.

"Rumours will be the downfall of this proud race of Trolls. If the Elves were intending war with Yea-Bor, then the Watch Wizard would know. It is as simple as that. I talked with the wizard but a few weeks ago. There was no mention of this supposed alliance between Elves and Dwarfs. I travel to Follonday as a peacemaker. We want all the races on the western side of the Great Eastern Divide to live in harmony. This you must believe," said Sarratt with a passion, his black hooded cloak revealing but a shadow of the face that looked down on the council of the Trolls. However he did not tell the Trolls present everything he knew. He had to leave them with hope.

"And what of our families, Wizard?" shouted another.

"Thousands of lives hang by a thread. What protection will you give us, Wizard?" asked one who had started to walk towards the wizard, his hand reaching for his sword.

Three of the seated Trolls actually tried to stop the enraged Troll, but they were beaten out of the way. His sword out and in the open, his intentions were made quite clear for all to see. Denjom, the head of the council, could only watch in sadness as the Troll came towards the wizard. He could not act as he was still concussed, though the blood had finally stopped flowing from the gash on the side of his head. Sarratt let the Troll stride towards him, his thoughts saddened by his actions. Even as the Troll lifted his mighty sword, the young wizard waited, giving the Troll the chance to change his mind. But such was the hatred that had found its way into the very soul of the Troll, that he swung at the figure of the wizard. But the wizard did not act. He remained perfectly still. The actions of the bloodied Troll that stood behind the wizard, saved the life of the attacking Troll, for a silent spell had formed on the lips of the wizard: a spell that would have changed the appearance of the Troll for eternity. The deafening crunch of Henthorn's sword rang out around the debating chamber.

"You fool! Have you any idea what you attack?" spat the Troll.

"A wizard is a wizard, how can you stand before him?" asked the other Troll, his shoulder smashed with the force of the impact of Henthorn's charge.

"I would gladly give my life for Sarratt, for he would do likewise. Have any of you looked at the drawings? Well, he swept them away as if they were a mere dust cloud. He is our saviour. Sarratt will see that the race of the Trolls survives this dark period." said Henthorn, his foot resting down on the chest of the fallen Troll. Sarratt then thought of what the Watch Wizard had told him, the alliance of the Elves and Dwarfs, the awakening of the evil one, rumours within the race of Trolls: a stark reality within other chambers.

"Henthorn speaks the truth. I will continue on my way as I had planned. I will travel first though to the northern lands of the Elves. Here I will see for myself what threatens these lands. Trolls of Yea-Bor, you have only the one path to tread. Send your scouts to the western borders. See what army, if any, faces you."

The debating chamber roared with approval. The Troll that had tried to attack the wizard hurried from the chamber, grasping his broken shoulder, his last glance at the wizard filled with hatred. He wanted the wizard dead. After an hour had passed, only five remained within the great hall that was called the debating chamber. Laid out upon the ancient table were the drawings that Bugram had done. The wizard was bent over them, studying in detail the creatures he had never seen before. He saw that they appeared to be dressed as wizards, but they were not; of this, he was sure., Bugram had drawn so skillfully that the wizard felt at times he was looking through a magical window where he could gaze upon whatever was within its view. The pouches of the so- called wizards were of the same colour: yellow, a weak colour within the world of magic, for these pouches could only offer simple protection spells. Sarratt tapped his finger on the colourful drawing.

"Denjom!"

"Yes?"

"Send as many running units as you can. Sending only a few could end in tragedy. If you are caught out in the open on the Plains of Desire, I fear that if there are only twenty or so of you, you will be overcome. Do it tonight. I will come with you until we reach the outer wall, then I must travel as fast as I can. May luck and good judgment stay with you."

"If only we had a King who could rally his nation, then the weeks ahead would not feel as if they were our last," said Denjom mournfully.

"The King of Yea-Bor died a long time ago," added Henthorn ruefully.

"The King has not been allowed to fight in battle for how many years? It is true that within the last few years he has fallen away from the city of Yea-Bor, but can you not see the pain he goes through when he is merely a figure head? At least within the Golden Valley he can observe what he was the best at: killing. I would give back the pride that I too was guilty of taking away from him, put him back within the first running unit, for you will need a leader of power if battle comes to Yea-Bor," replied the wizard, thinking of the consequences of his actions all those years ago.

"But he is twice the size he was!" exclaimed Henthorn in disgust.

"Yea-Bor needs the return of the King," replied Sarratt.

"The wizard speaks the truth. We will do as you advise, but the King refuses to leave the Golden Valley," said the head of the council, his head shaking slowly from side to side.

"He will be within the outer walls within the week. Now I must ask you to get ready the running units. My work here is finished for the time being. May all the goodness of the ages be with the race of the Trolls these coming months," stated Sarratt, who had already started to make his way from the debating chamber.

The parting of the wizard and the Trolls was a sad affair. The Trolls waited for the arrival of the majestic horse, which seemed to be part of the wizard as the two met, such was the love each showed for the other. Denjom was there, his lit torch illuminating his grim face. Behind him waited the running units, eager to be on their way. All in all, thirty three thousand Trolls waited for the watch tower bells to ring. This would also give notice to the rest of the population that many of their own were setting off to war: thirty three thousand Trolls who would gladly give their life for the sake of Yea-Bor.

"The King is the key to your future. Welcome him with his sword and uniform, he will be ready," promised the wizard, who had silently spoken with Stormbreaker, the great black stallion rearing up on its hind legs before galloping off into the bleak night.

The running units were not so quick to depart. Breaking into arrow- shaped formations, they broke forth from the outer walls of Yea-Bor. The only sound coming forth was the stamping of their feet upon the edge of the Plains of Desire, a grassland region where no trees or shrubs grew.

The expanse of the grasslands travelled by the running units in two weeks was travelled by the wizard in two days. The horse hardly ever touched the long grasses of the Plains of Desire. Like a shooting arrow, they travelled at speeds that made the world around them but a blur, though it must be said that the great black stallion known as Stormbreaker came to no ill health because of the magic performed by the wizard.

As the Sun dawned on that new day, the wizard and the horse returned to the ground, the horse at first galloping, then slowing up until he was merely cantering. Sarratt scanned the distant horizons for any signs of Goblins, Hobgoblins or the beings that, to all intents and purposes, looked like wizards, but nothing could be seen. What Sarratt had somehow overlooked, however, was the fact that the land dipped away suddenly some ten miles away from where the two were moving. But as the grasslands showed no difference in appearance, the error would have been made by almost anyone who looked upon the scenery; such was the deceptive nature of the contours of the land. So as the morning hours drifted away, the wizard studied the blackness of the distant clouds. They seemed too low to be real. He sensed an evil within the blackness and when he saw clouds moving above the stationary blackness he shuddered; a sudden fear gripped him. Stormbreaker sensed the wizard's mood and stamped his hooves nervously upon the sodden grasslands. He neighed loudly, not wanting to take another step forwards, but the gentle reassurances of the wizard calmed the great black stallion down. Then he saw what he had hoped he would never set eyes upon: an army of such great size it covered some ten miles in width, the blackness of it mirroring the clouds that hung above it. Two miles at most separated the wizard from Marsukia's army, a lone figure looking upon the millions that surely gathered. The wizard thought of the hope of which he had spoken with the Trolls of Yea-Bor and wondered if hope was merely the end of a rainbow: unattainable. Even as he looked upon the hordes of creatures that did not belong in his world, he noticed far to the right, a large group detach itself from the millions, surging to the east. Sarratt quickly sized up the numbers and thought of what the Trolls would be fighting within the week. He shuddered once more before he brought the frightened horse around and headed for the lands of the Elf.

Henthorn, being the head of the second running unit, was at the front of the huge advancing army of Trolls. He had drilled his unit so hard that none questioned his word. This was the case in all of the running units; a strict code was laid down with an iron fist. This brought order to the thousands that ran on the Plains of Desire that autumn day. They had been away from Yea-Bor for ten days and their spirits were high. Henthorn had instilled a confidence within the thousands that followed him. Most would have called him the real King if they were allowed, but such thoughts were kept private. Scouts who had been sent on ahead the previous day returned with grim faces. One of the scouts was a Troll who went by the name of Argost. He came to Henthorn.

"An army of blackness is but a few miles to the west. Thousands I saw, and they are a terrible sight to behold, my leader."

"Then we will defeat this tide of evil once and for all. They will never get within three miles of our city," said the defiant Troll, his mind already forming the battle plans he would instruct his running units to perform.

"They number three times as many as we, Henthorn," said Argost plainly, giving no sign of fear..

"Tell running units seven hundred onwards to travel to the north. We will try and slice them in two as they move east. Then in the confusion, we will flatten this black army. Go now, Argost. But return to my side as quickly as you can, for that is where you belong," ordered Henthorn, a shallow smile spreading across his rugged face. His braided hair was bare of all bones; Henthorn had decided that many new bones of war would be gained on this journey. As he ran, he looked to the north and saw the hundreds of running units run to the position he had spoken of to Argost. To the south, hundreds more running units had copied the running units of the north, while the main arrow- shaped army of Trolls ran to meet the evil which threatened their very existence.

A mile separated the two armies; each could see the other. Henthorn reached for the battle bell he carried into all battles and rang it high above his head. Hundreds of other Trolls did likewise, the ringing of the bells sounding out towards the Goblins and Hobgoblins that had now seen the advancing Trolls. They screamed high- pitched shrieks of war, the Goblins galloping like the horses that normally roamed the plains and the Hobgoblins sprinting as fast as they could. But they were not as quick as their smaller cousins. With the gap closing to five hundred paces, Henthorn dropped the ringing war bell. If he survived the clash with these hideous creatures, he would search out his bell and treasure it until the next time it was needed. Thousands of the small bells hit the Plains of Desire. The musical chants of battle fell silent. The Trolls prepared themselves for the battle ahead. Some had already withdrawn their swords, while others had primed their long bows, running all the time towards the evil army.

To the surprise of the leader of the Trolls, it was the Goblins who killed first. They unleashed the eight sided throwing spheres, hundreds of them screeching through the midday sky. The Trolls had been caught completely off guard, for their shields were at their sides. As the spheres hit the Trolls' bodies, they pierced the leather tunics, entering some with so much force that the stricken Trolls were lifted into the air, their backs arching in the final throes of death. It seemed that the advancing army of Goblins had cut a hole in the Trolls' running units, so many Trolls had been cut down with the lethal throwing spheres the Goblins had thrown. But the running units to the south and the north had now started to attack the Goblins and Hobgoblins with a vengeance, killing hundreds within a few minutes.

No screams or yells of war came forth from the Trolls. They were silent as they slaughtered the creatures that had attacked their own, making sure that each had been put to death. In some cases, several Trolls plunged their swords deep within the bodies of the Goblins or Hobgoblins that had already put to death many of the friends they had once known. The scene of battle was hectic. Trolls which never should have died, did do in the battle frenzy.. The Trolls which fought that day on the Plains of Desire and survived, would never forget the agonies which their own suffered. Within twenty minutes, the leader of the running units realised that he was in danger of losing every single Troll, such were the numbers they were fighting, relentless creatures that did not even regard their own lives as important. So he shouted as loudly as he could,

"Back to Yea-Bor."

Some heard the shout of Henthorn, but several running units which had been cut off by the hundreds of Goblins and Hobgoblins had no choice but to fight. It was the actions of Argost that bloody day that would change the course of the battle.

"Do as I do. Use your shields to protect yourselves against the weapons they throw; form into groups of three; kill every single last creature; charge for the sake of our homeland. I for one will give my life if it means our families are safe."

They then responded to the young Troll by doing exactly what he had told them. They shouted at the tops of their voices, denouncing the evil which would surely kill them on this sad day for the race of Trolls. Like spearheads slicing through water, the small groups of running units made sweeping attacks right into the heart of the advancing army. This had a profound effect upon the Goblins, for they were unable to unleash their throwing spheres. A panic quickly spread through the hundreds of Hobgoblins too. Some had even started to attack one another; the tide had apparently been stopped. One hour had now passed since the start of the battle. Henthorn had watched in disbelief as the trapped Trolls had counter attacked with such devastating results. He shouted immediately for the rest of the running units to copy what Argost and the others had done. Shattered to the core, the remaining Trolls looked upon the thousands of dead bodies that lay upon the Plains of Desire. Some had dropped to their knees, though this was to shed tears of sadness over the tremendous losses the Trolls had suffered that day.

"How many are left, Argost?" gasped Henthorn, whose whole body was covered in the blood of the creatures he had slain. His shield had at least two dozen of the weapons the Goblins had thrown at him embedded within its surface.

"We have lost nearly half. I have sent scouts to the west. We must head back to Yea-Bor, the council must be told of the losses we have suffered this sad day," replied the Troll.

"But we have just saved our homelands from the evil which threatened it. When we return, I will proclaim the success we have achieved," corrected the head of the running unit.

Argost knew not to argue with Henthorn, but he sensed that they had merely scratched the surface of the army that had been assembled to destroy the Trolls. That was why he had sent out two of the quickest scouts the Trolls had. These two were also the same scouts who had travelled with Henthorn all the way to the Rainbow Valley and had nearly died on their way back. If it was courage that was needed of the Troll race, then these two Trolls would show the way, for they had not hesitated when ordered to travel west to scout the very edges of the Plains of Desire, where the thick unnatural storm clouds had been a constant source of torment for the Trolls. But as the pair ran, they soon realised that another few thousand Goblins and Hobgoblins were on the distant horizon, the blackness of the creatures making them stand out against the setting sun, which had just reached the top of the storm clouds the three wizards had formed: a blackness that unnerved the two friends.

"Which way are they heading?" asked Bugram who had already sketched the scene with a charcoal stick.

"North," replied Browfell, who had taken a mouthful of water.

"The new settlers live to the north!" exclaimed the Troll, putting the scroll of paper back within his backpack.

"I know. Come, let us see if there are any more to the south, then we must return to the council as soon as possible," said the Troll as he stared towards the southern regions of the Plains of Desire.

Another hour passed before they set eyes on the main army of the three wizards. A mere five miles separated them, but such was the size of the army that they stopped dead in their tracks. It was like looking at a sea full of small bright lights, each bobbing with the rhythm of the tide. Even at this distance, they could hear the distant rumbles. From the far north to the southern horizon they looked in horror at the tide of bobbing lights.

"This cannot be true!" gasped Bugram, who had hastily started to draw what he was seeing.

"A devil's army I look upon this sad day, a beginning that signals the end," said the other Troll more to himself than to Bugram.

"There are millions upon millions. I am scared, Browfell," admitted the Troll.

"So you should be, for we are looking upon the army of the devil. It is written within the mountain scrolls that we would one day be faced with the force of the devil, that he himself would ascend and walk amongst our kind, eating upon our very souls," replied Browfell, who had suddenly noticed that he had begun to tremble.

"But the tale you talk of is but a tale from our ancestors. They did not know then where the race of the Trolls would be living. They told us many things, Browfell, most of which we laugh at today. You are mistaken, surely?"

Then in the gloom of the setting Sun, another few hundred thousand Goblins and Hobgoblins detached themselves from the sea of evil. The two trolls watched those head south for some five minutes, but then the advancing battalion of evil turned directly east, their torches bobbing up and down as they ran.

No words were spoken as the two friends turned and headed back to their homeland, their hearts beating like they had never beaten before. A fear had descended upon them, a fear which would not let them stop until they saw the massive outer walls of Yea-Bor. But even as they ran, they seemed to know that they would never make the safety of their own kind.

Chapter Eleven

The wizard watched as the figure of the Brethren entered his decaying fortress, the gaping holes in the roof of the keep of no importance to the powerful wizard. What he desired was not within this building or for that matter, upon these lands.

"The golden seeds, how many did you find?" asked Marsukia, his hand reaching out for the items he so desperately wanted.

The Brethren did not speak as he had none to give his master. The wizard asked once more, but the silence of the creature he had created told him the grave news he was dreading. Prestersfordle had entered just behind the massive figure of the Brethren, his head shaking wearily from side to side.

"Then I take it you know of what happened within the wooded place?" he asked, his shadowed face not visible to the pair who were looking at him.

"Not only did they not find any golden wood pearls, they did not even find any of the common type. It has been a disaster!" exclaimed Prestersfordle, making a point in pushing away the standing figure of the Brethren.

"Gnomes!" he exclaimed in his own defense, the Brethren giving Prestersfordle a look of hatred.

"Gnomes!" exclaimed Marsukia, his mind going over what it knew of the lowest race that lived within the lands of Ursalane.

"We know it was Gnomes. The dying Dwarf told us so, said that they stole what they could and burned the rest. No golden pearls within that place," explained the Brethren flatly, his eyes fixed squarely on the hidden face of his master.

"Leave," ordered Marsukia.

The Brethren turned and left the two wizards alone. Prestersfordle walked over to the gaping hole that was once a window, wondering what Marsukia would say now, his gaze falling on the black storm clouds he had helped to create. He thought of the lost years he had spent learning the art of the dark way and how a tiny group of Gnomes could shatter his dreams of life ever after. It was Marsukia who spoke first, his voice rasping into the damp air.

"Be ready to leave for the stinking homelands of the Gnome. We travel the black path, so be prepared to protect yourself."

A shiver ran down the spine of the wizard. This path was the quickest way in which to travel, but the horrors they would encounter would test even his sinister side. Step from the path and he would be devoured by the tortured souls that had no place in which to rest. It was a place meant for no mere mortal.. It had been the powers of Marsukia that had mastered the dark dangerous paths, so many times he had come close to death he had lost count. But the rewards of avoiding time were enormous for the evil wizard. He had used it frequently; so much so that the King of the human race of the east, beyond the Great Eastern Divide, trusted the mage as he called him; so much so that every suggestion of the wizard was taken up without question: something to which the wizards of Witches Watch were oblivious.

"I will follow your every step," said the worried wizard.

"Then let us prepare for the short journey," replied Marsukia.

Prestersfordle followed Marsukia down into the dungeons, where they had turned the deep cells into a massive cavern, with a huge furnace set on the north wall. It was only the magic of Marsukia that allowed the crumbling keep to remain standing. Several of the supporting walls had been taken out, leaving a space big enough for the Hobgoblins to work in. But there were no Hobgoblins there now. They had all set off to war. The furnace though burned just as brightly, the heat of it taking the breath away from Prestersfordle, for what burned within the furnace were wood pearls: wood pearls the wizard had purchased over the past ten years. This was a trade the small wooded community was glad of, but knew not of the buyer nor destination. The Dwarfs had simply delivered them to Wooded Hood. A farmer stored them; the Dwarfs cared not who bought them. But even so, some awkward questions had been asked of the said farmer. He replied by telling the Dwarfs that they were for his personal use and threatened to stop trading with them. This said, the Dwarfs simply delivered the sacks as the farmer ordered them.

Sweat poured from the brow of Prestersfordle. He disliked heat immensely, much preferring the cold bitter winds of the Fingertip Mountains. Marsukia, on the other hand, was happiest within the cavernous chamber. The heat licked at his being, enticing him to stand as close as he dared. He had mastered the art of handling fire many years previously, so when he reached out his hand and stroked the fires, his whole body seemed to relax. Prestersfordle coughed loudly.

"See how the fire tries to caress my body. But time is against us; we will now leave."

Suddenly there appeared an opening within the flames, a blackness that shunned all light, a nothingness that was filled with terror. As Marsukia entered the blackness, he stroked the flames one last time. Prestersfordle ducked his head, his arms tucked into his chest. He entered the chasm as though he were a child, trying to avoid a spider's web, fear making itself blatantly obvious to the other wizard.

"Rid yourself of the fear you carry."

Prestersfordle freed the thoughts that had made him tremble.

"Do it now! As you know, fear will not endure the journey we are going on."

"It has gone," came the flat, toned response, for he knew of what lingered within this blackness.

All in all, the journey took but a few minutes, for when they appeared upon the lava flow at the bottom of the volcanic mountain range that was the Gnomes' homeland, the Sun had hardly moved from its hidden position to the east. But within the blackness of the void, many hours had passed, many dangerous paths the pair had trod, many questions had they answered to the blackness and the nothingness. Marsukia being the one who confronted every question with a question, he himself gave the soulless creatures a fear they had never experienced before. But even as they cowered away from the figure of the leading wizard, they found comfort in the knowledge that the one who followed was not of the same ilk,, that deep within this one there was a fear. They had come close to dragging him into their netherworld on several occasions, but Marsukia had always come to the aid of the other wizard. The beings of the nether world knew that one day their chance would come; then they would feast upon the souls of the unwanted visitors to their lands.

As soon as the two wizards stepped into the bright, sunlit morning, they smelled the toxic fumes of the volcanoes. In some places giant plumes of sulphuric gas could be seen spiralling upwards to the cloudless skies. The lava flow they had stepped onto was old. It had long since cooled down, but even here, on the outskirts of Gutox, they could sense the heat of the lands. The mountains in the distance shimmered through this heat. They walked as one towards the home of the Gnomes. After an hour of walking, he saw what he had been looking for: a large hole in the crust of the lava. They jumped down into the lands of the Gnome, Marsukia landing without sound, while Prestersfordle landed with a thud.

"Come, we will be approached shortly, be ready!" warned the wizard, his long flowing cloak wrapped tightly about his person.

The wizard had of course been right, for within moments, several Gnomes appeared before them, swords drawn in front of them.

"You have stepped into the lands of Gutox. You are not welcome, wizards," said the leading Gnome.

Marsukia acted without his lesser wizard. Dropping onto his right knee, he rasped out but one word. But the instant he had said it, the leading Gnome seemed to implode. Within a fraction of a second he had disappeared. So quick the wizard had been that the other Gnomes did not seem to know exactly what had happened. When they did realise, it was too late, for Prestersfordle had decided to unleash his own form of retribution. Standing upright he spoke many words, twisting and turning them into but a couple of words. These were heard by no one except the two wizards, but the remaining six Gnomes were lifted suddenly at a great speed, their heads crushed against the smooth, curved ceiling of the lava tunnel.

"You still have much to learn, lesser one," commented Marsukia without emotion, his red eyes unblinking in the dim light.

"I hold sway over most of the races. Even yourself cannot use your spells upon the Elves. I learn more as each second passes, Marsukia," replied Prestersfordle, a hint of anger within his voice.

"The Elves do not worry me. They are chasing the same city as I. Then we will see if I have become all engrossing, for I will stand before the Elves and cast them asunder. You misjudge my art, Prestersfordle, but you shall see what I have become when the Sun finally disappears from these lands."

With the moment gone, the two wizards walked openly into the very heart of Gutox. Here, there were hundreds of Gnomes, their yellow faces peering at the two with a hatred Marsukia respected. He brought forth his hands and whispered into the minds of each and every Gnome that stood within the boundaries of Gutox. Some were several miles away, but they still heard the rasping threats the wizard was making.

The result was that within the hour, the hundreds had turned into several hundred, each trying to cram into the vast cavern that was the heart of their homeland. He spoke again, though no sound came from his thin, bloodless lips.

"I will start killing ten of you every minute until the head of your race stands before me."

Some of the Gnomes had put their hands over their ears,

trying in vain to stop the whispering voice within their heads. Most though thought the wizard was lying when he had threatened to kill them, so none came forward.

As the first minute passed, the air inside the vast cavern seemed to be sucked towards the standing wizards. Silence dominated the hundreds of gathered Gnomes. But as the silence came to an end, so did the lives of ten Gnomes, their bodies lifted high into the air. They fell to their deaths in front of the stunned onlookers.

"The second minute is but a few seconds away!" warned the wizard, who could feel the effects of the poisonous gases that filled the cavern; his throat was beginning to feel tight and stretched.

From the darkness of one of the many smaller caverns, a Gnome appeared, pushing his way to the front.

"I am who you seek. Speak of what you desire," said Kinaki, his yellow face a mask of hatred.

"Speak the truth, Gnome, or you will become lifeless like the ones who lay before you," replied Marsukia, his hand coming up to his mouth.

"I will," came the quick reply.

"We seek the wood pearls that you stole from the area known as Tarsit. Give them to us."

"May you search every inch of Gutox; no wood pearls are kept here," answered Kinaki honestly.

Marsukia felt the truth. If the Gnome had indeed been lying, then the wizard would have known instantly. However, this did not make him feel any better.

"Tell me of the last raiding party that left for that area," ordered Marsukia, who had felt the urge to cough, such was the sickening smell of the gases that were constantly breathing into the cavern from deep below where they stood.

Prestersfordle though was feeling worse. He had already started coughing. His face had twisted itself into a grimace, his sleeve had gone to his face, his head was feeling light and his vision was beginning to blur a little. He knew that within the next few minutes he would no longer be able to stand. Even worse, he thought, he would not be able to cast any spells. This was what the other wizard had spoken of, when he had said that one must confront the realities of one's death and not be afraid. Prestersfordle was now thinking of the prospect of that eventuality. He looked sideways at Marsukia and was shocked to see the more powerful wizard starting to cough as well.

"This is true," admitted Kinaki.

"Then where are they? When are they expected back within this stinking place?" asked the wizard, who had only now realised that Prestersfordle was nearing the brink of losing his balance. He reached out his hand to steady the other wizard, but missed the wizard's arm by a good two feet. He staggered a little, a spell of death coming to his lips at once, but no Gnome moved towards them. They merely watched as the two wizards crumpled to their knees.

"They were expected back two days ago. We assume by their absence that they were caught and did not escape the Dwarfs of Tarsit. We are saddened by this, Wizard, as we are saddened by your arrival within our lands. You kill openly, yet we do not attack you now as you struggle. Leave us be like all the other races of this world have done," said Kinaki, his fingers clicking a different tune, for they had sent out several messages to attack the hideous wizards when they saw him move back towards the cavern of the Gnome chieftain, his brother.

"You speak the truth once more, Gnome, but order no attack. We may be on our knees, but still have enough power to wipe every Gnome off the face of this world, so be warned," said Marsukia, whose eyesight had left him. With his senses failing, he knew that he had risked everything coming this far, but the wood pearls were the key to his eternal journey. So as he reached out blindly for the other wizard, he suddenly felt as if he had been given the news that was to become his life for the coming weeks.

"We leave as one, Prestersfordle. Say with me the spells of the damned, let us depart without the need of our legs."

"I am ready, but I cannot see and I have lost all feeling in my legs, so I agree," said the wizard without any movement from his lips, which had turned pale yellow.

As the two wizards spoke words the charging Gnomes had never heard before, they vanished completely from the cavern of the Gnome chieftain, leaving the Gnomes startled but relieved. They instantly went to the dead bodies of the Gnomes, lifted them off the hot floor and carried them away. Within the chieftain's cavern, a much smaller space than the huge one, Flutox gave his brother a hug. A tear had formed at the corner of his right eye, his fingers clicked softly.

"Why?" he asked Kinaki.

"They seek the four who went south to Follonday," replied Kinaki, who had not stopped patting his brother on the back.

"Who are these four?" asked Flutox, breaking away from the tight hug.

"Treak, Crikken, Kellek and Akkia. They travelled south through the lower bramble, then headed west onto the southern farmlands, then onto Follonday."

"They chase the treasure of the earth, how many have we lost?"

"Treak, as you know, is an experienced raider. He has always brought back great treasures from the Elves. As you know, these give us the only trade we have with the Trolls of Yea-Bor. He thinks only of the Gnomes' welfare," added Kinaki.

"Trade with the Trolls! They send the weakest of their animals. They suffer us only because of the state of war with the city of Pavelem. We need no trade with any of the races. Gutox is our home, we want for nothing," argued his brother, who had sat down on a natural volcanic ledge at the back of the cavern.

"We must trade, Flutox. You would have it like this always, would you? Hunted down by the Elves as if we were mere animals, killed on the spot by Dwarfs, shunned by the Trolls who think we are but thieves. This is not the way forward," snapped Kinaki, who had pointed his finger menacingly at his brother.

"We stay within our lands, brother. Others are moving upon the lands; we are safe within the caverns. Even the wizards felt the air upon their chests. Order all Gnomes within the lower and higher bramble to return to Gutox, that is my wish," replied the Gnome king.

"As you know, brother, your wish will be my command, but it is folly just to hide away. You must think long and hard of the consequences your decisions will have in the long run."

"Send the scouts out to the furthest reaches of the bramble. I want to make sure Gutox is safeguarded against another visit from the wizards. Do it now, brother," ordered Flutox, who had not stopped clicking his fingers as he spoke heatedly with his brother.

The two wizards appeared upon the Plains of Desire. Lying on their backs, they each felt as if a great weight was upon them, for they could not move any of their limbs. As the hours passed, they talked briefly, but even this proved too great an effort. Marsukia simply stared up at the scattered clouds and thought of the storm cloud that was gathering to the west. This thought calmed the wizard down. It was not often he had put himself this close to death, but somehow the feeling had tested his resolve; he knew then that he would face the ultimate test. Prestersfordle, on the other hand, had closed his eyes and had fallen into a light, troubled sleep. Death scared him; he wanted life. He dreamt of his early years when he was but a boy, how happy he had been. But as he dreamed he saw the way in which his parents had been killed at the hands of several Dwarfs. He awoke sweating.

For two days they lay there, silent and in pain, but Marsukia rose when the Sun reached them from over the Great Eastern Divide and started to walk slowly off into the west. Prestersfordle shouted after the wizard for him to stop.

"You are of no use to me or the cause if you cannot follow me. Pull all your strength together and let us return with haste to the keep; we have much to do," replied the distant figure of the wizard.

It was a sight rarely seen upon the Plains of Desire: two dark wizards limping and staggering towards the west. Marsukia had found the mental strength to call out for assistance, his voice travelling at the speed of light to the gathering of his armies. Each and every Brethren heard the call for help. Several set off to the east at once, their muscular physique rippling as they sprinted as fast as they could in the direction of the voice. They ran as the grasses of the Great Eastern Divide were perfect for running. It was at the Alluvia that they slowed. They had been warned of the Elven rivers. They skirted the banks of the great river until they came across one of the slender bridges that the Dwarfs had built for the Elves. The Brethren also knew that even the bridges carried danger. They took great care while crossing it, their eyes fixed upon the fast moving current of the Alluvia.

Each had been told in no uncertain terms that if any of them were to fall into any of the Elven rivers, their life would almost certainly be lost. Once over the bridge, the Brethren shouted out for their master.

"Over here," came the silent reply.

The Brethren then spotted the two wizards, way to the east on the horizon, smoking volcanoes as their back drop, the black smoke trailing wildly to the east. All in all, it took the Brethren three whole days to carry the two wizards back to the ancient keep. Here they were welcomed by the scowling figure of Fastanes. He had been alone for what seemed like a lifetime. Within his hands he held out two cups of elixir, which the pair drank in one gulp. This had the effect of taking away all tiredness and injuries to the limbs and mind. Prestersfordle patted the smaller wizard gently upon the shoulder.

"A fine mixture you serve, Fastanes. It is pleasant to be waited on by you," he quipped.

Fastanes turned his back and scurried back to his rooms, he too was tired and wanted his bed.

"We have work to do. We must create another creature, you and I," said Marsukia, as he felt the tingle travel up and down his body.

"Yet more?" moaned Prestersfordle.

"You wish to travel the dark paths again? We need to travel great distances if we are to rid the lands of the lesser races."

"Admittedly, I have no wish to walk those paths. But we have no need of any more Brethren," argued the wizard, who had started to walk away from the other wizard.

"Never walk away from me," warned Marsukia.

"Then speak of what you intend to create, that is if we have the strength left; I have never felt this weak before," replied Prestersfordle.

"You and I will summon the creature that will dominate the skies of Ursalane. We will bring forth the Sentry, long since forgotten Dragons. They are dormant now within the netherworld. I know the way into their world, come," said Marsukia, as he headed for the dungeons.

As ever, the dungeons were stifling, the heat seemed to be constant; Marsukia entered and pointed his finger at the gaping black hole he had opened only a few days previously. One word was spoken and the hole vanished.

"These Sentry we are bringing up from the depths of the world, will they know us as their masters?" asked the other wizard.

"You worry too much," replied Marsukia, his voice rasping in the heat of the dungeon.

"We are still recovering from that stinking place," said Prestersfordle in his own defence.

Marsukia ignored the other wizard and proceeded to mark out the twelve sided star that was required to reach into the netherworld. This was where they had brought forth the demon that was at the moment a pile of blood and guts on the wizard's floor. Marsukia beckoned Prestersfordle into the star. Here they reached out and clasped each other's hands. No words were spoken, just evil thoughts mixed with the highest form of magic: a state of mind only a few had achieved. A wizard from the past had reached this state, but had perished as he had been pulled into the chasm that was now appearing at the feet of the two wizards. Swirling white mists could be seen miles below them. To the right lay what Marsukia had called the forgotten mountain range, its snowy peaks just visible through the mists.

"The damned will make themselves known. We are seeking the Sentry; their assistance is needed for a short while. I, master of all the upper worlds, command these creatures to my service. Standing next to me is the light of the stars, he will be as I, your new master," ordered Marsukia, sprinkling as he spoke a dust from the red pouch which was tied onto the inside of his cloak.

Time seemed to stand still for the two wizards thought the time they had waited was but a few minutes, while in reality, they had waited four hours. The ancient Dragons suddenly appeared through the mists, their black bodies shining brilliantly as they soared through the air of the netherworld. Great roaring cries could be heard as they approached. The two wizards actually gasped at the sight. Four in all came towards the pair, their eyes completely black, their snouts long and filled with razor sharp teeth.

Marsukia let go of the other wizard and reached into his cloak. He produced yet more handfuls of magical dust. As he sprinkled the Sentry, he spoke several languages at once, ordering the Sentry to stay within his lands. Prestersfordle did the same, though his dust had come not from a red pouch, but from the one of lesser power: the blue one. He too spoke the exact words Marsukia had spoken, his spirits lifted by the sight of the flying Dragons.

What the two wizards had not considered was how the Sentry were going to get out of the dungeons. Up they came, their massive wings folding inwards as they flew through the gaping chasm. Up they roared, their eyes fixed on the two wizards, but they did not stop within the tight confines of the dungeons, they smashed through the ceiling with so much force that the entire Keep shook. Its very foundations were at breaking point, large rocks rained down on the two wizards. The second and third dragons followed the first without incident, but the fourth smashed its body into two of the supporting columns. Now the building was in danger of collapsing. Marsukia grimaced as he realised the stupid mistake he had made, though he did not once panic or feel threatened by the chaotic scenes around him. Words left his mouth silently, words never heard before by any living creature. His power was all encompassing. As the dust settled he turned to the other wizard.

"Let us look upon the Sentry."

Prestersfordle showed no outward signs of shock, but his mind was in turmoil. He knew that he should have perished at that moment; he saw his entire life pass before him, but he was here within what were the dungeons of the keep: alive.

"You have grown into a power that I thought not possible for mere mortals; I will follow you to my death in our pursuit of eternal life."

"You have seen but a glimpse of the power I hold, come!" said the wizard.

The blackness of the storm clouds seemed to add to the atmosphere, for as the four flying beasts landed, it was as if the thunder from the skies had boomed within the earth itself. Marsukia walked with Prestersfordle, the two wizards looking on in wonder at the massive beings that had come to serve them.

"We shall visit the wooded place known as Tarsit. I feel that there is something of great importance within the trees that the Brethren have overlooked," said Marsukia.

"Are we to travel together?" asked the other wizard, his eyes staring at the slime-ridden bodies of the Sentry.

Marsukia then uttered silent words of magic:

"We ride alone upon the saddles that will ensure our safe passage south," replied Marsukia, who had already mounted the nearest Sentry. Sitting high above the Plains of Desire, the wizard looked down at Prestersfordle. He was unsure of the wizard's future at that moment; somehow he had foreseen something that did not bother him.

"Let us ride the skies and survey our armies before we head for Tarsit," boomed the wizard, the Sentry screaming as it took to the blackness of the skies.

Chapter Twelve

The four Gnomes were tiring. The fields leading up to the river Alluvia were sodden, in some places they had sank up to their knees. Arrun was by now nearing the river, his eyes looking for a suitable boat in which he could navigate its strong currents. The sudden screams though brought him whirling around to see the four Gnomes being attacked by at least a dozen of the evil creatures he had fought only the other day. He unleashed several arrows within seconds, killing six of the Goblins instantly, but he knew that the Gnomes were easy prey while they struggled through the swamp- like grasslands.

The eight sided weapons the Goblins were throwing, screeched through the air. Several actually ripped the clothing of the Gnomes. Akkia was actually cut on the side, his screams of agony bringing Treak to his side within moments.

"I will not leave you, Akkia of Gutox. How badly are you hurt?"

"I am not injured badly, Treak my leader. It was the shock of seeing my blood that made me cry out," replied Akkia, who was looking at the creatures that were bounding towards them.

"Hurry!" exclaimed the Elf, "The ground is firm here, and then we shall turn and kill the creatures that hunt us."

Crikken and Kellek were the first to reach the Elf, their breathing hard and laboured.

"We are surely doomed!" gasped Crikken, his sword drawn in readiness for the coming battle.

"Always have hope, Crikken, master of the bramble," said Arrun, his bow unleashing yet more death amongst the enemy that was closing in.

"Hope is something the Gnomes do not believe in," spat Crikken.

Arrun suddenly leapt forward, the conversation lost in the frantic moments that followed. The Elf seemed to run without touching the earth, his speed as quick as a shot arrow. The two breathless Gnomes were in a desperate struggle, Akkia had been hit again by one of the Goblins throwing weapons. Treak also had been struck about his legs. All in all, twelve Goblins were closing in for the kill, their mouths open wide, craving the flesh of the hunted. But when all hope had left the souls of the two Gnomes, when they realised that the creatures that wanted their deaths were on top of them, there appeared the Elf, his two long daggers slashing the bodies he had come to loathe.

"The boats are but a few paces away, find the strength and hold onto your faith," said the Elf, as he killed with ease.

With the dead bodies of the Goblins hindering their path, the two Gnomes felt lost in a fear they had never experienced before. Panic seemed to wash over them, and it felt as if they were drowning in their own fear.

Arrun gave his hands to the injured Gnomes, helping them all he could, but in the distance he could hear the rasping screams of even more Goblins charging in their direction, the fizzing of their weapons quite clearly heard as they screamed past the heads of the fleeing group of friends.

Crikken and Kellek came to the side of the injured pair, putting their arms around them. The boat Arrun had chosen was a fishing boat, moored to the banks of the Alluvia by a long rope, which was tied simply to a wooden stake.

"We must be quick!" urged the Elf, who stood with his back to the river, calmly staring at the Goblins that were galloping towards them.

"Akkia is bleeding freely!" exclaimed Crikken, who had slipped on the muddy banks of the river, his head turning to see several Goblins charge over the brow of the riverbank.

Before he could react to the Goblins' attack, they were upon them, their snarling, open mouths bearing down on them. Wildly they sought to fight the creatures off, but with so many, their plight was as hopeless as a dying butterfly; death seemed a certainty.

Arrun the Elf was not their saviour in this moment; it was their leader, who was bleeding freely from an open gash on his left leg. He charged at the Goblins as if it were his last deed in life. Such was the ferocity of his attack, it saved the lives of his beloved kin. By the time he had entered the fight, the Elf and the Gnome known as Kellek had come to their aid, the Elf spinning wildly amongst the Goblins, his actions but a blur to the ones who saw his daggers enter their bodies. Kellek too was a crazed being, screaming at the top of his voice that the evil must be killed. Wildly he swung at the writhing forms of the Goblins, their flesh opening with each stab he made. In the confusion of the fight, the Elf sought calm. He knew that more could be heading their way and the river offered a safe passage for the moment.

"Get onto the boat! We must get onto the Alluvia, hurry!" he shouted.

As they rose from the death all around them, they made for the boat: a large Dwarven fishing boat, a vessel easily big enough for the five who tried to climb aboard. Arrun was the first to leap aboard, his eyes scanning the sodden fields that had spawned so much evil that day. He reached down and was helping Akkia when a screeching noise suddenly broke the relative silence of the moment. It tore into the right shoulder of the Gnome, making him gasp out aloud before falling silent. Crikken, Kellek and Treak turned as one and charged at the eight remaining Goblins, hatred meeting hatred in the sickening crunch of battle. Arrun killed the creatures like he had killed no other living thing. He tore into the Goblins and swept them away, the banks of the Alluvia were soaked with the deep red blood of the dead Goblins. He watched as the three Gnomes staggered to the fallen Akkia, his body twisted and limp. But even as he looked on, he sensed something to the rear of him. He let his eyes turn his head towards the direction from which he had sensed the fear. In the distance, there were at least two dozen Hobgoblins charging in his direction, their crooked spears pointing towards where he was standing.

"This is madness!" he exclaimed quietly.

Arrun reached for his arrows, but none were left. He raced to the boat, untying the rope from the small wooden stake.

"We must be quick. Here, give the wounded one to me, get onto the boat now!" he ordered, as he picked up the lifeless body of the Gnome. As he tumbled the stricken Gnome onto the deck of the boat, several spears were already airborne, heading straight for the Elf's back. Treak saw the spears and screamed a warning to him. Arrun took the warning gravely, turning his body to face the flying spears. Within that fraction of a second, he had pulled out his two daggers. His reflexes were like lightning as he deflected the long spears harmlessly away from his body, jumping instantly onto the deck of the moving vessel. He looked briefly at the staring figure of the Gnome.

"Like you said the other day, Treak, this is not the day I wish to die."

The Hobgoblins seemed to shrink away from the waters of the Alluvia. It was as if they sensed a great power from the flowing river, but that did not stop them from throwing everything they had in the direction of the large fishing boat, several daggers embedding themselves into the side of the boat. After they had done this, they headed back in the direction from which they had come.

"Treak!" said the Elf.

"I am still here," replied the standing Gnome.

"Give me your bow and arrows, quickly!" he ordered.

"Here," said the Gnome passing his bow and six remaining arrows to the Elf.

"You will not kill any of them from this distance, they must be at least a hundred paces away," said the sitting figure of Crikken, his face grimacing in pain. Blood was flowing from several deep cuts he had sustained in the battles he had just fought.

Arrun though angled his bow and let the six arrows scream into the midday skies within a couple of moments. Then he lay the bow down and watched as the retreating Hobgoblins started to drop to the grasslands.

"Five out of six is good. I only wish I had enough to wipe out the entire band of Hobgoblins. The remaining ones are sure to report to the being that I confronted within the woods. We will not be safe for some days, I am afraid," said the Elf, turning his attention to the steering of the fishing boat, for the river would not help the boat navigate its many twists and turns.

"The creature that you talk of, what is it?" asked Treak, who was still flat on his back and in some pain.

"It is not from the human race, of that I am sure. It belongs not in this world. I saw magic pouches tied around its waist, so wizards may hold the key to this mystery," replied the Elf, who had dropped the boat's anchor into the fast flowing river.

"I have never heard of a wizard being evil, so I can be no judge in the matter," said the Gnome quietly.

"Here, let me tend to you. I hold some healing knowledge," offered Arrun, who was happy that the boat had slowed sufficiently for him to leave it unattended for a while. He reached into his waist tunic and pulled forth a small bag; he emptied some of the contents into his hands and massaged them for a while.

"Show me where you are bleeding; I will halt the flow."

"I am fine. It is Akkia who needs your skills, not I," said the Gnome, who grimaced with pain from the many cuts his legs had suffered. But the Elf would have none of the Gnome's attempts to shake him off. He made Treak expose his legs; blood covered every inch of them. Arrun left the Gnome and went to the stores, a place where the Dwarfs kept the many items they would need for a weeks' fishing on the Alluvia. He saw what he was looking for and filled the water jug straight from the river.

"You are lucky on this day, Treak, for the waters of the Alluvia will cleanse your wounds and help them recover. Now this may sting," warned the Elf, who started to clean up the bloodied mess. Next he rubbed the ointment into the deep cuts, causing the Gnome to scream out loud.

"That surely is made from the breath of a Dragon," gasped Treak, his eyes watering with the sudden surge of heat into his thighs.

"It comes from the forests of Follonday, a simple plant found under the branches of Willow trees. Some herbs are added, but the goodness comes from the plant. The herbs merely take away the foul stench of the stewed leaf," explained the Elf, his eyes looking at the silent figures of the other three Gnomes.

"What is it called then?" asked Treak, who had not clicked his fingers at all during the short voyage.

"It is simply called Little Willow. You will start to feel better shortly; when you feel that you can stand, take up the steering of the boat. I am going to be busy for the next day at least tending to your friends."

"We hate the water. Every single Gnome alive today hates the water, and you want me to stand when I am surrounded by the stuff?" moaned Treak, hoping the Elf would just stop the vessel and let them get off on to solid ground.

"We will be safe when we pass Tarsit, then we may travel by other means. But it is the young one over there who worries me, for he has not stirred. My healing powers might not be enough to save him, but I will try."

Three hours had passed since the Elf and Treak had spoken. The fishing boat had barely moved, the anchor doing the job it was meant to do. Treak felt his legs, the pain had all but gone. He rubbed away some of the ointment the Elf had smeared on and gasped out loud, for there was no sign that he had been touched. He rubbed away some more, his heart beating a little quicker.

"Real Elf magic! Well, I never would have dreamt it in a million years. Arrun! Look! I can stand. You have performed a miracle upon my body, I owe you my life," laughed the Gnome, who even jumped up and down a few times to see if that would cause him any harm.

"If you are better, Treak, leader of this group of Gnomes, then pull up the anchor and let us drift into the west, before we are besieged by a thousand Hobgoblins," said the Elf, who did not look up from the work he was doing on the body of Crikken. Earlier he had done what he could for the limp body of Akkia, spreading the ointment in several places, but it was the wound the Gnome had taken in his shoulder that worried the Elf the most. He did not have the healing knowledge for such a wound. Little Willow was of no use to him, for he could see the embedded weapon that had entered the Gnome's shoulder quite clearly; he did not hold much hope for the youngest of the Gnomes.

Treak had hauled up the anchor and gripped the steering pole for dear life. They had picked up speed and the Gnome had nearly crashed the boat on several occasions, turning the rudder one way and the boat going the other, cursing silently all the time that this was no place for Gnomes. But as the day drifted into evening, Arrun came up to the Gnome and patted him on the back.

"I think we will drop the anchor; let us hope we are not spotted from the banks. You have negotiated the river well, Treak. It takes many years normally to learn to navigate such a water as this."

Treak stumbled over to his friends, the light of day almost gone; dark clouds had been rumbling across the skies all day, threatening them with rain. It was now they felt the first big drops of a downpour from above.

"Treak, help me with the covers," ordered Arrun, who was kneeling where all the storage boxes were kept.

"Covers?" asked the Gnome.

"Hurry, for we cannot afford for Akkia to get too wet, his body needs to be kept warm," said Arrun, who had already started to unravel the large waterproof canvas sheet.

"These Dwarfs were not as stupid as they looked!" exclaimed Treak, watching the Elf struggle with the heavy sheet.

"Hook the rings on to the wooden pegs, I will hoist the centre pole," ordered the Elf pleasantly.

Treak did as he was told and within minutes the back of the fishing boat was under cover. The distant thunder rumbled across the lands.

"Treak, give me two wood pearls."

Treak looked at the Elf in shock, he had completely forgotten about the treasure they hoarded. It also dawned on him that the Elf could quite easily have taken the wood pearls and left them to die.

"Where are they?" he asked in a high-pitched shriek.

"Over there in the corner. I removed all the sacks from your backs while you were suffering. Do not worry, Treak. The time has gone when I might have taken them away from you. I merely want to light a fire; the night is going to be bitter. Warmth is the only hope for the youngest Gnome. While you get the wood pearls, I will fetch a pearl carrier," replied the Elf in a gentle but firm manner.

The fishing boat had come to a complete stop within the soft currents of the Alluvia. Dwarven fishing boats were big, well- built and very well equipped. Several Dwarfs could spend several days away from Wooded Hood, such was the ample supply of provisions each boat carried. The one the Elf had picked was one of the biggest on the river. It even had fresh water, something which the Elf would use in the coming days.

The rain had become a downpour, pelting on top of the sheet which was covering the Elf and four Gnomes. Arrun closed the side flaps and opened a small canvas opening on the fair side of the boat. This would let out the poisonous fumes of the wood pearl, but not let in the weather.

"But I have no flint with me, Arrun," said Treak as he passed the two small wood pearls to the Elf.

Arrun smiled at the Gnome and brought forth two needle sharp flints. He placed the wood pearls on to the iron plate and set them alight within a few seconds. A bright light flared from them, a warmth instantly filled the space where they were sitting." These are indeed a treasure, Treak, for these two pearls left unattended would burn and lose none of their warmth for a whole season. We shall have some broth, I fancy: Dwarven broth, hearty and good for the being."

As they sat around the iron plate, which had already started to turn red at its centre, Arrun erected the cooking pots. This was a simple affair of a triangular set of iron rods which held the cooking pots at the desired height. Arrun then started to add the dried meat and fresh vegetables to the fishing boat's fresh water. From one of his many small pockets, he produced a tiny pouch full of crushed garlic seeds.

"What is that you are adding?" asked the bewildered Gnome.

"Treak, leader of the raiders, you will see."

By the time the broth had been cooked, Crikken and Kellek had managed to sit up. They had not spoken a word as yet, but the smells coming from the broth had them both craving something to eat.

The Dwarven bowls were big. Arrun handed out the servings to the three Gnomes and sat back down against the far side of the enclosed area. His back was resting gently against the canvas sheets; he felt safer sitting like this. The hour was late when they had finished the hearty broth. The bowls were handed back to the Elf. He shoved them out of the door flap and looked at the Gnomes, three of them sitting upright and looking quite at home on the Dwarven fishing boat. He then turned his gaze to the limp form of Akkia. A deep sadness came over him, for once Elves had made contact with a living creature, they never stopped caring for it, be it a wild Deer, a Stallion of the Plains of Desire, a simple field mouse or even Gnomes, thought Arrun, knowing that the bond he was making with the thieves of Gutox could not be broken by anyone or anything.

That night was as peaceful as it could be on a river full of water. The boat fared well and the rocking motion did not make the Gnomes any the worse for wear. They slept for long periods, tucked into their body wraps. Arrun though did not sleep.He had crawled over to the lifeless form of Akkia, where he did what he could for the stricken Gnome. As the light of a new day dawned, the rain stopped as abruptly as it had started. He woke Treak and told him to prepare for a long journey on the river Alluvia. As they were finishing putting away the canvas sheets, they heard in the distance the screams the Elf had been dreading all night.

"Pull the anchor, we will be the river's guests this new day," said Arrun, who was silently cursing himself for delaying their departure.

The boat seemed to be lifted as the anchor was hauled into its position; the current was strong. Arrun took hold of the steering rod and started to bring the fishing boat into the fastest part of the river. The deep guttural screams were near. He looked to his right and saw at least fifty Goblins and Hobgoblins heading in the direction of the Alluvia. Arrun quickly realised that they had a massive problem. He knew that there was an Elven bridge before they reached Tarsit. The creatures only he could see would reach the bridge before them. He did not speak to the Gnomes of what he had heard or seen. He checked his throwing daggers, twelve in all; these were all he had left apart from his cooking knife. He called for Treak.

"We are being hunted yet again."

"Where are they coming from and what do they want of us?" asked Treak, who looked in every direction, but could not see or hear the creatures that had already nearly killed him.

"They come from the north. Quickly are they moving. A bridge approaches that might give them a chance of catching us, let us prepare."

So they did. Treak went to Crikken and Kellek while Arrun steered the boat. He explained the situation and the two Gnomes looked shocked that they might have to fight yet again. In total, six arrows remained. These were given to the Elf. They possessed eight daggers, two taken from the limp figure of Akkia. The bridge suddenly appeared, albeit a smudge on the river's horizon. The three Gnomes peered into the fields that lay alongside the river. They saw nothing. With the bridge fast approaching they thought they may have reached the Elven bridge before the Goblins and Hobgoblins. The sound of the eight sided spheres hitting the side of the fishing boat brought them whirling around to see the horde of Goblins galloping just behind them. They knew then that these creatures would reach the Elven bridge before them.

"I will steer, Arrun, Elf of the fair forest," said Treak as he handed the Elf the bow and arrows.

"And I will kill, Treak," replied the grim- faced Elf.

The slender bridge arced its way across the river in a way that made it appear to be a living thing. The Elves had personally built the bridges a long time ago. Dozens were to be found on the four great rivers, though the Dwarfs of Pavelem had steered their trade routes well away from the magical bridges. The fishing boat was closing in on the bridge, which already had several Hobgoblins standing on its shiny surface.

"They will pay with their lives for having the nerve to set foot on one of our bridges," snapped the Elf, who was already preparing to let loose a hail of arrows in their direction.

"We have never stepped onto one of the Elf bridges. There are tales of woe for those who did, meeting terrible deaths at the hands of the Elf warriors who roam the Plains of Desire," said Treak, his hands remaining silent.

"No warriors roam the plains, Treak. They are here for a purpose, to rid the lands of….."

"Gnomes and the vermin that spread diseases!" finished the Gnome, his face grim.

Two dozen Hobgoblins were waiting for the fishing boat to go past them, their crooked spears reaching downwards. It seemed that all would be lost, for even more had climbed onto the beautiful bridge. But something started to happen: something of which the Hobgoblins had been warned.. Marsukia had made it clear that the bridges were to be treated with extreme caution. The wizard had even made the small army of

Goblins and Hobgoblins, led by the Brethren, take the route of the Great Eastern Divide when travelling to Tarsit, The bridge creaked softly, pieces of the slender arc dropping into the Alluvia. Even Treak watched in shock as the bridge suddenly disappeared from view. The whole bunch of Hobgoblins seemed for one brief moment to be standing in the air, the next second they had fallen in to the Alluvia, their deaths a certainty within the Elf's river, for the waters churned up and down until all the creatures had sunk to their watery graves.

"Bless the Elf Bridge!" cheered Crikken, who had come to see the river's anger.

"Bless the river!" added Kellek, who had begun to feel like his old self.

"Bless the Elf who stands in front of us, for he is like no other Elf," said Treak, his face breaking into a smile, his slanted eyes shutting.

Before Treak had opened his eyes, the Elf had unleashed the arrows from the bow, whistling through the air, hitting another group of the creatures that were still running towards them. The waters of the river once more became as they were before the bridge had collapsed. The fishing boat carried onwards, leaving the few Hobgoblins way behind.

Tarsit appeared to the south of them, black smoke spiralling into the scattered clouds, which were heading east towards the Great Eastern Divide.

"It is wrecked then," said the Elf, more to himself than to his new friends.

None of the Gnomes said anything as the boat was

swept along besides the woodland by the Alluvia. It was some way off, to the south of them, but all looked at the burning trees that would no longer yield the treasure they carried in their sacks. Small figures they saw too, hundreds of them, circling the entire wood.

"Pavelem will want revenge," stated the Elf, who had stepped backwards to hold the steering beam steady.

"Against who?" asked Crikken, who already knew that it would be the Gnomes who would suffer first at the hands of the Dwarfs.

"Their enemies," replied the Elf, not wanting to add that it would of course be the thieving race of Gnomes who would feel the iron fist of the massive Dwarf armies first. Then they would declare open war against the Trolls of Yea-Bor. He thought of the lesser races and sighed; they were going to pay heavily for something they had nothing to do with.

An hour later and the boat was drifting with the currents of the river. Tarsit had disappeared from view and the Plains of Desire were all that they could look upon: a green desert devoid of tree or shrub. The silence of the land filled the ears of the Gnomes; even the noises of birds could not be heard.

"This is a barren land, Elf. When are we to stop this voyage and head to the mountains in the east?" asked Treak.

"Treak, leader of this bunch of gnomes, you forget about the youngest here. He needs help!" replied the Elf, saddened by the Gnome's attitude.

"We have our ways, Arrun. Akkia is lucky that we are here with him. The treasures we now carry could give our race some real power. My instinct is to leave him be with nature; the hour has come to head home," said the Gnome, his eyes avoiding the Elf's.

"And you wonder why the Elves regard your race with the contempt they deserve."

"We serve the whole of our race. One who perishes trying to help the cause will, of course, be remembered. If the young one here dies, he dies, but his life will be honoured. He will live forever in the mind of our kind Elf. Do not try and judge us, as we do not judge you," said Treak, who had walked away from the Elf.

"We will do what we can for the young one here. I cherish life; I will not let you abandon one who needs our help," replied Arrun, his feelings hurt by the way Treak had forgotten about all he had already done for them. But to his amazement, it was the Gnome who had shown him real hatred when they had first met that spoke for the young Gnome's welfare:

"Treak, you are our leader, but I will not leave Akkia while he still breathes. I will follow the Elf, for he has proved to me that he does not care for the treasure we carry. If he did, he could quite easily have slain us. Arrun, I for one will not leave Akkia."

"And what of you, Kellek?" Treak asked, who had flown into a rage when Crikken had openly gone against what he had said.

"I will listen to the Elf, Treak, though you are still the

one I serve. But he cares for us; it is a good feeling to be cared for by an Elf," answered the Gnome, his head bowed in respect.

Treak stared onto the flat grasslands. He knew they were right. He cared for Akkia just as much as they did, but he cared for his kind more. He wanted his race of Gnomes to climb out of the stinking caves of the volcanoes, he wanted the Gnomes to be able to hold their heads high within the lands that Elves and the Dwarfs had taken for their own. His feelings had history, he thought of the hundreds that had been killed by the Dwarfs, killed trying to take something the Dwarfs did not own. He turned to the three and held his arms above his head.

"The Elf known to us as Arrun has shown us mercy. He has risked his own life protecting ours. I will agree that I was thinking only of our kind. Elf, accept my hand in the knowledge that I will follow you. Akkia is too young to die, let us bring him back from the netherworld."

Crikken and Kellek could not help themselves; they rushed to their leader and grasped him for long moments, their tears flowing freely. Arrun felt happy too: he had turned the views of a fanatic, a Gnome who was so set in his ways that he would have let his own brothers die for the cause. The Elf looked at the limp body of Akkia and shook his head; he seemed to be so close to death. Would the healers of the forest be of any use? To this, he did not have the answer.

Chapter Thirteen

The day Browfell and Bugram had looked upon the massive armies of the three wizards had been a day of terror for the two Troll scouts. They had seen huge numbers of Goblins and Hobgoblins detach themselves from the main army. For long hours they had run, but the gap between them and the Goblins, had if anything, closed slightly. The two running unit scouts halted in a dip in the grasslands. Looking back, they could see only the utter blackness of the storm clouds.

"We will not make Yea-Bor," said Browfell, his breath coming in short, sharp gulps. His hands had come to rest on his knees. This was a crucial time for the two Trolls, for if they did not recover their breathing, they would not be able to continue at the blistering pace at which they had run for most of that morning. Bugram sat with his head between his legs, taking in a massive mouthful of air before trying to reply to his close friend.

"I do not like it, Browfell," gasped Bugram.

"The Elf River is too far away."

"What about the northern territories, will they be safe? They are but a quick chase across the Plains of Desire." His face looked at Browfell's and all hope vanished as quickly as it had popped into his mind.

"The settlements are lost surely. The thousands that we saw head north would be reaching the outer regions about now," Browfell took several more deep breaths, his chest heaving up and down as he struggled to regain his composure.

"Our world is suffering," said Bugram.

"It is a sad day," was the simple reply.

As they were about to set off again, Browfell clapped his massive hands together. He took hold of Bugram's shoulders, his eyes having hope within them.

"I am a fool, that is true, but what are we running away for?"

"To save our skins from the monsters that hunt all Trolls," replied Bugram bitterly.

"We are scouts of the famed second running unit of the first age. We will dig down and let them carry on for a while, and then we can follow them at our own pace."

"The chances of our survival lying but inches below the surface of the grasslands, while those Goblins come trampling over us is nil," Bugram nearly laughed at the suggestion, but did not bother as he saw that Browfell was serious.

"There we will be safer, for if we are found here, they

may think we are already dead. Running on the Plains of Desire would be like throwing our lives away; that would be senseless. So let us get beneath the grasslands."

They worked together, taking the grass up in long strips, laying it to one side and then continuing to dig. The spoils from the dig were scattered over the surrounding areas. The skill of this was to lie in the shallow trenches with the turf laid on top of the body and remain there until the enemy had passed by. It had proved a success against the Dwarfs, who had fallen into many a trap laid by the running units of the Troll army. The hours they had spent making the appearance of their hiding place blend into sloping grasslands had been worth it, for even they who knew where to look, nodded their heads in approval. The distant sound of drums and great shouts brought reality crashing back into them. They ran to the brow of the slope and saw thousands upon thousands of Hobgoblins and their smaller cousins marching towards them. A terror filled them both for long moments. It was the loud screams to the right of them that brought them to their senses, each knowing that the army had sent out hundreds of scouts, something they had not thought the attacking army would think of. As quietly as they could, they started to crawl towards their hideaway, but the Hobgoblin was now just twenty paces away and closing in, his rasping, foul mouth uttering curses every second, threatening all that came before him and every Goblin that got in his way. He was naked except for the numerous belts that crisscrossed his twisted frame, his bald head full of warts and scars. He never saw the knife which entered his chest or the massive hands which strangled the life out of him. In but a split second, the bones of the spinal column shattered under the tremendous strength of the silent Troll.

"This is it then, my friend," said Bugram, who had retrieved the knife he had thrown at the Hobgoblin.

"Yes I know, but the smell will get better as the hours pass by," said the other Troll, who had already started to drag the lifeless body into the shallow pit, which like two unmade beds, still had the covers off.

"He lays with us, such horrors I never thought possible," spat the Troll, as he rushed to help his friend.

As they pulled the last strip of turf over them, they felt the ground shudder and heard foul language come to their ears. Now was the time when all was to be won or lost. The leading Goblins came past the two concealed Trolls at such a pace, they were gone within the briefest of moments. Several had touched the strips of turf, but none had heard the grunts of pain from beneath them, such was their haste in wanting to reach the city of the Trolls. Browfell and Bugram lay on their stomachs, with their heads tucked into their shoulders. They spoke the odd word or two, but on the whole they stayed with their own thoughts. The Hobgoblins came next, which were much slower in their progress. Some were walking even slower, stabbing their spears into the ground. This was mainly for support; little did they know that two of their enemy were but a few inches away from them. It seemed that they were within the blackness of the earth for hours, when in actual fact it had only been the two. Coming up was the scariest, for if they came up and there were still several Hobgoblins to come, their plan and lives would be lost.

When they did finally risk coming up from below, they were met with the blackness of the night. They were reluctant to stand, such was the fear that overcame them. Instead, they crawled for many long hours, expecting at any moment to be pounced upon by a stray Goblin. In the end, fatigue overtook the pair and they collapsed and fell into a short but troubled sleep.

Far to the east of Yea-Bor ran the King, his heavy breathing making him smile. He had shed many pounds in weight during the past two weeks. Something had altered his perception of what he was meant to be doing as King of the Trolls. No longer did he dwell within his massive tent, drinking the nights away until he could drink no more. The Troll known as Pig had been sent back to the city of Yea-Bor, his mood darkened by the way in which the King had dismissed him. He was on his own most nights now, sleeping rough amongst the lower slopes of the Great Eastern Divide. If he did manage to eat, it was because he had hunted the animal down and killed it with either bow or sword. The first few nights had been the worst of his life, but the last two had been the best, mainly because he had completed what every aspiring member of any running unit must do and that was to run for the morning, without stopping. Thengost was hungry, but he did not want to be waited on. He wanted to hunt down his meal of that day, like he had done for only three of the fourteen days since he had left the Golden Valley, a departure in itself which had caused panic and confusion amongst his own personal guard. Most had said amongst themselves that the sight of the fat King leaving would be the last, for he was in no fit state to fend for himself within the wilds of the Great Eastern Divide. So it had been Denth who had offered to track the King, making sure that he would be there for the King if he needed help. But so far Denth had merely watched in awe at the way his King had managed the wilderness.

Thengost had been resting for an hour when he spotted the wild pig some distance away, feeding within low-lying scrub. The King of the Trolls reacted at once, withdrawing one of his long daggers. He thought of using his bow for the briefest of moments, but he liked his daggers, liked the feel of them when he threw them. He slowly rose and went downwind of the unsuspecting animal. The pig died instantly as the dagger was thrown by the sprinting Troll, his speed taking him fifty paces past the dead pig. It was at this moment that the King of the Trolls knew he was ready to take his rightful place at the head of the legendary first running unit. Some distance away lying on his front was Denth. He had witnessed the lightning speed of the King, had seen him throw the dagger while running at a speed he knew he could never match and had seen the dagger enter the pig's neck with a force that had knocked the pig into the air and onto its side.

Yea-Bor though knew nothing of what the King was doing. The city was in a state of sorrow and deep grief at the news that they had lost so many Trolls on the Plains of Desire. The council had been in the debating chamber for the longest ever period of time without a break and the tempers of some had worn so thin that small fights had begun to break out. However, Henthorn was proclaiming that their losses were the saviour of the city.

"We must lift ourselves from the present gloom. We will endure," he shouted, banging his gloved hand onto the ancient long table.

"Argost, what is your judgment of the horrors you witnessed upon the Plains of Desire?" asked the head of the council, ignoring the last comment.

Argost rose from his seat, which was on the right side of the debating chamber. Behind him was a painting of the city of Yea-Bor, bathed in sunshine. His face though was grimacing as he thought of what he had just been through. The seated members of the council hushed as they looked at the bloodstained Troll approach the head of the table. Here he withdrew his mighty sword and plunged it into the table. What followed was an uproar so great, it needed Demjom, head of the council to hold back several Trolls that had risen in disgust. But the young Troll lifted his arms and shouted to the council.

"I pierce the wood of a mere table, yet I have seen the heart of our nation pierced with an evil so great that death they welcome. Even as we killed the hideous creatures that attacked us from every angle, they killed one another, such was the frenzy of the battle. They did not come to battle as a single force, of this, I am certain. "

"But we killed an army of such a huge size. Even the Dwarfs of Pavelem could not put an army of that size against us; the battle was won by the Trolls," argued Henthorn, not looking at the solemn face of Argost.

"Argost!" urged Denjom.

"A battle was won, this is true," answered Argost, who had turned to look upon his leader, the dried blood matting his hair in many places." But a war may already be lost."

"The Plains of Desire will tell us our future. Make ready for battle, Henthorn. Round up every single Troll who is still within the training camps to the north of Yea-Bor," ordered Denjom.

"But to panic is to lose the war against the Dwarfs. We have no enemies to the west of us now," replied the highly honoured Troll, his temper simmering just beneath the surface of his thoughts.

"Set up twelve new units, make Argost the head of one of them," said the head of the council, waving the Troll away.

"But have you forgotten the history of the Troll running units?" asked Henthorn, shocked at what he had just been told to do.

"History means nothing when we face this mounting evil," replied Denjom, not wanting to reveal his thoughts on the King.

"I assemble the running units as and when the ruling

King orders. So, that is the way," argued the shocked Troll, who had stood his ground.

"Do as the head of the council orders, Henthorn," said a distant voice from the bottom of the stairwell.

Many turned towards the direction of the voice and were shocked into a silence that would stay with them as the figure strode towards the head of the debating chamber. It was the rippling muscles of the upper arms that had some whispering of wizards ' magic, while others gasped at the sword the figure carried, for it was the very one the Troll kings of old had carried into battle.

"Head of the Troll council," said the figure flatly, "You may take your leave; the King has returned."

"My King," answered Denjom, who had dropped to his knees.

"My King," offered Argost, who had followed Denjom to his knees.

"My King," said Henthorn, doing likewise, his look of shock plain to see for the changed King.

"The King," roared the debating chamber, the deafening chorus lasting some time.

"As your King, I return to Yea-Bor, a city on the brink of a war we must not lose, for if we fail, the race of Trolls will end. I have spent long hours looking at the paintings and drawings of the running scouts of the second unit. They tell me one thing: war is coming to us."

Henthorn was the first to rise, taking the opportunity once more to claim he had seen off the threats from the west, but Thengost gripped the other's hands, squeezing them tightly as he spoke softly.

"You came to me less than a moon cycle ago. Tell me what you thought of me. No, do not bother with such talk, for I know what you thought: that there was a King who had forgotten his duty, had forsaken his family's great history, had sought comfort in the whiskey ale and food so readily available to one such as I. Well my dear friend, I felt something as you left that day. I knew my coming of age would have to happen sooner rather than later, but of this I am as certain as the dawning of the new day, that Argost here speaks the truth. The armies from the west come from beyond the Fingertip Mountains, you know of this place?" asked the King, who had pulled the other proud Troll close to him.

"I know nothing of the place you talk of, my King," replied Henthorn quietly, his eyes never leaving his King's intense stare.

"Then you are indeed lucky. Not many do. It was the late King who took me there. It is a place of great evil, where the ground itself has opened to reveal the depths of Hell. Millions I looked upon that day, millions upon millions of the creatures you yourself showed me when you came urging my return. I tossed you aside that night, my friend, for a nightmare that had been with me for the past ten years had come to show itself upon the blessed Plains of Desire, the very place our ancestors fought a great battle with the Elves of Follonday. Go now and do as the head of the council orders, he has my blessings"

241

finished Thengost, a single tear rolling down his rugged face. Henthorn left the debating chamber thinking of how many Trolls he had lost fighting: but a fraction of the army that was somewhere on the Plains of Desire. His mood was indeed dark knowing that the youngest of the Trolls had not lived a life as yet.

"So your father took you past the Fingertip Mountains, not many souls have seen past them," said Denjom in wonder.

"He thought it was so important for me to see what the wizard had shown him. It was a trip I blocked from my mind, such was the evil we looked upon. The Fingertip mountains are not a place for any living being to be upon, for they are as sharp as the sword I carry. You may rise, young Troll," said the King, his hand reaching down to help Argost up, the young Troll gripping his King's hand tightly.

"My King," acknowledged the young Troll.

"For the rest of you, arm yourselves and prepare for war. There will be no council meetings within this chamber until I say so. Well, what are you waiting for? Leave!" he ordered in a ferocious voice. The stunned Trolls left the debating chamber that day, most worrying about fighting. Some of them had not even picked up a knife before, let alone a sword.

"You really expect them to fight the creatures that threaten us?" asked Denjom in shock.

The King roared with laughter and added,

"No, of course I do not expect them to fight, but we

will not be troubled by the cowards who sit around this table, deciding the fate of our race when they know not of war and how to plan the counter attacks I have in mind."

Denjom relaxed a little. He went into the map room and brought forth several maps of the western approaches to the city. The King studied the maps for some minutes before he clenched his fist and slammed it into the ancient table, which still had the sword of the young troll embedded within its surface.

"One hundred and forty four running units will leave tonight. I will lead them. Then every hour on the hour until sunrise, send out eighteen running units at a time. But send them both to the south and to the north. If we are trapped in the middle, a surprise will be waiting for the creatures that do not belong on this earth. Argost!."

"Yes!" came the hurried reply.

"I want you to run alongside the King, advise me on the way they fight, tell of any weaknesses you have noticed while fighting them. The hour has come to rid the lands of the evil that threatens it," ordered the King, who had grasped the embedded sword, lifting it out of the table. Here he looked at it and waved it from side to side, seemingly admiring the weight of the blade.

"I offer you this sword, my King, for it has killed many of the creatures you talk of," said Argost, his mind whirling with what he was witnessing. After all, he was young, he had never even seen the King before, but the two of them seemed to be made of the same stuff.

"Thank you, Argost. But I wield only this sword, for

it is the sword of past Kings. You keep your sword safe, for I have not lifted many better," replied Thengost, who handed the sword back to the Troll who had impressed him like no other. There seemed to be a deep spirit about the Troll; he was looking forward to the coming days like no other day he could imagine.

In total, one hundred and forty four Troll running units left the city of Yea-Bor that night. As they left the inner sanctum of the city, crowds gathered to watch the departing Trolls, but no cheers rang out, for rumours had spread throughout the city that the King had returned to fight the final battle of the Troll race. A further two hundred and sixteen running units were at present getting themselves prepared to leave, but they would be leaving as separate units every hour as the King had ordered.

The midder wall loomed into view, Troll guards opening the second defensive gates that led into the outer section of the city: a place normally reserved for farming. But Denjom, the head of the council, had ordered hundreds of Trolls to start the laying down of the iron spikes that would act as a formidable defense if any enemy got past the outer wall. This was being fortified even as the King and the one hundred and forty four running units left through the massive wooden gates that faced directly into the setting Sun. He was at the front, with Argost running next to him. The pair were running quickly. their hearts beating wildly as they descended onto the flat grasslands of the Plains of Desire. The formation was that of a shooting arrow, their flight path heading for the thousands of Goblins and Hobgoblins that were stampeding towards them. Throughout the night they ran, silent and determined that they would seek out the evil creatures. As the Sun started to rise, a total of three thousand, four hundred and fifty six Trolls were running into battle upon the Plains of Desire. A little way to the west, a mile, maybe two, at least three hundred thousand of the enemy approached at speed. Little did they know that they would be facing the King of the Trolls on that infamous morning.

Thengost had sent out scouts earlier, which he could now see returning as fast as they could run. He lifted his bells and rang them once. All of the running units which were spread over a wide area stopped, their breathing hard and laboured. Each knew that the battle was only moments away. This was the time when they had to collect all their energy and hold onto it until the battle was won. They had been told earlier by the young Troll known as Argost that there were certain ways in which the creatures could be easily killed. They listened as if they were listening to the most important thing they had ever heard. The King ran from the southern tip of his army, touching each Troll upon the head, until he reached the Trolls in the north, a distance in itself of at least half a mile. . He was happy that his units were spread correctly for what he planned to do.

The distant screams and the shaking of the grasslands told each Troll that now was the time he either died or lived to be a hero within his homeland. They did not move a muscle as each stood in the way of the advancing army. As the fastest of the Goblins realised that a thin line of Troll warriors stood in their way, they did not slow down. In fact, there seemed to be a hatred so intense that the very first of the Goblins attacked where the King stood. The spheres he chucked screamed towards the Trolls,, but the shields had been raised, as the Goblin was within three feet of the King. It lost half of its body as Argost attacked from the side, the sword he had offered to his King slaying the Goblin with hatred in his eyes. Thengost held his nerve as he looked upon the sudden sight of the thousands that came into view. The smaller Goblins charged first, eager to get to the bodies of the Trolls.

"Hold," shouted the King, a message which was passed down the lines of Troll archers. Other yells could be heard, ordering the Trolls to hold fire.

The King looked at what his formidable Troll warriors had to fight. He was not scared for himself, but for the families that knew nothing of what attacked their homes. As he looked and waited, thirty to forty more Goblins were slain, each excepting death as a reward.

"Fire!" yelled the King.

"Fire!" shouted the leaders of the other running units. Within that first two minutes of battle, a total of twenty one thousand, seven hundred and twenty eight arrows had been unleashed into the oncoming tide of evil. Several hundred died instantly, while another three hundred were wounded. But onwards charged at least another two hundred thousand, some tripping over the dead and dying Goblins, hungry for the flesh of the waiting Trolls. It was at this moment that the King played his hand; he yelled into the sullen morning skies for his running units to form on their own and go forwards into battle. This had the effect of the two sides meeting in a sickening crunch, the first wave of battle leaving none of the Trolls fallen. They instantly regrouped as one large running unit and sprinted away to the north, the King hoping the other running units that had left after them had made the position on the map he had called for. Even as they ran, he could feel and hear the weapons that were hitting the shields that had been placed exactly where Argost had told them to put them.

The Hobgoblins numbered far less than the smaller Goblins. They being much slower too, they had suddenly realised that they had been stretched to a point where the Goblins had left them far behind, leaving them out in the open. It was now that the plan of the King was paying dividends, for the running units which had set off to the south were now closing in on the lumbering Hobgoblins, which were not suited for this type of battle. They were at their most dangerous within the small confined areas from whence they came, caves and narrow valleys, not out upon a grassland that would offer them no cover. So as the Trolls came on to them from every conceivable angle, several hundred or so died quickly at the hands of the members of the running units, they themselves not waiting, but running after the Goblins.

But the Goblins nearly had the King slain that bloody

morning. For some reason, the King had raced after a Goblin which in turn was bearing down upon a fleeing Troll. Even as the Goblin dug its razor sharp teeth into the left side of the Troll, the King ripped into the Goblin just as he had within the Golden Valley when he had hunted down the wild pig. As he rose to his feet, his body splashed with the thick red blood of the Goblin, he realised his mistake, for no other Troll had come with him, nor should they have done, for it was he himself who had ordered exactly where the running units should go, forgoing the fallen, as overall victory was the aim of the battle.

Thirty Goblins had seen the chase and had followed too, their screams of hatred washing over the King's head, for he did not run, but took his second bell of war from his side and rang it as loudly as he could. He cast it aside as the first of the Goblins reared up at the lone figure of the King of the Trolls.

Argost and the rest of the running units approached the other running units who had been waiting for the signal to unleash their arrows into the remaining hordes of attacking Goblins. But as they heard the distant ring of the King's bell, it was the young Troll known as Argost who charged away with such speed. He was but a blur to the Goblins that tried in vain to kill him. Several he cut down on his quest to search out the King of Yea-Bor. Henthorn rallied the rest of the Trolls and ordered the newly arrived warriors to fire upon the hundreds that still attacked them. Sickening wounds were beginning to be inflicted on the brave who stood their ground, the Goblins like crazed animals, circling the Trolls trying to pick away at them, not bothered if they lost their lives in the attempt to weaken the solid group of Trolls. Again, it was thanks in main to the foresight of the King, for five thousand Trolls that had slaughtered the hapless Hobgoblins had come from the south, their battle cries giving the others heart and even more courage. Within the hour, the entire army of Goblins had been either killed or chased away, but the King was missing.

Chapter Fourteen

Sarratt jumped from the great black stallion, telling him where to go next to assure his safety. Stormbreaker neighed loudly and was out of sight within minutes. This left the wizard within the fringe of Follonday, home of the Elves. The fringe was but a woodland that one would find almost anywhere upon Ursalane, but when one came past the fringe and surveyed the whole of the Follonday forests, fifteen hundred square miles of trees met the onlooker. Follonday itself lay miles away from where the wizard now stood, and was far below, on the last of three tiers, each filled with trees. Each of the great Elf rivers roared their way down to the basin, itself being some thirty miles in width, At the very bottom of the three tiers there was a lake, a lake of such size that it melted away into the Midlantic Oceans. The wizard never tired of treading the lands of the Elf, for they treated the trees like no other race could. He had seen mighty Oak trees, two hundred feet in height with a girth of fifty feet, with several Elf families living within the tree and living on top of the branches, but they were mainly in the southern forests. Where he stood now was more to the north, where Oaks were in abundance, but not as grand as their bigger cousins. Here he set his eyes on the Dragon trees, looking as if they were on fire at all times, and the Red Pine, its trunk reaching a height of eighty feet before spreading out a tiny fan of red and orange leaves: a tree favoured by the birds of prey that lived quite safely within the borders of Follonday.

The wizard though did not linger within the fringe; he hurried onwards towards the first of the three tiers. There were only certain ways down onto the lower tier. Some Elves actually used the trees, stepping from one to another as they descended, Sarratt though decided he would use the stairways the Dwarfs had built for the King of the Elves. This work of art was the end of the trade route and the Dwarfs had wanted to make the stairways as majestic as possible. As the wizard approached the beginnings of the descent he looked at the two stone Elf archers, their bows primed with an arrow. It had taken the stone masons many months to make the various statues that guarded the staircase all the way down to the bottom, some seven hundred feet.

"Peace to all creatures that intend no harm; hide from me not. I walk amongst you as a visitor, not a hunter," said the wizard quietly, his hand pointing to the north and then to the south. So it would be as he made his way down the first few steps. Not one animal scurried away into the bushes that hugged the steep sides of the first tier of Follonday. A mouse casually made its way in front of the wizard, not bothering to waste its energy on one of such goodness. Sarratt smiled as he always did when he saw the small animals of the wild, for he knew that their lives were in the balance for many hours of every day.

The second tier had a different feel to it than the fringe. The trees were tightly squeezed together, each climbing as high as it could to reach the fruit of the Sun. But even so, it was not a dark place, for the floor of the forest was carpeted the whole of the year with the Snowdrop, a vigorously growing hardy plant that did not mind being walked upon. In fact it seemed to relish the footprints of the wizard. But what amazed the wizard was the way each tree was so carefully looked after. The lower branches had been taken away at seven feet, allowing the Elven gardeners to walk without hindrance within their forests. He thought of the forests behind the Witches Watch and how thick and overgrown the trees were. He had spent sometime within them, but compared to this forest, Witches Watch forests were dark and cold. After ten miles of enjoying the atmosphere of the Elven forests, the wizard sensed the presence of a great army. Quickly he spoke several words as if they were one. With his hooded cloak wrapped tightly about his person, he wandered closer to the trade route, the cobbled pathway some fifteen feet in width. As he dropped to his right knee, he proceeded to look upon an army of at least fifteen thousand Elves marching by, their heads held high as they climbed onto the stairway.

For three hours the wizard watched the Elves. His hopes of the Elves marching onto the Plains of Desire to confront the millions of creatures fading quickly when at the very rear of the advancing Elves, he saw fifty or so Dwarfs, their battle axes resting over their shoulders.

"So you decide war is the only outcome, Esslestar," said the wizard to himself, who had already started to travel towards the last of the great Elven cliffs, this one sheer in its drop to the specks down below, which were mighty trees, some estimated at reaching heights of two hundred and fifty feet.

From here the trade route was the only way into the heart of Follonday. He could hear in the distance the deafening roars of the immense falls that stretched for some way, creating a permanent curtain of water in which the Dwarfs had actually interwoven the stairway. Even to the wizard, this was a magical place to walk down; behind some of the falling waters, the Dwarfs had dug into the cliffs, creating sitting areas in which the tired traveller could rest. But it was always the noise of the falls that drowned every other out. Sarratt reached out and felt at the water, cupping both of his hands together and taking a sip of the bubbling water.

By the time Sarratt had reached the bottom of the stairway, the Sun was already declining in the western skies, the redness of the clouds etching worry on the mind of the wizard. He hurried onwards, avoiding the numerous Elves that had no idea that a wizard was amongst them, each heading off to their respective homes. Some lived within certain trees, while others lived high up in intricately carved buildings that clung to the trees of the forest as if they were a living part, growing each season with the growth of the forests. As the wizard turned a tree-lined corner of the trade route he was confronted with the palaces of Esslestar, golden, silver and bronze in colour, massive domes with single turrets on each. With the Sun away behind them in the west, the sparkle of the precious metals glinted into the darkening skies, sending out singular shafts of coloured light: yet another wonder of his world, he thought, as he stepped within the tree-lined pathway, two miles of the most beautiful ground the wizard had ever walked upon.

The Elves had spent long periods in total peace, not at war with any of the lesser races, keeping their lives and their beliefs to themselves. But with each new era came a change, albeit small. For some reason, the start of this age - the cycle of Esslestar - had started almost immediately with war on the Plains of Desire, a bitter time for the wizards, who had watched the needless killing of thousands of Trolls. It had been the Watch Wizard who had brought the war to its close, ordering the Elves to care for the earth, not for the boundaries of others. Esslestar had listened to the wise wizard then; now it seemed it was the turn of the young wizard to try and talk sense into the Elven King's mind.

"Be seen and heard and declare your reasons for

treading within the grounds of Esslestar," ordered the Elf, who had drawn his sword.

Sarratt did not answer at first; he looked at the Elf and shook his head sadly as he approached.

"Be seen and heard and declare your reasons for treading within the grounds of Esslestar," repeated the Elf menacingly.

"There is no reason to take that tone, young Elf," said the wizard quietly, his voice soothing and pleasant. This had the guard confused; he had been given strict orders to stop and question anyone who tried to enter the King's palaces.

"Who are you?" asked the Elf, who had been joined by the other guard.

"I am from Witches Watch, a messenger from the Watch Wizard," replied Sarratt, removing his hood, his long black hair tumbling around his shoulders.

The two guards seemed at a loss. They knew of the wizards and knew that they visited their King on regular occasions, but they had been ordered by the King himself that no one under any circumstances could see him while he had the guests of Pavelem present.

"You will have to come another day; the King holds council," said the other guard, his lean face showing no signs of emotion. He simply had orders to carry out.

"The King will see me; I have the most urgent news. Tell him who waits, I will wait here," said the wizard calmly, but he was, to say the least, a little put out at the thought of being turned away.

An hour passed as the wizard stood before the golden gates of the palace. He thought of the poorer races that had spent years struggling to survive, how they had come to the wizards for help. This had put a great strain upon the relationships of both the Elves and the Dwarfs, neither wanting anything to do with the Trolls or the Gnomes, whom they regarded as mere vermin, killing them at every opportunity. The Elves had started to hunt the Gnomes, telling the wizards that too many had been allowed to mate. They were simply performing a necessary cull once every spring.

"The King says he is already in council; you are not welcome at the moment, Wizard," said the Elf as he approached the wizard.

"Then I will leave and return another day," said the wizard, though the tone of voice had deepened. It trembled within the air, causing the two Elven guards to shiver in fright.

Saaratt turned and walked away from the two Elves the way he had come, though the two guards never did hear the silent words of magic.

Sarratt approached the two guards once more. He opened his arms and asked again if he could see the King, though no reply was forthcoming, for the pair of guards could not see nor hear the wizard as he stepped by them and made his way quietly into the Golden palace of Esslestar.

Esslestar was sitting within the chair of Kings: a chair carved out of the trunk of Esslestar's favourite tree, the mighty Oak. He ran his fingers down the side, feeling the polished wood and nodded his head in agreement with the three Dwarfs who were standing before him, all attired in the battledress of Pavelem: a chainmail suit which seemed to protect every part of the Dwarf except for the head. They were holding their helmets in their left hand.

"The Troll city of Yea-Bor will fall within months. Their army grows thin on the eastern front, many hundreds have been seen leaving the Golden Valley," said the Dwarf as he stood awkwardly before Esslestar.

"And the Troll who is King, where is he?" asked Esslestar.

"He is within the Golden Valley, his flag still flies above his camp," answered the Dwarf.

"Though he is of no importance to the race of Trolls, without him, they would fall apart. The war would be won without too many losing their lives," replied Esslestar distantly. His thoughts were on the Plains of Desire. The grasslands belonged to the Elves; this was the reason why he had joined forces with the Dwarfs.

"The Trolls will fight to the last; that is their way. The Dwarfs will oblige, and they have killed thousands in their claim for the Golden Valley."

Sarratt watched from the doorway, his fury at the Dwarfs quite clear as he prepared to enter the room. But he was suddenly aware of an Elf standing next to him, a she Elf of great beauty. She was the daughter of the King and she was standing within the shadow of the wizard.

He held his breath as she seemed to sense she was not alone; a shiver ran down the length of her delicate frame. With arms folded, she entered.

"Allucia, the guides are waiting outside. They will take you across the Great Eastern Divide, have you prepared yourself?" he asked in a softly spoken tone. The love he had for Allucia was not to be found anywhere else in the world.

"I am ready. So are my guard, when do we leave?" she asked after she had kissed her father upon the forehead and had ran her slender fingers through his hair.

"Tonight, for I wish you to take control of the army that left these lands earlier today; make sure they are prepared for war," replied the King, who had risen from his chair. He gave the two Dwarfs a nod and they bowed in respect for the company they were keeping.

"King of the Elves, it has been wondrous to hold council with you. Forgehammer will want to extend his hand when the moment is right," said the Dwarf, his face beaming with pleasure. But the sight that caught his eye nearly made him scream out aloud.

"That moment, Thoregin, will never be the right moment, not while the wizards of the Watch are alive," said the wizard sharply, his tone of voice cold and harsh.

"I am in council, Wizard. What is this madness?" asked Esslestar, his whole frame whirling around to see the wizard stride past him towards where the Dwarfs were standing. He turned to face the Elf.

"This is no madness, Esslestar. I witness though a

meeting that has madness woven into every word."

"You enter my palace uninvited. . This is a serious matter, Wizard. You know that I would be within my rights to call for your head," warned Esslestar, his eyes fixed upon the wizard's eyes.

"Tell your guests that they are no longer welcome in my company, Esslestar. I am frightened that I might turn them into a pair of wild pigs. Then they might know what it is like to be the hunted. Do as I say," ordered Sarratt, who had woven into the spoken order a spell of great power, for it took over the mind of the Elf for the briefest of moments. The King looked at the Dwarfs and waved them away, his head nodding as he said.

"Leave us now. Return to your homelands. Time will soon come and go."

"But we were offered beds for the night, food and drink," moaned Thoregin, his hand reaching to stroke his silver beard.

"Listen to the King, for he shows you favour, not like I on the other hand, for I would break your necks right now. Leave!" ordered the wizard, his hand coming up to face them. He lifted the pair of Dwarfs off the palatial tiled floor and took them to the borders of the forest. Sarratt felt drained after he had performed this spell, for it had taken him the best part of an hour to take the kicking Dwarfs away from the King of the Elves.

Esslestar was seated upon his wooden chair as the wizard returned. Allucia was still unaware of the spell that had been cast. This was what the wizard had hoped for. The King on the other hand would want to know exactly what had been thrown about his thoughts, and the wizard came to the she Elf and smiled.

"Leave, Allucia, for you are needed elsewhere, I think."

"This is true, but the King still sits as if in a dream. I wanted to say farewell," replied the worried Elf.

"A lot is on the mind of your father. I will tell him that you wanted to stay; he will understand. He is after all a good father, is he not?"

"This is true and time presses on. My guard will be getting restless upon the horses of the plains," admitted Allucia, who still did not realise that the wizard had cast a small spell upon her father, the King of the Elves.

When the King finally woke from his dreams, he was surprised to see the wizard sitting at the window to his right.

"My daughter and my guests have gone wizard?"

"Well! The two dwarfs really did have to leave, they insisted. And your daughter was in such a hurry that I gave her leave in your absence. We need to talk, Esslestar," said the wizard frankly.

"We talked the last time you were here. The time for talking has long since departed. It is actions that are needed now," replied Esslestar, who was still rubbing his forehead.

"Yes! The time for action is right, but you are fighting in the wrong place at the wrong time. The real peril lies to the north of your forests."

"Nothing lies to the north," argued the King.

"When was the last time you sent scouts to the Fingertip Mountains?"

"They are of no importance to the Elves. They are but the end of our lands; beyond them lies a barren land devoid of any life," answered Esslestar, who had now walked over to where the wizard was still sitting, his head resting on the knuckles of his right hand.

"I will ask again: when was the last time you sent scouts to the north?"

Esslestar brought forth a simple wooden chair and seated himself next to the wizard. Though he did not like the young wizard much, he felt compelled to answer him as honestly as he could.

"One year ago, maybe two. But nothing stirs within the Fingertip Mountains. We know of the three wizards at the Keep, but they are quiet and keep themselves to themselves. As you know only too well, wizards cannot perform magic upon the fair race. We worry not about the northern Plains of Desire; it is from the west that we feel we have been robbed."

"Then you will not know of the threat!" exclaimed the wizard, who had hoped that the thousands of Elves he had seen leaving the forests had been in response to the millions of Goblins he had witnessed the other day.

"What are you talking about?" asked the bewildered Elf.

"That forces of such size and evil walk upon the Plains of Desire and you have no idea that it is happening.. The Dwarfs have surely kept your eyes and ears averted from the real threat of this world," gasped the wizard in shock.

"You talk in riddles, Wizard. You talk of monstrous armies that head where?" asked the Elf King mockingly.

"They are preparing to march on Yea-Bor. Time is running out for the Trolls, but even as I say this to you, I feel that you are relieved that the threat is not yet on your forest fringe, that you feel that the loss of the race of Trolls would do no real harm, seeing that they are one of the so- called lesser races. Well, the wizards of the Watch will not let the Trolls face this evil alone. What will you do for the Trolls, Esslestar?" asked the wizard heatedly.

Esslestar had turned his gaze from that of the wizard and was looking out towards the bay of Follonday, the waves relentless in their pursuit of the land. The golden sands shimmering against the last rays of the day's Sun, not many trees obstructed his view, for he had a love of the oceans that he could not explain. Deep within his mind he knew that one day he would set off on a voyage of discovery.

"I will not shed any tears if the Trolls of Yea-Bor fall. They came from another land and claimed the eastern Plains of Desire without question. They ignore all of our requests for them to leave peacefully. Maybe they are destined to fall, as are the small rodent-like Gnomes: another race who steal and scavenge off others. We live in a world full of evil. If an evil has moved upon the Plains of Desire to kill another evil, I will not move my army against one who seeks the same."

Sarratt shivered as he heard what the King of the fairest

race was saying. Everything he sought to achieve was being rubbished by this Elf. Slowly he rose, gathering his black cloak about his person, his hood pulled tight, so that his face was hidden from the King. As he prepared himself to leave, the King grasped his arm.

"Do not take what I say to heart, Wizard. You have much to learn about the structures of our world."

"Do not take what I say to heart, Elf, when I say that you are undermining the soul of your race and that you have strayed off your chosen path. The way things are moving, the leaves will begin to fall for good from the trees of your forest. I have nothing left to say to one of your making. I leave now, with you knowing that I too have become your enemy," replied Sarratt in disgust. Before the King could grab the wizard or pierce him with his sword, he had gone, as if the air itself had taken the wizard away. The King of the Elves pulled the rope in the tiny hole in the wall. Within minutes his personal guard were before him.

"The wizard leaves our forests this evening; seek him out and kill him," ordered the King, who had noticed that thin beads of sweat had formed upon his forehead. He wiped them away and shook his head in anger.

Sarratt spoke with the wind as he climbed the steps of the mighty trade route, the deafening noise of the waterfalls drowning out every other sound. But the tops of the trees were listening to the spells of the wizard, for many of their leaves had begun to fall, landing on the sodden steps of the stairways. The dozen or so Elves that had given chase slipped several times on the slippery leaves. In the end, they were forced to tread with great care. A fear had entered their beings too; not in a hundred years had the trees of the forest let go of their leaves. When the wizard had reached the top of the stairways, the Elves that had given chase were still on the first tier of the Forest. It would take them all of that night to climb to the fringes of the forest, by which time the wizard would have once more called silently for the great black stallion. He and Stormbreaker flew across the Plains of Desire at a speed none had travelled before.

Chapter Fifteen

Marsukia entered the woods of Tarsit in shock. The burning was so widespread, it seemed that every tree was alight. The heat was so intense that the ground itself had caught fire. Thick, black smoke billowed wildly into the skies, heading quickly towards the Great Eastern Divide, its distant peaks showing the first signs of the winter snows. Goblins and Hobgoblins were everywhere; some had scorch marks on their bodies, while others had given up on life and had fallen into heaps, burning slowly to their deaths. The Dwarf inhabitants of Tarsit had long since been taken prisoner. The Brethren had taken siege of the woodlands, circling the entire place, but they knew not of the importance of the trees for they had fired many in getting the Dwarfs to come out of their hiding places. Many had been burned to death and many had been slain as they ran from the burning inferno. But most of the Dwarfs had been taken on the long journey to the wizards' blood camps, where they would wait for the Demon to walk amongst them.

Marsukia did not feel threatened by the burning trees, for he had the power of the living flame. He did not hesitate in entering a burning tree. As the minutes went by, Prestersfordle watched on in some wonder. This was beyond his skills as a wizard; to keep back such heat would be an impossible task for him. So he walked away and sought out the Brethren, who would feel the wrath of his anger. Marsukia went into the depths of the mighty wood pearl tree, opening the hatch that would lead the wizard to the basement below. Black smoke billowed out from the opening, but the wizard ignored the choking smoke and climbed down the ladders. He soon realised that the roots of the tree were bare of wood pearls, and worse, the roots had been damaged beyond repair. This was no longer a living tree. He cursed silently as he exited the tree. In the distance he saw that the other wizard was putting one of the Brethren to death. He walked towards them with his blood at boiling point.

"The Brethren are better alive than dead, W izard," he said quickly, his hands moving over the bloodied form of the Brethren.

"A price had to be paid for their stupidity; I merely made an example of this one," came the angered reply.

"When one of these Brethren keeps in order thousands of our army, I wish to use our hard labour, not waste it in a petty vengeance. I know you struggle with these creatures," replied Marsukia, who had already begun to revive the Brethren.

"But they see you as their only leader, when there are three!" explained Prestersfordle, who had stepped closer to the other wizard.

"Do not count on Fastanes as a leader. He is merely a physician, he has no idea how the Brethren think. Maybe you do not either?"

"They are here for one purpose."

"Well, you should focus your mind on that fact and stop behaving in such a jealous manner. The Brethren look up to me for I was the one who spent many months teaching them; it is as simple as that," said the wizard.

The fallen Brethren slowly got to its feet, its eyes fixed upon its master.

"We did as we were told. We did not kill all the Dwarfs, but such was the way in which they attacked us, we did not hesitate in fighting. They withdrew into the darkness of this wood, so we fired the trees; have we done wrong?" asked the Brethren in a flat voice, the 'fatal' injuries it had received from the other wizard seemingly forgotten.

"To burn the whole of the woodland was needless, but you are still learning. Seek out the rest of the Brethren and come to me within the hour," ordered Marsukia in a cold, rasping voice.

"You show pity, a feeling which I thought had left you," commented Prestersfordle, his look of hatred towards the departing Brethren plain to see.

"You confuse pity with control. Come; we have many

trees to search," said the wizard, his gaze not once falling upon the other wizard. They spent many hours searching each tree for the illusive wood pearls, but none could be found. The trees which had survived the infernos which were still burning out of control, had already been harvested. The two wizards came out of the last tree empty- handed. Marsukia was in a rage.

"The thieving Gnomes are to be hunted down and killed instantly. We need the golden wood pearls; they must have at least seven hundred amongst their bounty. Time we spend here is time lost guiding our armies towards the walls of Yea-Bor. At the moment I am at a loss, Prestersfordle," admitted the wizard.

"We need to think, Marsukia, for I have never seen any of the golden wood pearls within the Keep. The Dwarfs must keep them for themselves."

"Let us rest and turn our minds towards the army that waits for its true master," suggested Marsukia, who was referring to the heap of guts that lay upon his floor within the Keep.

Fastanes had spent most of the day sleeping. His bed was the warmest thing around, seeing that most of the windows and doors no longer remained. He had fought Prestersfordle for the luxury of having a room with a ceiling, such was the state of the ancient Keep. On waking, he rubbed his eyes and thought of what he might do. He knew that he was supposed to seek out new spells from the thousands of books Marsukia had taken from the Witches Watch, but it seemed this was all he ever did. What the physician wanted was to be directly involved in the changing of the world. After all, he often thought to himself, that is why he had left the Watch and later the clerics of the Rainbow falls to have the chance to change the way he saw the lands. Along the path he had taken, something deep within him had told him to follow the chosen one. Marsukia had promised so much, even eternal life: a gift the podgy wizard simply could not refuse.

After he had eaten a hearty meal of cooked meats and stodgy bread, he suddenly thought of the chests that he had brought with him from the halls of the clerics. He threw aside the dozens of books that had collected dust and opened them. From nuggets of gold to very small stuffed rodents, he searched through, casting items aside as if they meant nothing to him. In fact, if the wizard were to sit down, he would have seen his life pass before him, from the mice he had stuffed when he was but a child to the ingots of gold he had created out of granite when he had mastered the art of deception. But such was the fury in his being, he thought nothing of his past life as he rummaged through the several chests that littered the floor of his room. When the sweat had become too much for the wizard, he slumped back against the cold stone walls of the Keep, his mind trying to recall where he had put that for which he was searching. Suddenly he remembered and fell sideways onto the cold slabs of the Keep. He crawled to the smallest of the chests, it being but a few inches in length and width, but it was locked. The wizard was in no mood to search for the smallest of keys, so he uttered a simple spell and the chest opened, its lid flipping all the way to the other side.

"Life eternal and eternal life, you are the key for everlasting life," he whispered, knowing he had found the answer.

From his covered room within the Keep, the small rounded wizard had to climb over rubble that had gathered within the various corridors and through the gaping holes the Trolls of Yea-Bor had made to reach the chambers of Marsukia. Here the very air seemed to be chilled; his breath could suddenly be seen within the air. No door stood on its hinges, keeping out unwanted guests. Marsukia had told the Trolls often enough that the evil that stirred from within would keep most from entering. As he entered, he noticed the sky above, the black sullen clouds heavy with the evil they carried, but the wizard was more interested in what lay on the cold slabs of Marsukia's room. The pile of blood and guts showed no visible signs that it could form the shape of a muscular horned being from the depths of hell, but Fastanes had been present when the hot blood of the Gnomes had been injected into it. What he had seen was a glimpse of evil itself, a power so great, not even all the wizards in the world could defeat it. Part of him though was petrified, albeit a small part. Even so, this was enough to cause him to break into a sweat when he walked by the misshapen pile of guts.

"Take your time, Fastanes, for time will mean nothing

and the future will become the past. The past will become the future and I will be part of the history that will change the world," whispered the wizard as he fumbled with the golden wood pearls, putting them on to the large desk in front of the gaping hole in the east facing wall.

From what he had read, he determined that the seeds had to be heated until they appeared to become unstable. He walked over to the large wall chests that stored various books and storage jars and rummaged around, casting aside items he knew to be of great importance to Marsukia. But the thought of what he was on the verge of opening was getting the better of him. Some jars smashed as they hit the floor, wild sparks igniting as the magic was unleashed, but the wizard continued, becoming frantic in his search. By the time he had cleared most of the shelves, he felt that all of his body had been covered in a fear he was just about managing to control. Stepping back, he wiped the sweat from his brow and looked at the empty shelves, hoping that he would see what he was searching for, stumbling backwards as he lost his balance. Fastanes the wizard fell onto the bloodied pile that lay in the middle of the chilled room, his heart quickening as he realized what he had fallen onto, But as he tried to escape from the demon, it spoke with his mind. No words could be heard, but Fastanes understood every word. After several seconds he found he was lying some distance away from the demon, but knew where he was to look. He crawled his way to the wall chest, his heart beating like it had never beaten before. Getting to his feet, he reached up to the top shelf, which still had everything placed where Marsukia had placed it. Fastanes though swept his fat, sweaty hands across the shelf, bringing every object falling onto his head and shoulders, but he instantly saw what the demon had told him to look for; it was a simple leather bound book, tattered at the corners.

Opening the book, he gasped at the flowing scripture. It was written in the oldest form of Elvish: a written word that could not be spoken, only translated if the reader knew the code. Fastanes took it to the table that looked upon the gaping, broken hole in the wall and read the contents several times before he uttered the first line of the small book.

Before his very eyes, as he was translating the Elfish code, the wood pearls began to glow, their golden colour turning red as they started to heat up. Fastanes continued his translation, watching as the golden wood pearls started to wobble and turn into a liquid state. As they were placed directly onto the wooden desk, they made the table set alight, but the wizard instantly spoke the words that calmed the surface of the table, enabling him to collect the wood pearls with a silver plate. The two metals fighting against each other as they were joined together, he quickly moved over to where the demon would soon be standing and looked to see if there were any openings into which he could pour the golden liquid. The mass of flesh that lay upon the wizard's floor resembled no living creature. Fastanes thought he had seen part of a hand, but this might be anything from a spinal column to part of the intestines. The wizard was well-known for his opening of various bodies, searching for answers to questions he often asked himself, but he had never worked on anything like this before. He trembled as he thought of what he had to do.

"Calm yourself down right now!" exclaimed Fastanes, his left hand grasping his right wrist, which was starting to shake violently. The sweat had started to run into his eyes; he smarted as the salty substance came into contact with his pupils. Squinting, he stepped closer to the waiting demon.

Reaching out, he delved his left hand into the mass of blood and guts, making a hole where he could pour the liquid wood pearls. As it started to drip off the silver plate and drop into the opening the wizard had just made, a hissing noise came forth, followed by the smell of burning flesh. Fastanes wanted to stop what he was doing, such was the sudden fear that had taken hold of him, but it was too late. The large pool of golden, simmering liquid suddenly poured over the rim of the silver plate and disappeared into the centre of the demon. He staggered backwards until his rounded frame touched the desk of Marsukia. He tried to imagine what might happen, but the wizard could not actually think of anything but the chilling fear that had entered the room.

The wizard watched as the demon started to rise from the cold slabs. He saw how the arms suddenly appeared, how the shoulders popped into view. The thickly-veined neck rose and the misshapen head looked up at him, the blood-red eyes staring at the small wizard, not letting the wizard look elsewhere. The first noise that entered the room was a deep booming cry of pain that shook the very foundations of the crumbling keep. This continued for some time. Large parts of the wall collapsed with the booming cries. Some of the slabs cracked in two. A bolt of lightning struck the demon directly on the top of its head, making it scream so loudly the wizard felt that his ears had been broken. Such was the noise that Elves within the north of the forest of Follonday looked to the skies, fearing a dreadful storm was on the way. They stood sheltered amongst the trees some fifty miles away, waiting for the storm that would not reach them.

"Wizard who has brought me here, tell me of pain?" asked the demon, its voice breaking even more of the walls of the keep. If it had not been for the spells of Marsukia, the entire keep would have fallen, killing the small, rounded wizard instantly, for he was in the grip of the worst fear he had ever imagined. He simply could not answer the demon.

"I will show you pain, Wizard," cried the demon as its head roared backwards in a scream of agony. Fastanes thought the being must die, for nothing could suffer the way this creature was suffering.

The black horn came forth from the demon's chest, puncturing the flesh with a cracking noise. Hot blood poured freely from the broken flesh. Another scream came from the distorted mouth of the monster that had the full attention of the petrified wizard. This continued for several minutes, scream after scream, horn after horn. More than a dozen black horns appeared on the front of the demon, but then the wizard was shocked again as the demon actually seemed to smile.

"This is the pain of the living world; without pain and suffering, there is nothing," said the demon. Its voice seemed too loud for this world, thought Fastanes as he desperately tried to remember the protection spells he had spent hours learning for this very moment. If he could not master this thing from the depths of evil, he would surely perish. He thought of the races that would be brought to their knees before it and he actually felt sorrow, a feeling which he could not let go. He looked at the ever-changing form but a few feet away and realised that the evil he had unleashed was wrong.

"How many of the seeds did you use, Wizard?" asked the demon.

Fastanes could not talk, but as he thought of the number of wood pearls he had used, the demonic figure shook its head from side to side, a rage entering the room of Marsukia which had Fastanes thinking of his own life and what it had meant to the world in which he lived. Looking death in the face was not something the wizard had ever done before. Death was upon him as he realised that the demon suffered no forgiveness for anything. Not a shred of goodness was to be found within the mind of Lucifer, as the demon now called itself, the name booming out of the keep and onto the Plains of Desire.

"The number I require for life eternal within the

living world is written within the writings of the Elves. You have read them, Wizard. Why bring torture to me when the number falls short by hundreds?" asked the demon, its voice not as loud as before. It seemed that the fear it had created was not everlasting. Suddenly the wizard felt as if a great weight had been taken off his mind; the fear had virtually gone and he prepared himself for the answer.

"Three golden wood pearls I used, Lucifer, for that is all we have."

"Sixty six golden seeds are needed for the briefest of lives within your world. Six hundred and sixty six of the golden seeds will give me a life everlasting; where are the roots of my evil to be found, Wizard?" asked the demon quietly, the force of its voice gone.

Fastanes moved his right leg and was relieved that it moved to the side. The fear had gone, the wild beating of his heart had calmed down, allowing him to think of his next step. Some kind of order had returned to his mind; several spells entered his thoughts, but were dispelled. He walked a bit closer to the immobile figure of the demon, knowing full well that he had survived the first contact with the most evil being that ever was.

"You know the place, Lucifer, for you tend the seeds yourself. From your roots of all evil comes wealth and warmth to the Dwarfs and Elves who farm them. It is this which will cause you the most pain," replied the ever more confident wizard.

Lucifer tried to scream, tried to reach for the wizard

and bring him towards it, but its arms stayed where they were. Its legs had not formed, so he could not step closer to the wizard. The pain was overwhelming, each bloodied black horn caused the demon a pain most mortals would not tolerate for one second, never mind several minutes.

"Death comes quickly, Wizard!" warned the demon, gasping as he took breaths of the room's chilled air.

"But you know of the trees that spawn the seeds, why threaten the one who can bring you into this world? If I were you, I would be considering an offer, something you may want to bargain with," replied Fastanes, his mood darkened by the presence of the demon.

"But you are but a servant, fat one. You will die if you do not get me out of this floor," spat the demon, wincing as even more black horns appeared, one coming through his throat, causing the monster great pain.

"The wars will fail without Fastanes. The two need to be three. I am just as important as the other two. Now leave this place before I summon the spell that would have you crying in agony."

Lucifer stared at the circling wizard with a hatred of such gravity that the demon actually reached out its right hand, tearing the flesh of its side as it ripped it upwards. The ripping noise made the wizard turn around instantly, but he was too late to avoid the grip of the devil. A coldness he had not thought possible entered his being. Shivering wildly, he let the first of the spells enter the room, but it had little effect upon the seething figure that now had hold of the wizard.

"Your life may want to carry on in an endless way. This is why I was summoned. Seek a way to get me to the grasslands and your wish will be granted by me, for I have the power of eternal life. Or die now within my arms and return with me to the depths of hell."

Fastanes held back as much as he could, but the strength of this being was just too great for him and the many spells he had delivered made no impact upon the writhing body. He spoke quickly and clearly, making sure he was crystal clear in what he was saying.

"Many of the wood pearls you require are to be found within the Dwarf kingdom of Pavelem. Send me down the pathways through which you allowed the other wizards to pass and I may return within a day or so."

"How many?" cried the demon. Its pain was becoming too much for even it to bear.

"Hundreds. If there are not enough, then I will enter each Kingdom and seek out what is required, for I desire eternal life more than anything else. One lifetime is not long enough."

Fastanes was suddenly tossed into the bookcase, his face whacking the corner of the wood. He fell like a felled tree and lay upon the cold slabs of Marsukia's room for over two hours. Lucifer though did not last that long. The wood pearls which had entered its being had started to come out near the bottom of his torso. Where it had felt the chill of the room, it now felt the searing heat of its own world. Its head folded in on itself, once more becoming just the pile of blood and guts that had lain there before. Upon the floor however, two golden wood pearls lay at its side, gleaming as if they had never been touched.

When Fastanes awoke, his head was banging. He stared at the demon and shook his head. He knew then that something within his soul had awoken; whatever goodness had been left had found its way into his thoughts. He thought of the journey he was about to make and trembled; the dark pathways were as treacherous as things got. Marsukia had often warned him and Prestersfordle that the evil from the depths fed upon the goodness of the souls that slipped into their darkness. Only an evil soul could hopefully cross the narrow pathways. This thought stayed with the wizard as he stumbled down into the dungeons, where the contrast in temperature was huge. Almost immediately he began to sweat; he now knew why he had never showed much interest in what the other two wizards were doing down in this inferno of a place. Fastanes stopped then and fell backwards as the opening of the dark hole appeared at the far side of the dungeon. Even from here he could hear the distant taunts of the wraiths and lost souls calling for him to walk the pathways of their world. Fastanes though had already made his choice as to which path he would take.

Chapter Sixteen

The days they had spent on the fishing boat numbered four. Each of the Gnomes had agreed to take it in turns too steer the large vessel, though Kellek had been petrified at the prospect of taking control of the Dwarf's fishing boat. It had been the Elf who had quickly taught the Gnome what he was meant to do.

"Is that all, Arrun?" he had laughed nervously.

"Just keep us within the centre of the current, Kellek. It is as simple as that," replied the Elf, who had given the Gnome a pat on the back. The Sun had not shown itself now for the past two days. The rain had poured relentlessly upon the southern Plains of Desire, causing the river to quicken slightly. But with the Elf on board, the three Gnomes were happy that they seemed to be travelling a little faster. Under the cover they had erected for Akkia, they had also rigged up the cooking and sleeping area. Treak and Crikken were busy cooking the fish the Elf had caught that morning. It had been a new taste for the Gnomes, for they had never eaten fish before. But with Arrun's persuasive words, they had tried the food reluctantly. To their utter surprise, the three Gnomes had gorged themselves upon the freshwater fish the Elf had dredged from the Alluvia. Arrun even left the boat one night for the sole purpose of collecting wild herbs, grasses and river mushrooms. When he returned, he explained to the three Gnomes how he cooked the fish and wild herbs together, but not the grasses and the river mushrooms; they had to be eaten as they had been found.

"We will see the fringe of Follonday within the hour. I want you both to look upon the greatest sight within these lands," said Arrun, who had knelt next to the limp form of Akkia.

"Trees are trees, Arrun!" exclaimed Crikken, who was stirring the boiling fish.

"We have seen many trees, Elf," added Treak, who was busy sorting out the portions of river mushrooms with which he had fallen in love. Each bite had given the Gnome a pleasure he had not thought possible when it came to food, so he had insisted to everyone that he would always serve out the meals.

"It is my homeland," replied Arrun flatly, touching Akkia's forehead, his look of disgust hidden by the hood of his cloak.

After they had eaten in silence, Arrun spent his time feeling the life pulse of Akkia. He had taken it upon himself to ensure that the young Gnome had a chance to live. To his disgust, the other three Gnomes had come nowhere near the stricken Gnome. But as he realised, having spent long hours talking to Treak, the weak and injured of his race were simply forgotten. Only the strongest carried on with the work which had to be done for Gutox to prosper.

"How is he?" asked Treak, who was wiping his lips, smacking them together as if they could get a little more of the river mushroom taste he so adored.

"Close to death, but you will carry on and forget about this stricken Gnome. Is that not the way of your race?" asked the Elf.

"I do care, Arrun. How close are we to Follonday?"

"Come, let us see," replied Arrun, who bent to kiss the forehead of Akkia before he left the shelter.

The tops of the trees came into view first, a thin smudge on the distant horizon. But as Treak looked, he realised then just how big was the forest of the Elves,, for he could not see a break to the north, or a break to the south. As the minutes went by, he gasped several times, lost in the wonder of Follonday.

"Crikken! Come here and look upon Arrun's homelands," said the Gnome excitedly.

"But they are only trees, Treak," replied Crikken, who was lying on his back thinking of his family. "And we have seen Follonday before."

"No, I want you to see this!" exclaimed Treak, his eyes looking north, then south in wonder.

The fringe as it was known to all Elves was the start of Follonday, a place where only wildlife lived, for the

Elves lived far below upon the lower tiers of their lands.

Crikken eventually crawled out from the shelter and joined the Elf and Treak at the front of the Dwarfs' fishing boat. As the minutes passed by, the fringe of the forest came a little closer. Crikken stared at the millions of trees that lined the fringe of the homelands of the Elf, unable to say anything as he had never seen so many trees before. He wondered how this forest of trees could accept the likes of his race, and he suddenly felt scared, as if he had been trapped by the Elf.

"This is madness, Treak. We do not belong amongst Arrun's kind, and the fair race will treat us as they have always done."

"While you are within the company of one of the King's personal guard, you will be treated with care. Do not worry, Crikken. Enjoy the trees as I do," replied the Elf, trying to reassure the scared Gnome.

"You are that close to the King?" asked Treak, his voice showing a fear it had not shown for some time.

"We have walked the silver-laden paths of the lower Alluvia. We know of each other, but I do not know Esslestar. He has spoken with me and told me certain things that have enriched my life, but I do not claim to have his attention. He has so many Elves which take their turn protecting him that it would be unfair to expect my King to remember me, but I am still proud that I spent two years in his service."

"I bless you, Elf," said Treak respectfully.

"I too bless you," said Crikken, his gaze shifting away from the fast-approaching forest of the Elves.

"I bless you as our saviour," added Kellek, who was at the rear of the fishing boat.

"I am not a saviour, Kellek and your blessings are beginning to wear thin. You have no need to bless anything. You are what you are. You bless this, that and anything that happens to do you any good; save all your blessings for yourself," said the Elf, his face having a look of sorrow etched into it.

"But it is well-mannered to bless the things which help the Gnomes with their daily lives. I would not dare criticise the Elves' habits. I do not think I will be able to stop with my blessings," replied Kellek as honestly as he could. In any case, what would the Gnomes say if he did not bless them when he returned? He smiled as he steered the fishing boat onwards towards the forest home of the Elves.

Within the hour the first of the fringe trees glided past them. The Elves tolerated other races wandering through the fringe. Not that any did. The trees were well-spaced out; the grasslands of the plains though had now long since been left behind, for here grew a multitude of wild flowers and ferns. Little streams left the main river on both sides, feeding the wilderness of the fringe with their rich supply of water. Treak gasped as he lost count of the different types of mushroom he had seen. He also noted the many smaller trees, heavy with the strange fruit they carried. He felt a love here he had never known existed. He smiled and blessed this forest, silently as he did not want Arrun bearing down on him. He thought of clicking his fingers, but since meeting the Elf, he had hardly ever used his fingers as a form of speech or command. Shaking his head, he continued to observe the magic of Follonday.

The noise came slowly out of the distance, a distant roaring; the Gnomes looked towards the Elf, who had taken over the helm of the fishing boat.

"The first of the three falls of the Alluvia! We are close," said the Elf, who had steered the boat towards the right of the fast flowing river. As the noise of the waterfall became louder, Arrun suddenly swung the fishing boat to the left, sending the Gnomes careering across the decks, cursing as they hit the side. But the Elf knew what he was doing. The Alluvia had three safe inlets, where the river widened and allowed boats to drift on the gentle currents. This was the first and Arrun wanted to be sure he made the boat as safe as possible. It would have been a disaster if he had allowed the Dwarven fishing boat to crash over the falls. Some wrecks had found their way down onto the bay of Follonday; that was why there were several small piers jutting out into the river. Three of them had smaller boats alongside, bobbing up and down in the gentle waters of the inlet.

"Help yourselves to the fruits of the forest. All are edible, it is the black mushroom one should avoid," said the Elf, who had jumped onto the lush floor of the fringe.

"Why?" asked Treak, who had closely followed Arrun.

"For they are not meant for eating. They are common around the fringe and you, being Gnomes, might be tempted. But be warned, they are deadly!" came the ominous reply.

"What are we to do now? Akkia is still within the boat. Shall we lift him out and care for him amongst the trees?" asked Crikken, his hand touching the bark of the Dragon tree.

"Under no circumstances shall you touch the stricken Gnome. I will travel to the place of the healers; they might know of a treatment that will bring him forth into the living again. I will be gone for two days; I will not let you down," said the Elf, who was looking far to the west, where the Sun had begun to dip into the western skies.

"But what of the other Elves who might come across a bunch of thieving Gnomes? Remember, Arrun, we are still hunted freely by your race," said Treak in shock.

Arrun had already set off on his way when Treak had made his reply. This stopped the Elf in his tracks; he had forgotten about the dangers these Gnomes faced, such was his haste in trying to save the life of Akkia.

"Then we must be quick. We will move Akkia to where you will be as safe as I can make you."

As the last rays of the Sun died away, the Elf darted off at such a speed that he was but a blur as he weaved in and out of the trees of the fringe.

Treak had never felt as scared as this before. He did not know these lands; if they were forced to flee, where would he lead them? No bramble grew within these lands: their saviour on so many occasions. As he slid within his body wrap, he thought of the treasure he carried and how it would help the Gnomes bargain with the Trolls of Yea-Bor, for they too sought the fuel just as much as the Elves and the Dwarfs. It would help to bring the Gnomes stature; that was why he was willing to sacrifice his life for the betterment of his race. As he lay there staring at the clouds that were rolling towards the Great Eastern Divide, he dreamed of the time when the Gnomes of Gutox would have a trade route too, leading in every direction, even over the mountains to where the rarely sighted human race lived. He had ambitions as he fell into a deep, untroubled sleep.

Arrun though did not sleep that night. Like the wind itself, he brushed the trees, a sense of urgency within his mind. Time would run out for the Gnomes, for the fringe was a place the Elves adored. If they did stumble across the so-called rodents of the lands, they would not hesitate in killing them. As he reached the cliffs of the fringe, he had already decided that he was not going to waste time running down the many hundreds of steps that wound their way down the sheer cliff face. Instead, Arrun quickened his pace as he reached the end of the fringe. Below him were the mighty trees of the second tier: huge fully grown trees, some reaching heights of eighty feet or more. He jumped into the blackness of the night sky as if he were a bird. He felt no fear, just the thought of reaching his destination as quickly as he could. Hurtling through the air at a fearsome pace, the Elf looked at the closing upper branches of the mighty trees. Such was the speed of his reactions that he readied himself for the impact. The trees were kind to the falling Elf, cushioning his fall, but they did not stop Arrun completely. Still he fell downwards, but he was constantly aware of what was behind him, what was beside him and what was ahead of him. As the ground rushed towards him, Arrun picked the branch he knew would bend with his fall. The many small cuts he had suffered upon his upper body and arms meant nothing to the Elf, once he had grabbed hold of the long thin branch of the Ash tree. This brought Arrun to the height of around twenty feet. Letting go, he dropped not to the next branch, but to the one lowest to the floor. With his feet but a few inches away from the leaf laden floor of the second tier, he released his grip, gently falling as if he had taken the first step of a stairway.

The next cliff though was too high for the Elf to risk his life, so he charged down the final stairway. But even Arrun had to take care as there was nothing to stop the Elf from falling over the edge if he misjudged a single step. The blackness of the night brought the Elf to the slow, steady thousand last steps which would lead him to the southern parts of the Elven Kingdom. By the time he had reached the bottom of the last tier, the first light of a new day had begun to lighten up the dark forests. Arrun again ran through the trees with a speed that not many of the hunted animals could keep up with. The place to which he was going was a well-known area to every Elf, for the healers lived here, spending every hour possible in the pursuit of healing.

The Elven clerics were already busy tending their gardens, lovingly seeing to the plants that helped them heal the sick and the wounded. They saw themselves as a race apart from the Kingdom of Esslestar; in some isolated areas, the clerics wrote the way of the ancient Elfish code, a language unspoken.

"Where is Leanderstall?" asked Arrun of the quiet Elven gardeners.

"Who asks of Leanderstall?" asked a cleric who was on his knees, picking the leaves off a small shrub that was used in the healing of tiredness.

Arrun strode forwards with his sword withdrawn, showing the clerics the mark of the King.

"Before you stands Arrun, once a member of the King's guard. Tell me where he bides his time," ordered Arrun, his menacing tone of voice having the desired effect,, for they did not hesitate in pointing to where the head of the clerics could be found.

"Tell me, why me? Why do you seek out my services? You do not appear ill nor wounded. The scratches upon your person do not threaten your life. Why have you come?" asked Leanderstall.

"I seek your help, for one of my friends is at the doorway of death. So ill is he, I fear he might even be lost to us. I come seeking your aid, Leanderstall," replied Arrun, who had been as honest as he had wanted to be.

"Where is the stricken Elf?" asked Leanderstall, concern showing on his tanned face.

"Within the fringe."

"Who tends to his ailments while you travel down to the gardens of the healers?"

"He is laid beneath the Dragon tree; three others are tending to his injuries."

"Which are?" asked the Elven cleric.

"Injuries caused by the evil which walks the Plains of Desire. He is close to death; his side bleeds while he sleeps. I fear even now that we are too late."

"Then I and the clerics will come with haste, for we have also heard rumours of attacks further to the north. Some are saying that the Hobgoblins once more roam the Plains of Desire. It is sad when travellers fear for their lives," said the cleric, his white robes showing the star of Esslestar upon the right breast.

"It is true, for I have fought against them. They are evil in the extreme," added Arrun, his face a mask of worry.

The Elven cleric travelled with three other Elves, their robes though were a pale green colour. Arrun led the way up the many hundreds of steps. They slept upon the second tier for a brief period of time, but Arrun stayed awake, anxious that time was running out for the Gnome. With each of the giant tiers being ten miles in width, their journey through the scented forests was at times slow, but the Elves who healed lived at their own pace. Not once did they run; a brisk walk was as fast as they moved.

As the Sun was setting on the second day of the Elf's departure, Treak had become worried that they had risked everything in trusting the Elf. He had nearly convinced himself that the Elf had actually gone to fetch Elven warriors. In which case, their lives would be lost within seconds. Pacing up and down, he had started to click his fingers again and they were telling him that it might be better if he and the other two Gnomes were to scarper with the treasure they had risked their lives in obtaining. Kellek and Crikken had spent the last few hours of daylight tending to the wood pearls. Each sack had been opened and the contents carefully wiped and polished. Kellek had laughed nervously when he had finished his sack full. He still could not believe they had got away with it. Each of the four sacks held dozens of the small wood pearls: a treasure worth more to the races of Ursalane than even Gold.

"I am not happy that we are to be alone for yet another night in these strange lands," said their leader who had stopped his pacing. The clicking though was continuous.

"Then what would you have us do, Treak?" asked Crikken, rubbing the last of the seeds that would make him a hero within Gutox.

"Leave straight away," he said, his fingers clicking exactly the same thing.

"What of Akkia? We promised we would not leave him," replied Kellek, his hand reaching out to touch the fallen Gnome.

"If what the Elf says is true, then Akkia will be treated, but if the Elf has decided that the wood pearls would be better off within these lands, then we will almost certainly die trying to stop the Elves from taking what is now rightfully ours," replied Treak, his mind set on the departure.

"Then we leave and have not only the Elves hunting

us, but those hideous creatures that would eat us alive if they got the chance," commented Crikken, reluctant to leave the fringe of the Elven forests. He had felt safe here; beyond the fringe lay death.

"But we might be cut down without having the chance to run for it; I think we should leave now," argued Treak, unaware that he was being looked upon.

"We will leave. Treak, when we have made certain Akkia is going to be safe," said Arrun, who had run as fast as he could as soon as he had made the fringe.

"When did you return?" asked Treak, startled by the sudden appearance of the Elf.

"That does not matter. What matters is that you do not say a word when the Elves get here; they still do not know a Gnome lies here. I am trusting they will feel bound to help this stricken one, for they are the healers of Follonday."

Arrun had been right about the response of the healers; they had at first been disgusted that they had travelled so far to see to a mere animal. This had nearly caused Crikken to shout back at the healers, but Treak had put his clicking fingers against the lips of the angered Gnome, silencing him before he had even spoken.

After some time, the healers finally agreed to take the limp body of the Gnome back down the many hundreds of steps to their houses of healing.

"And where does the Elf, Arrun, travel with these thieves?" asked the cleric sternly.

"It is best you do not know," he replied, defensively.

"Then take heed of the rumours. Travel south of the river; the southern farms might give some cover. I will see you when you return," said the cleric, who had already sent his helpers away with the body of the Gnome.

As the Elf and three Gnomes set off on their long journey, Crikken approached the Elf and handed him the sack full of wood pearls Akkia had been carrying.

"I think these are yours," he offered.

"I will choose to carry them for the absent Gnome, but they are not mine, Crikken. That time will come soon enough in front of the Chieftain of the Gnomes; then we will see if I have made the right decision in trusting Treak."

Chapter Seventeen

The King was missing.

"Then where have you searched?" yelled Denth, furious that the King had been allowed to disappear upon the battlefield.

"We are still fighting to the north," said Stemmer, head of the tenth running unit, his blood stained face showing he had not cowered in battle.

"Then search for the King; we cannot lose him here," ordered Denth.

Argost had found the King lying face down upon the Plains of Desire. He had thought the worst at first; dropping his mighty sword and kneeling at the side of the fallen King of the Trolls, he cried out with a pain he thought he would never possess.

"Argost!" exclaimed the King.

"My King!" he replied, startled.

"Have we succeeded in defeating the evil that threatened our homelands?"

"There is still a fierce battle to the north of where we talk."

"Then we must make haste, Argost," said the King urgently, trying to get to his feet as he spoke. But his legs would not let him; they had lost all of their strength.

"You are bleeding, my King, upon the side of the head. Let me help you," offered the young Troll.

"Leave me be, Argost," said the King as he managed to get on to his knees. Slowly he rose, the blood flowing freely from the gash he had suffered when he had tripped and fallen onto a Hobgoblin's spear.

"At least let me aid you into battle," pleaded Argost, who did not like to see his King suffering. But the King would have no help from Argost. He took off his battle dress which was a leather jacket interlaced with metal rings. Beneath it he wore a simple white shirt; he ripped off the right sleeve and wrapped it as tightly as he could around his head. Instantly the deep red blood of the King stained the whiteness of the shirt.

"You may help me on with my jacket," said the King, his smile weak in the circumstances.

The Brethren had spent a great amount of time planning this battle. They knew thousands would be lost, but that did not matter when they had millions waiting for the chance to attack the races they so hated. The first wave they had sent was merely a token force, sent out to inflict as much damage as possible. The second wave of Goblins and Hobgoblins had been sent north, where they had already killed hundreds of Trolls who had made their homes upon the northern edges of the Plains of Desire, where they tended to the livestock that fed the huge city. Other settlements which had been wiped off the face of Ursalane had been the simple farmers: Trolls, which had never even been taught how to fight. Having gorged themselves upon the hundreds of Trolls and thousands of cattle and sheep, the hideous creatures had slowed in their hunger for battle; this is one of the reasons why the Troll running units stood a chance, for their hunger for battle still remained.

Browfell and Bugram had followed the enormous army for two days and two nights. They were fatigued and weak, but the sight of the running units attacking the evil lifted their spirits to such a degree, that they forgot about the lack of sleep and food, running as fast as they could to join the fierce battle that was on the distant horizon.

"The running units are defeating them!" exclaimed Browfell, panting heavily as he ran towards the battle.

"We will be too late," said Bugram, who had already withdrawn his sword.

"Let us hope we do not have to fight a thousand Goblins," remarked Browfell lightheartedly.

"One thousand Goblins do not worry me. It is Denjom and what he is going to say when he looks upon what we have seen, that I am scared of," replied Bugram, his sideways glance telling him that Browfell had not lost his sense of humour, as he was laughing.

Three hours had passed and the two scouts saw that the battlefield was littered with Trolls, Goblins and

Hobgoblins, the latter outnumbering the Trolls by at least two hundred to one. But even so, many good Trolls had died here.

They could now see two figures running away to the north. They then saw what the two Trolls were running towards, a sight they had dreaded since they had seen the army of the wizards split into two.

"The settlements are lost then," said Browfell quietly, his tone of voice showing signs of hatred towards the creatures upon which he now looked.

"Let us run for the saviour of Yea-Bor," cried Bugram, who had already started to quicken his pace.

On the whole, the Plains of Desire were an area of flat grasslands. But even here on the approaches to the city of Yea-Bor, there were dips and rises of several feet or more. It was up one of these rises in the plains that the two Trolls had climbed when they saw the distant outer walls of Yea-Bor, a mere speck on the horizon; but it was this sight that made them call out for the deaths of those who attacked them.

"Did you hear that?" asked the King, looking back towards the west.

"Yes," replied Argost, who was watching the coming together of the two opposing armies.

"I see two distant figures on the brow of a rise."

"You wish to wait for them, my King?" asked Argost, knowing that his King was in terrible pain.

"Yes, I do," said the King, who staggered as he slowed to a walking pace.

Argost put his hands upon his knees as he had been taught, breathing deeply, trying to regain his composure as quickly as possible. Within a minute or so he had pulled himself together. Standing up, he noticed that his King was on his knees again, his breathing hard and laboured.

The distant figures soon became the familiar faces Argost knew and respected.

"So it is not as we feared," he said as the scouts came to a halt, getting into the recovery position as soon as they had stopped.

"We became part of the plains," gasped Browfell, who was taking massive gulps of air.

"What did you see?" asked the injured King of Yea-Bor.

"An army of such size that it filled all of the lands to the west of the Plains of Desire; but they are killed easily,my King," replied Browfell, trying not to sound too despondent.

"Give me a few moments and we will enter another battle; they will not defeat us," declared the King, who had finally recovered his breathing.

"Argost."

"My King!"

"You go forwards into battle; these two will see that I reach the safety of our walls. I fear that I am too weak to lift even my sword," ordered the King, who had finally realised that he would be far more effective as a living King than a dead one.

"I go forth into battle with your blessing; I will not fail

you," said the departing Troll, his sword held within his right hand.

The battle to the north was a bloodbath. Having eaten, the Goblins had become sluggish in their movements. This had been the saviour of the Troll running units that awful day, and they had entered the fight as crazed beings, offering no mercy as they hacked at the small animal- like Goblins. In total, the various battles took less than seven hours. A few of the Goblins still roamed the Plains of Desire, but many thousands had been slain, certain parts of the grasslands turning red with the blood spilt. It was mainly due to the leadership of Denth; he had screamed the orders that had proved such a success, splitting many of the running units into four. This meant that they had more freedom where they ran, for running was the key to the effectiveness of the running units. But as Denth had screamed, the four had to stay as a unit, protecting each other as they met their enemy. Their shields were just as important as their swords, for as the Goblins screamed up towards the sullen skies, they started to throw the only weapons they possessed, these being eight sided razor sharp spheres. But the running units had also started to gain confidence as they shielded themselves against the first of several volleys of the deadly weapon. From then on, the battle had become very one- sided, with the much larger Troll hacking at the small Goblins' bodies, causing fatal wounds with every swing of their mighty swords.

Argost had joined near the end of the battle, running like the wind as he cut his way into more than a dozen of the screaming Goblins. They died easily, too easily, thought the Troll as he plunged his sword deep into the head of the nearest Goblin.

"Denth, they want to die!" exclaimed Argost.

"Then let us help them on their way; let us make this a day we rid the lands of this evil. Yea-Bor will rejoice," replied Denth, who had run over to the young Troll.

"I cannot see us rejoicing, Denth. There are too many dead and injured Trolls for the city to be uplifted by the events of this day."

"Then I will drink on my own, for I have been part of our long history on this blood ridden day. A few hundred against the many thousands that attacked us; it is nearly the work of wizards that we have done!" he exclaimed, wiping the blood of the many Goblins he had killed off his sword.

"I am no messenger of the King, so I would seek his counsel if I were you; do not celebrate a victory that means nothing," said Argost as bluntly as he could.

"Then you more than I, Argost. Tell me what you have heard. The King will be hard to see in the coming days if he is injured; the healers from the bell towers will keep out all those who do not know him closely."

"The two scouts that were sent out into the western Plains of Desire saw what we fought today."

"Then they have seen them die also!" interrupted Denth, who had waved away the three Trolls who had been trying to recover from the battle.

"They saw two groups detach themselves from an army

which they say is a thousand times bigger than what we encountered. These Goblins died easily, too easily."

"Then we must retreat to the safety of the outer walls, which is still many miles to the east. If they are right, Argost, then I will not rejoice. Instead I will start to prepare for the defense of our city," said the big Troll passionately.

Suddenly from the west, they could see six running units running as fast as possible. Seeing the figure of Denth, they came directly to his side, their breathing hard and laboured.

"Even more we have just now spotted upon the western horizons; my eyes had to look again as they did not believe the size of the advancing army," gasped the leader of the seventh running unit, a Troll highly respected throughout the city.

"Is it the Goblins that charge forth?" asked Argost urgently.

"None of the rodent-like creatures did we see; those which advance are much larger, marching in rows of at least a hundred," replied Rethost.

"Hobgoblins. It is as I feared, Denth. We have been set a simple trap," said Argost in a flat tone.

"Then let us call every running unit to our side. We run as one. If any fall, they will be carried; no more Trolls will die on this day," ordered Denth, who had already started to ring his bells.

Within the city, the King had just arrived with the two scouts. They helped the King towards the healers' houses, which were to be found underneath the bell towers.

"Do not dare take me to those meddlers. Take me to the debating chamber; the council will look upon the sights you have seen. I want Denjom brought to me first," ordered the King, pushing away the two scouts. They went rushing away to the north of the city, while the King tried to walk down the steep stairwells of the debating chamber. But the King of the Trolls knew that he had suffered a severe wound; he had become lightheaded and his eyes suddenly could not focus on anything. Swaying backwards and forwards, the King knew then that he might never see another living Troll.

"Let me take your hand, King of Yea-Bor. I will see to you now," said a soft, friendly voice.

The King though had already closed his eyes, his mind falling into a troubled sleep.

The debating chamber was empty as the body of the King was laid upon its floor. The figure, which was in shadow, tended quickly to the wounds of the King, words flowing over the body of Thengost, healing both his body and mind within minutes. He was suddenly awake again, staring at the familiar face of Sarratt, the wizard.

"I hoped that I would see you, King of Yea-Bor," said the wizard, a thin smile spreading across his rugged face.

"Then you have also seen our fate?"

"It is worse than you could ever imagine," replied Sarratt, who had seated himself heavily down onto one of the hundred chairs that surrounded the debating table.

"It can get no worse, Wizard. The army that spreads across the Plains of Desire is coming to the walls of Yea-Bor."

"I went from the Plains of Desire to see Esslestar. He gave me news that I dreaded, and he has already sent a formidable force to join the Dwarfs within the Golden Valley."

"Then we are doomed, Wizard, for we cannot fight two wars at the same time," said the King in dismay, his head coming to rest within his massive hands.

"I have many days of travel ahead of me, Thengost. I will be with you in thought, but such are the troubles that lay ahead in the coming weeks, I have to start my preparations for war. I will not fail you, Thengost, nor would I fail any of the so-called lesser races, but you must defend the outer walls with courage. Do not leave the safety of Yea-Bor until I return," said the wizard who had laid his hand upon the King's shoulder.

"But the Elves could take us within a day or so; you know this, Wizard. They are as quick as a lightning bolt when they strike. I witnessed a killing a few years ago to the south of the main trade route; the dozen hunted Gnomes were dead within seconds. They move as if they were in two places at the same time. We are living out our sentence of death, Sarratt. What can I say to the council? That we have the aid of two wizards? They will not want to hear such words."

"Then tell the council that it must be them who save Yea-Bor. I will leave now, you will see me when it is your darkest hour."

The wizard left as he had come, swiftly and quietly. He returned to the Plains of Desire to find that Stormbreaker was waiting for him.

"Come, Stormbreaker. We seek out the Watch Wizard; he will be our salvation."

The wizard galloped as fast as the horse could run before whispering the silent spells from deep within himself. The horse neighed loudly, such was his joy at being in the company of one whose love for him was undying.

During their time together Stormbreaker had watched and listened intently, for the wisdom of the wizard was a great thing. The horse had picked up many of the wizard's moods. He would take this knowledge back to the Plains of Desire and shepherd his family in the same manner of the wizard. . The wizard had other darker thoughts on his mind: would he be able to save the Trolls from total annihilation?

Epilogue

Peter Miller rubbed his eyes as he looked at the stranger who had arranged this meeting. He did not know if he was going to laugh or cry. What he had just been told was a tale of fancy, which had no part in his regimented life, a life which had so far been meticulously planned out. Everything Peter Miller did, he did for a reason. That was why he had moved up the ladder of success at a high rate of knots. Something within his mind was shouting at him to get rid of this young punk. Maybe he was a robber, maybe even a murderer. A headache was forming too. He glanced at his watch and realised he had been sat there listening to this young lad for one hour; it seemed far longer. As he was about to say as much to the stranger, he found himself again listening to that high-pitched voice. During the time he had closed his eyes while listening, he had felt at times that musical sounds had replaced the voice of this yob.

"I realise, Peter Miller, that my tale may sound silly to you, but what I have so far told you actually happened. I wish I had more time to spend with you, but others are waiting for me; I must leave you."

"Fucking Hell! Is that it then? I receive a message through my letter box, telling me to travel nearly the length of the country. Well, guess what, whoever you are! I can drop by any library in this country and read stuff which is a lot better than what I have just heard. I am a busy man and I do not like to be taken for a fool," said Miller, his anger plain to see.

"Goodbye, Peter Miller. Six of your months will pass by before I continue my tale," replied the stranger, who was making himself ready to leave; he had even turned the mobile phone on again.

"Wait!" said the reporter, his hands still rubbing his tired eyes.

"For a few minutes only," came the soft reply.

"Where are these friends of yours?"

"Within the trees right in front of us. You won't be able to see them; the light has left us for the day."

"But wizards and Goblins, Elves and Gnomes, on a Continent known as Ursalane, I am at a loss with this, why me?" asked the reporter, who had turned to stare at the wooded area once more. But as he did so, a series of lightning bolts lit the surrounding area as if someone had switched on a set of floodlights. Within the trees right in front of his car, away across the car park, stood three figures. He blinked and they were gone. He gasped in shock, for it had really spooked him to see anyone who would be foolish enough to stand amongst a bunch of trees whilst a storm raged.

"For you are the right person," answered the stranger.

"Then at least tell me who you are. That will give me something to think about when you have left…, your name at least, otherwise I leave here tonight thinking that I have had a trick played upon me," pleaded Miller.

"I can only tell you this, Peter Miller. I chose to contact you, for you are the right one. Go and visit your Father, he will talk to you of what happened during the dark days of the second world war. But I also fear for his life; nothing more can I tell you. I must leave now, for we still have many miles to run before this night is through. "You dare leave now! My Father lies on his death bed; he has not got much time left," warned the reporter, his head now banging with the headache which had slowly crept upon him. The hooded stranger reached within his green camouflaged jacket and pulled out another sealed golden envelope. He passed it to the reporter, who looked at the red wax seal with the acorn adorning it, and then looked back at the hooded stranger.

But the stranger had already left. Such was his speed of movement that the reporter saw only a blur going across the car park. As if it had been meant to be, another series of lightning bolts lit up the service station. What he saw was a vision that would stay with him for the coming days: four figures running onto the M6 motorway at such a speed that they were gone before the light had left the area, a blur of figures that moved as if they were part of the wind, gusting as they vanished into the area that led to the M6 motorway. Astonished that they had risked their lives in this suicidal direction, he rushed from the comfort of his pride and joy and went to the verge of the motorway. He saw nothing in the darkness but the speeding cars that raced past him every second he watched. He then turned back to his car and thought of what he had been told. He got into his range rover sport and decided that he would travel south. He made a couple of phone calls, cancelling the tour around the new studios, telling his wife of his father's situation. He felt really emotional; a lump had formed within his throat. All the while, his hands toyed with the golden sealed letter.

"Fucking Hell!"

He eventually opened the letter and read the contents, gasping out loud as he did so.

Peter Miller

Time is running out.

You need to sort out your personal fitness.

This you need to do.

"Fuck off!" yelled Peter Miller.

Before you can start to run you must first walk..

Walk five miles each and every day, walk it as fast as you can.

I will measure your fitness the next time we meet.

Your life depends on you becoming a runner of the lands of your country.

Acorn.

Peter Miller swore three more times as he screwed the letter up in disgust and threw it in to the back of his car.

He drove away from the service station a changed man; he now knew that his father was close to death, he now realised at the age of forty nine how unfit he really was. Something within his mind had also changed, but he could not put his finger on it. A slight change had happened, something good though, he thought, something positive. The rain was still pouring down as he drove away from his first meeting with the stranger of whom he could not stop thinking.

"How the fuck am I going to get fit? How can I stop myself from fucking swearing? And how can I stop my Dad from dying? Fuck.!"

Lightning Source UK Ltd.
Milton Keynes UK
UKOW051134211012

200872UK00002B/3/P